I0527256

REIGN FROM HEAVEN

BOOK 2 OF THE WAR OF THE GODS SERIES

DAVID GEARING

AKUSAI
PUBLISHING

1

A snapped tree completes its slow fall to the ground in a bustling thud of cracking branches and squawking ducks.

The least intelligent of the local waterfowl decide it's finally high time to heed the warnings and head into the blue lake, away from cries and laughter, away from the would-be battle field.

"Is that all you got?" screams Herakles. His oversized shoulders just barely scrape by the patch of deciduous trees that line the border between the shimmering blue lake and the park benches. He grabs his left shoulder and rubs it, trying to hide any reaction he may have to the bruises with a smile. The large behemoth of a man adjusts the lion's cowl that lies just slightly over his shoulder. "Good shot, kid."

A crowd of people smartly walks around the cracked tree that accidentally got in Herakles's way mid-throw while the ex-god flew through the air mid-throw.

This spring, it seems to be perfect sparring weather. Cool winds to dry away the sweat, the soft green grass—almost blue—by the small blue lake that fed into the Thurmond River.

Well, not a river, but maybe a stream. A big stream.

Brad stands with his legs a shoulders' length apart, his hands each throbbing red and cracking. His shorts used to be beige before the two began sparring. That was only fifteen minutes ago. Now deep, dark grass stains cover nearly every available inch of the fabric.

What isn't covered in green chlorophyll is pressed with dirt. Brad checks his shorts, socks, and his shoes.

Herakles could already hear Sophie screaming at him about having to clean more grass stains out her son's clothing.

"Wait a sec, Herc" Brad says. He kneels down and grabs his laces. "My shoes are untied."

Herakles jerks his head over each shoulder, cracking his neck in too many places to count. He smirks and winks.

"I said wait!" says Brad. Still kneeling, he holds his little ten-year-old hands out in front of him, as if he could stop the two-hundred and fifty pounds of pure muscle running at him with the power of a bullet train.

Herc cracks each of his knuckles and forms tight fists, holding them to his side as if wings.

"That's no fair!" screams Brad.

When Brad closes his eyes and feels the blast of warmth come over his face and chest. When he opens his eyes, he watches an old couple fly past him.

Or was he flying past them?

"No fair!" Brad extends a hand out to grab a tree branch, but he's too late. The best he can do is grab the leaves right off, scraping them off in an explosion of green and brown wood chips.

Brad's tumbles head over heels over head, stopping on his shoulder. He takes in a deep breath and focuses his attention to the pain.

Breathe it out. Breathe in air. Slow. Deep. Just like Herc taught him.

"Are you okay?" Herc shouts clear across the park.

From where Brad sits, even Herc's humongous shoulders look no wider than a piece of paper. He nods and holds his head.

"Dear God, boy, are you okay?"

Brad looks up. The same elderly couple stands by his frayed

body. He feels the freeze along his back through the frayed edges of his shirt, his shorts nearly pulled off of his behind from the force of the blow.

"Yeah, yeah, this is nothing," Brad says. He stands up and dusts himself off. "I'm fine. Serious."

The old man stretches his neck out and checks along Brad's back and arms. He reminds Brad of an old, slow talking turtle from a movie he saw just last year. Never ending something or another.

"Are you sure?" the man says out of quivering, wrinkled lips.

"Ya, ya, I'm fine." Brad pulls his shirt up near his shoulder. "But he ripped my shirt." He waves over to Herc. "You ripped my shirt, you jerk!"

"Should we call the police?" the woman asks. The old woman's purse seems to eat her hand as she rattles through a bunch of plastic-who-knows-what in there.

Brad scoffs. "What? No, no. He's my brother."

The man adjusts his glasses and peers over at Herc, who waves and roars with laughter. "Brother?"

Brad pats the man on the shoulder hand. "Thanks for checking on me, mister." He smiles and runs back for more beatings.

"You need to be more careful," says Brad. "You ripped my shirt. My mom's going to be pissed."

Herc cringes. "Your mom will be mad at you if she hears you talking like that." He raises his fists to his face and shadow boxes into the air. "Ready for round two?"

Brad adjusts his torn shirt, pulls at his collar to extend it over his collarbone. "Bring it," he says.

"When is your mom supposed to be here?" says Herc. He begins the dance, taking slow steps to his left.

Brad responds by taking a step to right. Same pace. Same distance.

"I dunno. When she's done with whatever she's doing with Hermes, I guess."

He holds a thumb against one nostril and blows a snot rocket onto the ground. "You think he likes her?" says Herc.

Brad's lips begin to snarl. "Ew, gross."

Herc smiles. "It's not gross. I think it's rather adorable," he says. "It's pretty obvious he likes her. Are you going to make a move or what?"

"He doesn't like her," says Brad. "I would know."

Herc stops and stands up, his hands on his hips. "And you would know because?" He strokes his short, dark brown beard. "You're like what? Eight?"

Brad smiles. "You know I'm ten."

"You will be ten. You aren't ten yet."

"Almost," says Brad. He smirks as a thought comes to his head. "Do you like anyone?"

Herc's eyes widen, taken off guard by the question. "What? No. I've been, um, busy."

"Well, when are you going to get a girlfriend?"

"When are you going to?" mocks Herc.

"I'm only ten," says Brad. "Mom says I have time for girls."

"Then hurry up and hit me, old man. You're not getting any younger." Herc snorts back some laughter and puts on his game face on, full snarl, baring teeth.

Brad pulls up his imaginary sleeves and readies his fists. "You ready?"

Herc holds his index finger out to Brad. "Okay, new lesson. First, you never—oof!"

Brad's head rams into Herc's hips, forcing him to the ground.

Dirt and sod fly into the air as Herc's massive shoulders dig into the dirt around him, carving out a shallow hole. "Whoa there, boy. I wasn't—" Herc freezes and then grabs the top of Brad's head. "That's my boy! You're getting better at that."

"Are you okay?" Brad checks Herc's body and chest for injuries.

"Ya, ya, I'm fine." Herc picks up Brad off his chest and sets him off to the side.

"Are you sure?" Brad's eyes begin to tear up, his lower lip quivers.

"Yes, yes, I'm fine." Herc tries to stand up, but he winces and takes in a sharp breath. "See?" he says. He holds his hands out as if going in for a hug. "All good."

Brad raises an eyebrow and inspects Herc's dirt-ridden shirt and sweat shorts. "Okay, I guess."

Herc brings Brad to his side and goes in for a hug.

Brad closes his eyes and wraps his hands around Herc's comparatively thin waist. He doesn't even begin to squeeze when he feels the air escape Herc's chest and he flinches in a quick jolt.

"Easy there, buddy," says Herc. He nudges Brad along the side with his giant bear paw of a hand. "I'm tender."

Brad wipes away a tear not yet quite formed. "I'm sorry."

"For what?" says Herc. "You have nothing to worry about."

"But I—"

Sophie climbs up the low hill that served as their battle grounds. "What did you do to your shirt?"

Brad releases Herc's side and points at him. "He did it."

"Herc," says Sophie. She can't finish the sentence, lost in the fact that two of her fingers fit through the sizable holes in her son's shirt. "This thing's ruined."

She holds her son's head in her hands. "Are you okay at least?"

Herc sighs. "Why is everyone asking that?"

Sophie eyes Herc. "Brad, honey?"

Brad lowers his head. "Yes, mom. I'm okay."

"Well, now we have to clean up before we go shopping." She taps the back of Brad's head and points toward the downtown. "Come on," she says. "We have your birthday to plan." Brad begins a slow walk like a death march toward the road. "And you, mister. We'll deal with how you're going to pay for his shirt when we get back."

Herc lowers his eyes and kicks the fresh pile of dark, wet soil he pushed up earlier. "Okay," he mumbles.

2

Sophie holds the bright blue and white box of cupcake mix directly into her son's line of sight. "But it has sprinkles," she says. "You love sprinkles."

"Sprinkles are for mortals," says Brad. He shoves her hand aside and pushes the empty cart with a single, child-sized finger.

"The hell is that supposed to mean?" says Sophie. She drops the box into the cart and rests her hand on the side of the cart, stopping it though it takes a little bit of strength and focus to overcome her son.

"It means that I'm not a little kid anymore."

"No, no. Don't go changing the conversation on me, little man. I gave birth to you, I know when there's something bothering you." Sophie pushes her hair behind her ears, which just falls back into place anyway. Though she likes her recent hair cut because it doesn't require a lot of upkeep, the downside is, well, there's not a lot she can do with it.

"Nothing, mom."

"That's a load and you know it." Sophie leans over the cart, meeting her son eye to eye. "What's going on?"

"I'm not mortal, mom. Sprinkles are for mortals."

"Well, this mortal likes sprinkles, so she's getting sprinkles. And you, Sir Too Big For His Britches, is going to like it."

"Fine," he says.

"And put that lip away. You know I can't say no to that lip." Sophie pretends to stare forward, directing her son's cart to the next aisle over. As she steers the cart from the front, she notices a significant lack of smiling in her son.

"What else do we need?" mutters Brad.

Sophie lets out a deep, steady breath. "A different type of cupcake mix," she says.

Brad holds still, eyebrow raised, mouth just barely open.

Sophie rolls her eyes. "Fine, my little demi-god, you can pick the cupcakes that are fit for a god."

Brad's lips form the beginnings of a smile before falling down like the London Bridge. "But I'm not a god, either, mom."

Sophie feels her chest tighten. She drops the blue box of cake mix and grabs her son's shoulders for a mini-hug. "I know, honey. And I wish I knew how to help, but this whole half-man, half-god thing didn't come with an instruction manual."

"I know," says Brad under his breath.

Sophie grins. "Besides, even if they did, you know how I like reading instruction books."

"You don't."

"That's right. I don't." She squeezes her son extra hard. "So what kind of cupcakes do you want for your birthday?" she says.

Brad pauses and taps his chin as he looks up at her. "Hrm," he hums.

Sophie holds her hand casually over her hand, trying not to laugh her son imitate his older step-brother.

"How about sprinkles?" he says.

Sophie nods. "Sprinkles it is." She taps the side of the cart. "And we're set."

"No," says Brad. "We need frosting."

"Quite right," she says. "Can't have cupcakes without frosting." She twirls the cart around and drags it down the aisle again. "Which kind?"

Silence, as they both stare at the bright red, blue, and green boxes, teasing them with delicious treats and promises of smiles and cake.

"Well, duh," says Brad. "Sprinkles."

One hundred dollars later, Sophie hands the heavy paper grocery bags to her son.

"Just how much milk are you drinking?" she says.

Brad hauls one of the bags on top of his left shoulder with a grunt and turns his head. "What does that mean?"

"The commercial?" Sophie flexes a bicep and grimaces like a constipated bodybuilder.

Brad shrugs.

"Really? You watch all that TV and you haven't seen this commercial?"

"Maybe it's an old commercial," says Brad. He manages to carry all four bags by himself.

"I will pretend you didn't say that. Are you sure you don't want any help?"

"Nope." Brad's steps get bigger, confident. He steps forward, swinging his shoulders and feet in big steps. "I got it."

Sophie watches with awe, remembering the time when she had to pick her son up from Head Start when he was four. He cried all day, waiting by the doors for her to return. It broke her heart to see him when she returned. Puffy faced and red, glassy eyes from the nonstop tears.

The words "holy" and "terror" may have been used when the nice ladies at the school described his day.

As she watches her almost-ten-year-old son balance nearly sixty pounds of food and supplies in and on his arms, her heart begins to break again.

Every mother wants her son to be someone special. Able to change the world.

But no mother dreams she will see that happen before her son has his first kiss.

A strong blast of cool air from the automatic doors throws her short hair into disarray and brings Sophie back into the real world.

Her son continues his confident strides to the edge of the big gray building where he stops and turns around. "Mom, stop being so slow."

As she reaches the corner of the building, she reaches her arms out and takes a bag off of her son's shoulders. "Let me at least look like I'm helping," she says.

"But mom, I've got it," Brad says. He takes a step to the side away from his mom.

An old man shuffles from his spot, seated cross-legged in the shade cast from the building onto the sidewalk.

"Excuse me," says the man. He holds out a dirty hand. What looks like white chapped skin, dry cracks, line every crease in his palm. "Do you have any change you can spare?"

Sophie shifts the bag of ham and canned corn from one hip to the other. "I might have something," she says. She takes her free hand and fishes out a dollar and offers it over.

The man bows and takes the dollar. He sniffs it, holding it up and then crumples it up into a pocket in his loose-fitting green cargo pants. "Do you have any more?" he says.

Brad takes a step backwards, hiding behind his mother.

"I'm sorry," she says. "I don't. Nothing more to spare." She nudges Brad along in front of her. "Good luck, sir."

"But I asked nicely," said the man.

Sophie feels the homeless fellow get closer behind them. She tries to pick up the pace, but her son blocks her.

She turns around. She thanks the gods that she's holding a bag of groceries, or her shaking would be embarrassingly obvious. "Listen, sir, I gave you everything I could give you. Please leave us alone."

The man holds out a steak knife. Its wide blade held directly at Sophie's chest, his hand clutching the thick wooden handle so hard his white knuckles shake. "But I asked. I asked nicely."

"Mom!" Brad drops his bags and rushes to her side.

"Yes, you did," says Sophie. She takes a step back. With her free hand, she feels for her son's chest and pushes him backwards in pace with hers.

"But you have more money," the man says. "You all have more. I can smell it."

"Okay," says Sophie. "But I think you need to calm down. I have a son, and you're scaring him."

Brad's hands grip the back of her pants. His shivers travel up her spine. Sophie feels her heart beat through her ears, her breath short and shallow.

"Give me the money."

"I don't have anything."

The man thrusts forward with the knife.

Sophie drops the paper bag in her hand and clutches at the man's dark sleeves. Her hands wrap around completely, squeezing. Pushing. Pulling.

Seeing what he did, the man looks left, then right and takes a step back. "Give me the money," he says.

Sophie feels strange on her neck. Something flows down her neck and chest, warm as bathwater.

"Mom!" Brad screams.

When Sophie realizes she's bleeding, her knees give out and she falls into her son's arms.

3

B rad struggles to keep his mother on his tiny shoulders as he attempts—not successfully—to wipe his brow. He takes to the backstreets to keep from anyone asking questions. The small one-story buildings that line the streets serve two roles—cover from the sun and cover from questioning and wandering eyes.

The first is a matter of survival. Ninety degree heat and ninety-three percent humidity is nothing to laugh at. Even for a demigod.

The second is a matter of avoiding annoyances. Right now, if someone were to ask, he couldn't say the truth without crying. Because to say it out loud might make it true.

His mother might be dying. And it might be his fault.

He looks down at his shirt. Blood everywhere.

"I'm so sorry, mom," he says.

She mumbles something, but then goes right back to sleep. Her body feels heavy, dragging him down along his narrow shoulders. Only four feet off the ground, he finds balancing his mother not as easy as he thought. He is a boy just developing his magnificent Olympian strength. He is nowhere near as strong as his step-brother Herc.

A thought that only makes him wish he were faster, stronger. Better. Maybe smarter.

Anything to keep his mother breathing.

He listens for her breath in his right ear. The sky is cloudy and the backstreets are quiet. The only sound his feet dragging along the loose rocks of gravel that cling to the ridges of his sneakers.

He begins to realize that his frequent breaks to adjust her weight on his neck and shoulders is a good thing.

If he stops enough, he can check her for breathing.

His back feels warm, then cold and slick. His shirt moves when he pulls his mother left. Then right to stabilize her.

All the while, he feels the itchy tears along his cheeks and chin. They drip off his chin, the stream drying between sobs.

His thoughts are lost in the future. Will she live? Die?

Is it bad luck to even think that she will die?

Why couldn't the homeless man stabbed him instead of her? He could take it.

He's immortal.

He thinks. Or is he? Why is he spared?

"C'mon, mom," he says. "We can make it. We're almost there."

Sophie groans. Red spit dribbles down his neck.

Brad shiver. The wetness catches him by surprises and he jumps in his own skin.

"Eww, mom."

He shifts his mother over his shoulder once more and pauses. He still has two more streets to cross.

He can do it.

Brad holds his breath and measures the distance again.

His arm strong. But is he leg strong?

"I'm sorry, mom. This is going to be shaky."

His mother says nothing.

"Mommy? Did you hear me?"

He shakes his shoulders left to right. "Mom?"

Her legs twitch along his left side, pushing his hands away from her thigh.

Brad lets out a smile and the air that gathered into his chest like a balloon.

"Hermes can help us, mom. Just hold on."

Brad kicks off with the front of his feet and runs. The air pulls at his hair. The little boy slows down only so long as to get a better grip onto his mother's arm and thigh.

"Almost there," he mutters to himself again.

He looks down at the ground and watches his feet. Even to him, they look like white and blue blurs along the black-gray rocky road.

And then he spots the blood. Dark red. Fresh.

He must clean that off. Get all of it off. It's proof he did something. Something wrong.

Hide it. Away from Hermes. From Herc. From his mom.

Brad runs down the streets and passes by the light blue house of his neighbors and tries to stop.

Except he doesn't know how. His legs stop moving because that's the only thing he can manage to think to do.

And when he does, he rolls along the grassy lawn that his mom makes him mow every three weeks.

Brad tucks in his arms along his side. His nose burns, scraping it along the asphalt driveway three, four, five times. Too many to count.

His entire head feels warm, scraped up.

He peels the tiny specks of rock that press into his skin. Not breaking it. Not bleeding, but pushed in from the rolling and the stopping.

But as he looks at his hands, he realizes he was once holding something.

"Oh my God. Mom?"

Sophie lays next to the apartment's cement steps, curled up and legs kicked out in front of her.

Her head sits twisted in Brad's direction, her eyes half-open. She looks asleep, Brad thinks.

The thought kicks him in the gut. He feels like his throat wants to close up all the way.

He clasps the ground, crawls toward his mother.

"Mom?" he says. He grabs the collar of her shirt. The blood gushes up out of the fabric and bubbles around the crevices of his fingers. "Mom? Wake up."

Brad's chest begins to heave into heavy and quick sobs. He fights back the tears, but his hands shake.

The shaking moves to his elbows to his shoulders.

Soon it travels down his spine and he clutches his mother's shirt and pulls her closer to him. He kisses her on the forehead the way she did every night before bed.

"Please, mom. Wake up."

When she grunts, Brad lets himself smile for only a moment.

He pulls himself to his feet and grabs both of her armpits and drags her along the gravel to the front door of the apartment complex.

Brad's baby-god strength slams the door open so hard it stays open, swinging loose and quivering along the busted hinges.

Thin red streaks trace the path from the front door to his step-brothers' apartment.

He opens the door. It bounces off the wall and back into his little shoulders. He shoves it off and brings his mother inside the apartment and drops her gently on the floor.

Herc comes out of the kitchen, his hands covered in cloth and drying a glass. "If you don't stop doing that, you know Hermes will kill you."

Brad's lips quiver too much for him to talk. He opens his mouth but doesn't know what to say.

So he lets his hands, covered in half-dried, sticky blood do the talking.

His mother squirms at his side. Her head turns, nudging against his sneakers.

Herc reaches behind and into the kitchen to place the glass on the kitchen counter. He misses, shattering glass on the linoleum floor.

Brad gulps. "My mom needs help."

4

The large room pulses with a crystalline glow when Gabriel walks into the room. He is followed by Michael, a sandy blond-haired angel clad in white and silver clothes.

Gabriel, taller than Michael by nearly half a head, peers down at the little angel and nods.

The room's alabaster white walls reflect the pure white light that pulses from deep within the room. The glow is almost warm and soft, the way light reflects off the surface of a lake.

Above the angels' heads is a vaulted ceiling, similar to what Michael had seen in Gothic churches, minus the beautiful, if not sometimes gaudy colored glass windows.

Michael follows the command and closes the door behind him. He knew this day would come, but if he were asked his honest opinion, it would be maybe a few hundred years from now.

Not in the early twenty-first century. Not one of the Archangels could have predicted that.

Gabriel seats himself in his white chair at the end of the table. The chair is padded and made of something like wood, but shimmers as if more celestial. The frame bends with Gabriel's weight and cushions around his legs and back as he rests backwards.

It appears the perfect chair for a commander hard at work in the war room of Heaven. One of many created over the last thousand years. Gabriel had once described it as a war throne. When accusations grew of his desire for the real Silver Throne, he quickly denied as rumors.

Rumors, he attributed to Michael himself.

This is the room in which the great Archangels deliberated, deciding that yes, Dante and Virgil needed passage into Hell. Gabriel himself had sent Michael to ensure Dante and Virgil's entrance into the City of Dis.

"Is this really the wisest option?" says Michael. He adjusts his dark, gun-metal belt and shifts his weight from one leg to the other. "I mean, we cannot confirm anything just yet." His hands twitch behind him.

"But what better way to claim victory than to actually declare that victory in front of millions?" Gabriel folds his hands in his lap and smiles.

His golden hair falls over his forehead as he tilts his head forward, staring at the ground. He speaks as if talking to the floor. Concentrating on the image of victory in his mind's eye.

"The sooner we make the move and win this war, the sooner we can rest, Michael. We serve Him, after all. We deserve this victory."

Michael fidgets with the paper map in his hands. He fears that his sweaty, nervous palms will make the paper brittle and difficult to read. He relinquishes it to the table.

It unrolls with a wave of Gabriel's hand. "You are sure that we have checked all available entrances?" he asks.

Michael nods. "As you have commanded."

Gabriel nods. At no time does his eyes meet Michael's, a fact that is not lost to the little angel. While he feels the need to catch his commander's attention, get a little recognition, he hardly feels that it is his right to do so.

Gabriel could be somewhat—intimidating—was the best word.

Especially since The Silence nearly one year ago.

"And we are sure that none have come in or out?"

"Not in the last eighteen months." Michael begins to pull out a chair, but Gabriel raises an eyebrow.

Michael releases the chair and, feeling guilty, decides to push it back under the table.

Gabriel rests his feet on the chair that Michael just pushed in. "Then it is time that I speak as the Voice to the people of the Earth realm. Let them know that they are saved. Once and for all."

"But is this really the proper recourse? You know they have their Bibles. It does not say that things will end up in this manner."

"Does it ever?" Gabriel says. He rests his hands behind his head and leans backwards in the chair. "I mean this as an honest question. Does it, ever?"

Michael shuffles through the thought in his head. At the tip of his tongue is the word yes, but he swallows it down.

"So then we are in agreement. We won."

"I never said we agreed sir." Michael's voice trails off to a whisper when he sees the scolding stare of Gabriel's golden hazel eyes.

"I never asked if you said it, Michael. I asked if we were in agreement."

"I never said I agree." Michael's fingers twitch so he rests them behind his back. "I mean, yes. Yes, we do agree."

Gabriel stands up and pushes in the chair. "Excellent," he says with a smile. "Then we make the statement that Man is now saved. That should be a nice way of saying that we're now in charge of the Earth realm."

"You cannot be serious, Gabriel. In charge?"

"In charge," says Gabriel softly. "The humans need our help, do they not?"

"But what if Hell really is not…"

"On hiatus?" Gabriel says, eyebrows raised and the corners of his mouth beginning to curl upwards. "Fortune favors the bold, as the humans say. And I am bold enough to seize fortune by the throat and take what is mine."

"Then I recommend that we post guards at the entrances and exits of Hell and Hades, Gabriel. Just in case."

"Always the cautious one, Michael."

"That cautious quirk of mine saved your wings in the War for the Throne. Never forget that, commander."

Gabriel motions toward the office door with an open palm. He only half smiles. "You will never let me forget that, will you?"

"Not on your life."

5

Hermes lifts Sophie into his arms and covers the bleeding wound on her neck with his hands. "What the hell happened?"

"She got hurt," says Brad. His hands fidget from in front of him to behind him in his pockets.

Hermes' face turns red, pulsing heat. "Yes, I know she got hurt. What happened?"

Hermes rests Sophie's body on the couch. His hand slips off her neck, his wrist now covering the gushing wound.

Herakles towers behind Hermes, his shadow casting over Sophie and clear up to the wall behind the couch. "We need to get her to a hospital, Herm."

"We can fix this," says Hermes.

"Not without magic," says Herc. "And you know it."

"Then we get a healer."

"We don't have time. That type of wound will not suffer too much time." Herc rests a hand on his friend's head. "We should move fast."

Hermes feels the itching sensation of tears welling up inside his eyelids. He dares not to blink.

To cry means to show fear. To show fear means to admit that something could go wrong.

Hermes feels the tickling punch in his gut.

"No, nothing can go wrong."

Hermes' fearful paralysis is suddenly dropped when he feels a slap to the back of his head. He turns toward Herc. "What was that for?"

"If you aren't going to do it for Sophie," says Herc. "Do it for him."

He points in the small dining room just off the northern end of the living room. There, at the glass table with his head buried in his arms, sits Brad, head down and sobbing.

"Fine," says Hermes. "I'll be the fastest. I will take her."

Herc pats him on the back. "Good luck. May the wind blow behind your back."

HERMES THROWS his caution to the wind as he runs with the help of his winged sandals. They push the wind along, guiding him down the street and toward the tiny, one story hospital at the edge of the town.

Herc and Hermes never had a reason to own a vehicle. Prior to living in Saraday, they were teleporters. Anything they needed was merely a blink away.

Hermes squints to block the sun from his eyes. The white single-story building appears as a fast approaching dot on the horizon.

He looks down at Sophie.

She has not moved in nearly twenty minutes. From picking her up to moving her to the couch, nothing seems to get her to talk, or groan, or mumble.

Trusting in his winged sandals to guide him to the hospital, he peers down at Sophie's pale face.

"You can hang in there. For Brad. For Herc." His throat nearly closes on him. "For me."

Sophie's head turns away from Hermes' chest.

Amidst the chaos of the moment, Hermes works a pathetic smile and tenses his leg muscles, pushing himself to move faster.

The mechanical doors could not move fast enough to let Hermes and Sophie into the hospital.

The doors blast open from the force of Hermes' shoulders, one of the doors falling off the hinges and onto the ground.

The nurses and doctors in the emergency room gasp in unison amidst the explosion of glass and metal.

A male nurse approaches the "Sir, you cannot just barge in here." He motions toward the shattered door with no words. Just a face as angry and twisted as the door frame lying on the ground.

"She's hurt," says Hermes. "I need one of your doctors."

When Hermes releases his hand from Sophie's neck, a thin red river of blood trickles down her neck and onto the ground.

The male nurse takes Hermes' shoulder and pushes him toward the two large coffee-brown doors that lead down a brightly lit hallway.

The back of the building has a tiled floor that reflects the buzzing white lights like a mirror. The lights shine a bright white that almost appears baby blue at first glance.

The light hurts Hermes' eyes and he squints to keep his balance and focus on the nurse's directions.

"Here," he says.

Hermes places her lightly on a gurney and feels the nurse's hand push him backwards.

He resists at first, his hands reach out to Sophie as she gets wheeled away down the long hallway.

A frustrated roar bellows from behind the doors into the emergency room's waiting area.

"Sir!" shouts a poor hapless nurse. "Sir, you cannot go in there without—"

The words soon disappear behind a shuffling of people and a scream for security.

Hermes feels wind from the swinging of the door behind him.

"Is she okay?" asks Herc.

Hermes hears Herc, but cannot pull his eyes away from the door at the end of the hall.

Surgery. Where Sophie's life may hang in the balance.

His heart wanted to say "Yes, yes, she will be all right."

But his brain saw the wound. The dark red, almost black, blood that poured out of her wound.

She had bled all the way to the hospital. He had felt the warmth all over his chest. Down his sides.

A quick glance at Hermes' shirt and it would be hard to convince yourself that Sophie was still alive.

"No," says Hermes.

Herc steps in front of Hermes and shakes him out of his trance. "What do you mean no?"

Hermes blinks twice. The massive image of a bearded tower of muscle gradually comes into view.

"I do not know," Hermes says. "The blood. So much blood."

"We don't know human anatomy that well," says Herc. He whispers as he gently clasps his hands on both of Hermes' cheeks. "Maybe she is good. Maybe that's normal."

Hermes buries his fists into Herc's chest. Each punch feels like slamming his knuckles into the sidewalk.

"Normal?" he grunts. "That blood. That is not normal. It cannot be."

Hermes hits harder with each punch, hoping that Herc will do something about it. With each hit, he stops if only for a second, waiting to be hit back.

To feel pain. Warmth. Bruises.

When he can barely hold his own shoulders up, Hermes steps backwards and rests along the padded bench up against the wall.

"Feel better?" says Herc. He sits next to him and wraps his hairy, muscled arm around Hermes' comparatively small shoulders.

"No." Hermes sniffs back tears. "Where is Brad?"

Herc nods toward the door. "He didn't want to come in."

Hermes nods and stands up. His legs wobble underneath him. "I am being selfish," he says.

Herc takes the seat of Hermes' pants and yanks him back to sit down. "You stay here. I'll tend to the kid."

"But," says Hermes, but he has nothing. No words. No worries. Just a mixture of feelings and confusion.

"Yeah," says Herc. He rests his hands on his buddy's shoulder with a tight pinch. "Yeah, I know."

6

Hermes' short stature, curly brown hair, meadow green eyes and olive skin only confuse the nurse as she approaches him in the hallway.

"So you are not the patient's family?"

Hermes shakes his head. "Not really. It is complicated at best. Confusing at worst."

The nurse ushers him out of the emergency room hallway, through the coffee-brown flapping doors and into the waiting room. "Then you can stay out here. Family only."

Herc stands up and crosses his arms. As he does so, he catches the attention of damn near every woman—and some men—in the waiting room. Tall enough to touch the ceiling with the top of his head if he were to jump, he thinks this is the best time to flaunt his size.

"What's going on here?"

"We cannot go in," says Hermes. He turns away and runs his hands through his hair. "She says we aren't family."

"What the hell is that supposed to mean?" Herc steps forward between the nurse and his best friend. "If my friend needs to be back there, he needs to be back there. Sophie needs us. He loves her."

"And that's fine and dandy," says the nurse. She slaps the clipboard against her hip as she shifts her weight into pure sass mode. "But if you aren't related to her, we cannot have you back there. State law."

"That's a bunch of bullshit," says Herc.

"And if you continue with that mouth, you'll never get back there again."

Herc's face goes white, then red with rage. "Listen to me, and listen closely," he says. He takes a step forward to get into the nurse's face.

She does not blink or twitch a muscle in the face of such an intimidating face.

"Stop it." Brad sits up from the waiting room chair and grabs hold of Herc's elbow. "This is my brother, and that's my mom in there."

The nurse's face softens, her grimace makes a gradual shift into a smile. "I'm sorry for your loss," she says.

Hermes feels his hands ball into tight fists. Herc grabs the woman's shoulders and shakes her as he yells. "What do you mean loss?"

The nurse tries to wrap her hands around Herc's massive wrists, but they are shaken off as fast as she can seize a grip. "I didn't mean. What did I say?"

Brad speaks up. "You said loss." His lower lip quivers and the color drops out of his face. "She's dead?"

"I—I saw the wounds. The doctors were not very hopeful. But if you are her son," the nurse says softly, "then you are allowed to be in there when she's out of surgery."

Brad sits down. "I—I can't."

"I'll let the front desk know about you," says the nurse. She sends the evil eye to both Hermes and Herc, who stand behind Brad's body, gradually melting into a sad ball of fear and frustration.

"But you really should," says Hermes. "Let us know what's going on."

"She needs you, buddy."

Brad gulps and stares at the doors down the hallway. "I don't want to see her."

His feet shuffle, turning left, right, then finally turning around on his heels. He marches through the doors, which flap open like big wooden wings hanging off the walls.

Herc says, "He's really not going to see his mother?"

Hermes shakes his head. "Would you want to watch your mother die right in front of you?"

Herc clears his throat.

"Right, I forgot." Hermes marches forward through the flapping doors.

The lights seem duller in the waiting room. The smell of antiseptic gel and too much chlorine tickle the outside of his nose and burrows deep within his chest.

Hermes sits next to his little brother, whose legs kick off the ground and into the air the way a little boy kicks forward and back on a swing set.

"Are you sure?" says Hermes.

Brad turns to face the muted television. A woman with blond hair lifted completely off her face mouths something, looking like she's chewing a piece of steak on camera. Underneath, the words "Worldwide Aurora Borealis?" scrolls through on a dark blue ribbon.

"I'm sorry," whispers Brad.

Hermes wraps his arms around Brad's shoulders, still stuck in a stoic pose and focused on the television. "It's okay," says Hermes. "I promise."

Herc's shadow covers them both. "We could always just ask for Hell's help."

A woman and her son—no bigger than Brad, Hermes thinks— flashes them a confused look and two raised eyebrows.

"We were cast out," says Hermes. "We can't possibly do that."

"Sure we can," says Herc. "We sneak back in the way we snuck out the last time."

The woman gets up and moves two seats over. When her son doesn't follow, she grabs his hands and leads him over next to her, furthest away from the three godlings.

"Lucifer ordered us out of there. We are not to return," says Hermes. "Nice try."

"But you heard the lady. If she cannot fix the wound herself, then we can try magic."

Brad's ears perk up. He turns his head into the conversation. "Can that work?"

Hermes rests his hands on Brad's shoulders. "If we had access to magic. Sure, it's possible. But up here, we're too weak."

Herc's face perks up with a hopeful smile. "What about Demeter? Hecate?"

"Do you know where they are?"

Herc blinks twice, then shrugs. "No."

"Then we're back to square one."

"Well, let me go," says Brad. His eyes stay fixed on the television as he says this.

Herc shrugs. "Why not?"

"Why not?" Hermes stands up, whispering. "Because we were banned from entering. You included."

"But that's bullshit," says Brad.

"Language," says Hermes. "And yes, yes it is."

Herc grabs Hermes by the shoulder and hauls him off the chair. He keeps yanking, tugging at Hermes' arm until they are nearly half the room away. Brad watches with a raised eyebrow.

Of course he's not fooled. He knows they're talking about him.

"Why are you being such a dick?" says Herc.

"Me?" Hermes scoffs. "I'm not being a dick."

"You're being a serious downer."

"Downer?" says Hermes. "You have been up here too long. Stay away from the mall, will you?"

"Jokes are not going to get you out of this one so fast," says

Herc. "That boy over there, he wants to save his mother, and he needs to prove himself."

"He does not have to prove anything to me," says Hermes.

"That's not the point, and you know it. He wants to feel helpful. Why can't we let him?"

"We cannot just let him waltz into Hell without any supervision. He does not know the area, he does not know who to find, nor does he have any idea where to get into Hell. We need someone who is more experienced."

"Well, you were the messenger god."

"I was a trickster god, too, but I hardly fit that definition anymore."

Herc sighs. Hermes feels the warm, spicy-meat filled breath from his best friend.

Hermes holds his breath and takes a small step backwards.

Brad sits on the chair, his legs kicking back and forth. His hands fidget with each other, then the handles of the chair.

"Fine," says Hermes. "I will go. I have the best chance of making in and out without being detected."

"Your size is finally going to be an asset," says Herc.

Hermes looks forward and immediately sees his point, though he hates to admit it. The pointed view of Herc's left nipple pokes out at him from underneath his Ed Hardy shirt.

"Why do you say these things?" says Hermes. He turns and walks toward Brad, who lies around on the seats. His arms and body crunched up like he's lying in a metal hammock. His arms swing from side to side while he stares at the ceiling. His face holds still, seemingly preoccupied by something.

Hermes wishes he knew the feeling well, but if he's going to do this, he needs to do it well and do it fast.

For his brother and the woman he...likes.

7

What both of the godlings assume to be a doctor comes out of the back room where Sophie was wheeled back.

He stands with his hands over his hips, then folded across his chest, then back down by his side.

Hermes nudges at Herc's chest. He nods at the doctor. "He looks nervous," he says.

The doctor detects Herc across the walkway and takes a step back, surprised. He wipes his forehead and walks briskly toward them. The doctor stands before Herc and peers upwards, almost hesitating to look up to him. "Are you here for the stabbing?" he says.

"Sophie," says Hermes. "Her name is Sophie."

The doctor nods. "Right. Sorry." He clears his throat, staring at the ground. As he looks back up, he catches eyes with Brad, tucked behind Hermes's back. "There are some complications," he says. "In short," he says, "she's hurt and she's hurt bad. She's bleeding and not responding to getting stitched up." He decides to just rest his hands in his pockets. "I can't explain it, really. It's unusual."

Brad tugs on Hermes' jacket. "Is she going to die?"

The doctor smiles at Brad's glassy blue eyes. "We're going to do everything we can to keep that from happening," he says. To Hermes he says, "But for now, I just wanted to let you know, she's bleeding profusely, but she's not bleeding out. It's strange."

"So what does that mean?" asks Hermes.

"It means that we don't know what's happening. I've never seen this happen before." He shrugs. "I can keep you posted, but we don't know when she will stabilize. I'm sorry," he says. The doctor friendly hazel eyes offer Brad a hopeful smile and returns back behind the coffee brown swinging doors.

"So what does this mean?" says Herc.

"It means that I have to move fast," says Hermes. He kneels down in front of Brad.

Brad's lightning blue eyes drip thin streams of tears down his cheeks. He sniffles and wipes his nose with the back of his hand.

Hermes wipes the rest of the tears away with his thumbs and kisses him on the forehead. "We're going to do everything we can, okay?" He feels the tugging of tears behind his eyes. He lets out a long, smooth breath.

He can't cry now. If he cries, then Brad will know that they're in trouble.

When the electric sliding doors part, Hermes feels the sudden need to check his clock.

"Is there supposed to be a meteor shower?" he asks a woman hobbling into the emergency room.

She looks at him, smiles and bats her eyelashes. Though she walks in on a set of crutches, she stands tall in her shorts and flowered Hawaiian shirt. "I don't think so," she says with a smile.

Hermes pats her on the back and steps out to get a better look.

Long streaks of light stretch from the heavens, bursting from the clouds like search lights and shooting stars. The light itself appears golden, not yellow. Not sunlight. Brighter than any sun.

Hermes feels a pinch in his stomach. The lights remind him of the ethereal lighting of Hell. Only brighter. Cheerier. Warmer.

Brad pops his head out of the walkway. "Someone said something about a shooting star," he says.

The rest of the crowd stops what they're doing.

A female nurse pushes her wheelchair-bound patient to a small white van. The electric metal ramp lowers down with a motorized hum, but the nurse forgets to secure the man. "My shit," she says.

Soon, the wheelchair bound man and the driver, everyone is looking up, pointing at the sky.

"Superman?" says the driver.

"Those are really pretty," says Brad. It's the first time Hermes has heard his step-brother sound not depressed all day.

"Yes," says Hermes. "Yes, they are." At the end of each shooting star, he spots a dark orange dot. The orbs move as if dragging through the air the way jets look when they tear through the clouds.

"What are they?" Brad asks.

Hermes feels the breeze of the insides blast at the back of his shoulders and head. The blast of air disappears as fast as it appears.

"What the hell is that?" asks Herc.

"Your guess is as good as mine," says Hermes. He takes a step forward, but stops and holds his hand out to Brad. "Stay here."

"But I wanna see," he says.

Of course Brad doesn't pay attention to his commands. He stays tight against Hermes's legs, nearly hugging them with his shoulders.

"Is this from Hell?" he says.

Hermes looks down at him. The thought had never crossed his mind. Something his beautiful, this magnificent didn't seem like a Hell kind of feat.

Herc stands near the both of them, dwarfing his two step-siblings. "Why would Hell be attacking from above?" he asks.

"They wouldn't be," says Hermes.

"Is it an Olympian? Apollo?" Herc asks. "Is Zeus out?"

"Apollo would never make such a grand entrance. He's too full of himself. And Zeus? He would come find me. Probably for revenge."

Brad's hands grip the pockets of Hermes's pants and squeeze. Hermes feels the faint tug against his hips and he shakes his brother loose. "I'm sure there's nothing to be afraid of."

"Where are they going?" asks Brad.

Hermes traces the orbs' paths with his finger. He counts five of them thus far, but more come shooting from the clouds higher up. Each one explodes anew as if fired by the sun itself.

Hermes' fingers end over to the east. He looks upwards. "Europe, maybe?"

"Acheron?" asks Herc.

Hermes shrugs. "Maybe."

"Are they be from Heaven? You said they aren't from Hell."

Hermes smiles. "I would not worry about that, buddy." He rubs the top of Brad's head, messing up his hair. "Go back in and check on your mom. Stay with her and let me know if anything happens."

"Where are you going?" Brad tugs on Hermes's hand. "You need to stay."

"I need to get back into Hell. Maybe someone can help your mom."

Brad wraps his arms around Hermes's short legs. "Don't go." He feels the gradual pull of Brad dragging his body backwards, back into the hospital.

"But I have to go," he says.

Brad collapses to the ground in a mess of tears and sobs. His chest heaves up and down as he tries to speak, words that Hermes can only guess are variations of "Don't," "go," and "please."

Hermes tries to lift Brad up from the ground, but is interrupted by tapping on his back.

"Dude, you gotta come inside and see this."

8

Hermes struggles to keep Brad on his shoulders as he and about fifty other people try to watch the television in the emergency room.

The crowd in the room gets chatty, asking questions and speaking amongst themselves.

"What's going on?"

"Where are they?"

"Are we going to die?"

The same questions get thrown around like tennis balls, served from one person to the next without a single answer among them.

Hermes can feel the panic in the room, so thick that someone could—what was that phrase Sophie used all the time? Cutting it?

"Oh my gods will you people just shut the fuck up?" roars Herc.

The humans go silent instantly.

"Thank you," says Hermes. He tries to step on Herc's feet to get a better view of the television, which sat up in the corner of the room on a black metal arm extended from the wall.

Across the bottom of the screen flashes the words "Celestial" and "lights"

"We go now to correspondent at the scene, Brant Proctor. Brant, can you tell us what we're seeing right now?"

The newscast cuts to a scene of a man in a dark blue suit, his tie fluttering in the mild wind that whipped across South Carolina at the same time the lights came down. He holds onto the microphone like someone is going to steal it.

All of this, Hermes notices, and his hair is immaculate.

"We're here just outside of Columbia and witnesses claim that they saw what could best be described as alien spacecraft landing in the fields."

A group of Columbia locals gathers behind Brant and wave to the camera, smiling and giggling.

"However, our investigation has not recovered any spacecraft of any kind. In fact, our radars and weather services indicate that the lights are in fact not natural."

After the man says this, the television cuts off and the screen goes into bars of maroon, blue, and green.

A piercing, long beep streams from the television. Herc and Hermes both slam their hands against their ears.

"What is this?" says Hermes.

"It's the TV," says Brad. "It's not working anymore."

"What the fuck was that?" shouts one of the patients. He holds his respirator at his side while waving a weak fist at the television.

"It's a government cover up," says someone else, a woman's voice.

The girl who came in earlier holding her elbow like it was broken, the whole arm a deep blue-maroon bruise screams the word aliens.

Hermes latches onto Brad's legs and tries to flip him off his shoulders.

Herc grabs hold of the boy and lifts him off with ease.

"We need to get out of here," says Hermes. "These humans are going to go crazy and tear this place apart. It's like Gomorra all over again."

Herc nods with a smile. "Let me," he says.

Herc stomps onto the ground. Tables rattle and even Brad stumbles backward.

Any of the humans close enough to a doorway gets inside it and braces both walls. "Earthquake!" someone shouts.

"There's your walkway," says Herc. He motions toward the doorway with an open hand.

Hermes takes Brad's hand and helps himself to the hallway with the examining rooms.

"Have a seat," says Hermes.

Brad sits down. He tucks his hands between his legs and sits still.

"Can you watch him?" Hermes says.

Herc nods. "Yeah, I got the little man, don't you worry."

"I do not know how long this will take," says Hermes. "Promise me you will keep an eye on her."

Herc nods. Hermes can see that he understands everything that Hermes just can't say right now. "Don't you worry. I got this."

Hermes nods and heads for the chaos of the emergency room's waiting area.

9

Hermes follows the lights that rip through the sky, cutting through the clouds and landing somewhere in the distant horizon. It seems no matter how far he flies, Hermes cannot find the true destination of these balls of light.

Near as he can tell, however, they land somewhere over the Southern Europe.

Hermes hopes that he also needs to go to Southern Europe is just a coincidence.

At the speed of sound that Hermes travels, the balls of light travel slower through the air. This makes it easier to keep an eye on them.

Unfortunately for him, he finds it difficult to see exactly what they are. The balls glow with such fiery brightness that it's like staring into Apollo's chariot.

Instead, Hermes directs his eyes downward into toward the ground. The balls seem to want to land somewhere north of him.

Italy. Maybe Switzerland.

He'll have to reserve time to check this out later. Now, Sophie's life hangs in the balance. Everything he cares for depends on him.

. . .

HERMES'S SANDALS touch down on the moist, sandy beaches of the River Acheron. The river's reeds appear to have grown somewhat back into place, but there's more noise here.

Not human noise. No boats or motors. No fishermen or hunters yelling at each other.

No, this is a dialect he hasn't heard in years. Maybe even centuries.

Hermes' wings flutter him over the water's edge to the long grasses that drape over the edge of the river. He kneels down and peers through the thick reeds.

He spots the source of the commotion at the rocky wall that hides the entrance to the Underworld.

Tall winged men and women—white with golden yellow and orange hair—stand around in groups of two or three. Their clothing suggests official military. But their suits are white with silver trimmings and etchings along the sides that look like feathers.

A single fancy chestpiece covers each of their torsos, glimmering in the sunlight when they turn to listen to the more decorated one's orders.

"And we're to make sure that no one gets in or out," he says. His sandy blond hair is cut short around his ears and temples. His armor has the markings of a golden eagle across the chest, with the wings stretching clear around the chest piece to the back.

Hermes studies the eagle crest. "Oh shit," he whispers to himself.

He's seen that crest before. The only other person he knew to have white and golden armor: Lucifer the Lightbringer. The original general of Heaven's army before the War for the Throne.

"Sir," says a young-looking angel. Maybe still a teenager by human standards. She's smaller than the other angels, but has nearly twice the energy. Her quick steps take him from the doorway to Hell to the leader's position in only a few seconds. "I believe we can secure this entrance. There is no sign of movement from inside."

"Have we entered to find out?" says the leader. His gaze is intense, serious.

"Well, no, but—"

"Then guess what I'm going to say next, Jamaerah?"

"Yes, Michael, sir," the young angel says. She clicks her heels together and gives a spirited, but shallow bow. "We'll be right on it." She begins to march away from the one she called Michael.

Michael quickly turns his attention toward the doorway and says something to another angel, something Hermes doesn't quite catch.

For now, his attention stays fixed on the youngest angel. She has sharp features despite her young age, smooth complexion with large sea green eyes that commanded allegiance.

Hermes checks behind him. The coast is still clear. The angels lie before him, guarding the entrance through the River Acheron.

The others, he imagines, are still covered by the other angels.

Hell is officially off limits.

Not that they weren't banned or anything.

He stands up and tiptoes backwards so as to not gather any attention.

This, however, doesn't seem to work.

"Michael! Jamaerah! Up there!"

Hermes runs only a few steps before taking flight.

The angel's armors rustle and clatter behind Hermes before he hears flapping of much, much larger wings.

"Dammit all to hell," Hermes says.

His wings pick up speed, flapping enough to give Hermes a lead that he's not sure he can maintain.

The angels, being warriors, are fast. Almost too fast for the type of armor they carry. They haven't, however, pulled weapons.

Yet.

Maybe they just want to talk.

Maybe they don't know who he is.

Like there are tons of other gods who fly around with winged sandals.

Dammit, Hermes, you blew your cover, he thinks.

Flying somewhere over the island of Sicily, he hears the female angel they call Jamaerah bark orders.

Something, something flank.

Hermes sighs. He knows what that means.

Hermes slaps his hands next to his torso and makes himself into a thin human-sized bullet. Gradually he drops his height until he's just above the Atlantic Ocean. If he were to stick his tongue out he could get a taste of the briny goodness of the waters.

"Come on," he says. "Give it up."

Hermes dares not look behind him. He still hears their flaps, but they seemed to be slower, quieter.

He slows his speed down and notices that the wings don't catch up with him.

The female angel shouts something to her soldiers. Orders.

So Hermes decides that it's time to play a little game.

10

_____

Over the blue waves of the Atlantic Ocean the salty breeze blows through Hermes's hair. His cheeks burn from the cold wind that whips past his ears.

Fast approaching in front of him, a series of green specks. Islands. Somewhere near the Equator in the New World.

The angels that follow him from behind appear to match his speed. The frequency of their flapping tells him that they speed up and slow down when he does.

He grins. Why not just ask him where he's going? It's not like he would lie.

Hermes's flapping ankle wings slow down to a crawl. He flies so slowly it appears that he walks along the surface of the water.

The island of something or another lies just a few hundred meters in front of him.

If the angels want to play hardball, Hermes is ready to bat.

Hermes imagines himself to be Jesus, walking along the surface of the Dead Sea. He holds out his hands to get the natives' attention. Arms outstretched like the cross that Jesus was nailed upon.

He takes steady, confident, religious steps toward the surface.

If the angels want to pursue, they'll have to risk exposing themselves.

Hermes extends a bright smile to a little boy playing in the water. His dark, caramel-colored skin contrasts with the pale hazel eyes he uses to watch Hermes touch ground onto the white sandy beach.

He turns around to watch the surface of the water. No waves. No flapping wings.

Has he won or are they simply waiting out of sight?

The boy drops his pail and plastic shovel and watches Hermes hover over the earth.

Hermes waves. "I hope you were a good boy this year," he says.

The boy nods his head up and down. "Si."

Hermes smiles back. "Good." He waves goodbye and takes to the air again.

It's in his best interest to save his hide, lay low. Keep from being spotted.

But whatever is going down, it's bigger than they thought.

The humans, they'll never understand what just happened. But Herc and Brad and Sophie.

Oh, shit. Sophie.

His wings pick up speed and carry him off across the waters toward Florida and up the Everglades. He knows he risks humans watching him fly, but today he's not in the mood to play it safe.

Brad. Herakles. They have to know what's going on.

And the closer he remains to the humans, the less he'll see of his pursuers.

Or ex-pursuers.

Hermes extends his hands back behind his head and relaxes, flying backwards. He turns around to face the bright, baby blue sky that reminds him of the poorly painted sky in Brad's room. Narrowing his eyes a little, he identifies three specks of black among the clouds, small V-shaped shadows hovering just above him.

"You clever bastards," he says with a smile.

Sure, this was stressful. Lives are on the line.

But it's not every day Hermes gets to flee from someone who can fly as well as he can. A race is a race, even if it's for one's life.

Hermes keeps his pace, climbing up the coast of Florida and just off the beaches of Georgia until he recognizes the South Carolina lowlands. The swampy emerald green smells of moss and mud, even from out here.

Returning home is too risky.

Going too far inland means Hermes will direct them to the cities.

Good for trying to get rid of them. But that would be calling their bluff.

Hermes runs the odds in his head. While he is a god who could gamble with the rest of them, he sees no positive end in sight, especially with the chaos breaking out.

Sophie and Brad. They needed his protection. At all costs.

It's almost too late to take the angels some place else when Hermes comes back to the reality of the chase.

The dots hover just above the clouds from where Hermes can see them. Most humans won't bother to look up.

What they are doing is smart.

But Hermes? He's much smarter.

He directs his flight to just around the town of Saraday. His path circles around in the skies until he flies among the branches of the thick forests that borders the town.

He slows his pace just long enough to hear the rustling of the branches behind him.

The angels are noisier than the largest birds. Sloppy and loud like an elephant with wings.

But Hermes, small and light, maneuvers among the branches with a quick speed that Brad would call "ninja."

Hermes's eyes meet a large boulder buried into the ground. The top stretches out into the air and rounds out like a small hut.

This was where they came out of Hell nearly a year ago. When he rescued Sophie from the long, slender grips of Death the first time.

He uses what little magic he has left to blend into the

surroundings around him. To the naked human eye, he appears blurry and colorful. A breeze among the trees.

To the angels, well, he's not sure.

But it's worth a guess.

He lands on top of the rock and waits, standing upright and proud. He rests his loose fists on his hips and stares up and out into the trees.

The branches crack and rustle with the heavy, stumbling angels. Guess there are no trees in Heaven, Hermes thinks and smiles.

He imagines just what he sees on television when watching cartoons with Brad. Cloudy fluffs like marshmallow cream. Bouncing from cloud to cloud while wearing curtains and looking like a Roman senator from ages ago.

Something large cracks behind Hermes. He figures it's time to go.

He leaps off the rock and curves his trajectory with his wings to fly into the rock.

Except just as he expects to feel the cool breeze of the dark tunnel, he feels nothing but a warm set of knuckles along his back.

"Where do you think you're going?" The girl they call Jamaerah smiles with a disarming smile.

"Go to Hell," says Hermes. He smirks as he enjoys the wordplay.

One of the angels peers into the cavern and looks back at Jamaerah. "He isn't kidding," the angels says. His voice is deep, hurried.

None of the angels sound out of breath.

If he could reach around, Hermes would kick himself.

He was outclassed all along.

They were just following him. Seeing where he was going.

"It's another doorway," says the angel.

Jamaerah nods at the others and says, "Get Michael."

"Save your energy," Michael says from above. He extends his arms out and lands in a soft thud next to Hermes's frozen position. "Who are you?" he asks.

Hermes spits on the ground and grins.

Michael peers down the cave while Jamaerah shakes Hermes in place. "Is this what I think it is?" he asks. Michael's eyes—golden eyes—meet Hermes's as he hangs upside down by Jamaerah's powerful grip. "Where does this go, exactly?"

"I believe it goes to Hell," says Jamaerah.

Michael massages his chin for a moment and then turns to face the other angels. "Guard this exit as well. Nothing gets out of that hole alive. Nothing goes in without my permission first."

"But sir," says Jamaerah, "if we just go in, we can make sure that no one comes out."

Michael clicks his heels. "We are not starting a war, Jamaerah. We are ending one." He turns to Hermes. "Now who are you?"

"Fuck you," says Hermes.

Jamaerah's grip loosens on Hermes as she shakes him yet again. "You will treat him with respect. Watch your tone."

The woman's grip is tight around his foot yet again.

"The better question is, who are you?" Hermes asks.

"So it does talk," says Jamaerah.

"Indeed it does, you rat with wings."

Michael clicks his tongue and then kneels down to meet Hermes at eye level. "If you just answer us this one question, we can go ahead and let you go."

"Why are you here?" says Hermes.

"Do you even know who we are?"

"Let's see. Wings on your back. White and silver armor." Hermes hrms and haws for a moment before widening his eyes with a great big smile. "Are you from the circus?"

Jamaerah looks to Micheal. "Please? One more time?"

Michael shakes his head. "Let him go."

"But…"

"Let him go," says Michael. "He's not going to answer us, and I am not in the business of taking prisoners. He is on Earth and therefore in our jurisdiction." He pauses and looks to Hermes. "Let's just keep an eye on him for a while."

Hermes feels the sudden wet cold of the grass against his cheek.

The rest of his body folds over his shoulders and soon he's lying, face-planted into the moist soil.

"If he becomes a problem, then we'll deal with him."

"But he was spying on us."

"We don't know that," says Michael. "Nor do I care. We won the war," he says with a concerned smile. "It is best we show mercy upon our new subjects."

11

When Hermes arrives at the hospital doors, he finds himself limping yet again. The landing part was no problem.

That time he was held by his ankle by an overzealous angel?

That could have gone better in his opinion.

The outsides of the one-story building that the natives called the hospital is completely empty. Devoid of people and of sounds. Even the birds refused to chirp. Something about those lights brought everyone to their knees, hiding in cellars and churches and praying for forgiveness.

The afternoon creeps up on Hermes as he checks the skies for more angels. In his travels he had counted hundreds of them. At the moment they appear as rare as true shooting stars.

And now with the purple-pink along the edge of the horizon, the lights now shine white and blue against the darker indigo of the afternoon skies.

Hermes gets that feeling in the back of his head, like he's being watched from afar.

"What do you want?" says Hermes. He stops at the front door entrance to the hospital emergency room. While it's quiet outside, the insides hustle with running doctors and panicking nurses.

The doors glide, slow and steady, to their resting, closed state. In the reflection of the glass he spots a woman with long black hair pulled over her shoulder. She wears a dress that fits so tight she could have only been poured into it like pancake batter.

"Nice to see you, too, sexy." Lilith rests her dark manicured hand on Hermes's still shoulders.

"How did you get out?" says Hermes.

"Out?" she says.

Hermes turns around and stares directly into Lilith's forehead. Searching her in the eyes—to Lilith at least—will only antagonize her, make her think that maybe there's something still to be had.

"Yes, out." Hermes shoves her hand off his shoulder. "What do you want?"

"I wanted to tell you I'm sorry for what happened to Sophie." She sounds sincere in her apology, but she's from Hell. Lying is practically currency down there.

"Bullshit," he says. "What do you really want? Did you do it?"

Lilith gasps and makes a slow, dramatic clasp toward her chest. "Me? You seem quick to judge."

"You seem quick to forget," says Hermes. "We're over. Extinguished. Done."

"And I can't just be nice? Send my condolences?"

"I do not need your condolences, woman. She is not dead yet."

"That's what I came to talk about," says Lilith. "We've got problems."

Hermes doesn't catch the rest of Lilith's comments. His brain swims with a fierce need to reach the edges of his memory, to remember everything he heard and seen just today.

Lilith's presence, well, it just makes it too difficult to think about anything other than revenge. Maybe violence. Maybe some yelling for good measure.

"Are you even listening to me?"

Hermes storms past the crying and praying crowd in the waiting room. He is followed by Lilith, who stops momentarily to take note of the forty or fifty people still kneeling, heads nodded forward and mumbling something to themselves.

"Seriously?" she says.

Hermes ignores her. The doors thwap closed behind him.

Soon, another slap of Lilith's hand against the swinging doors opens them up.

"Do not just walk away from me," Lilith commands.

Hermes goes through the second door.

Again, the doors slap open behind him. "

"What the hell is your problem?"

Hermes had expected that a doctor would stop her any second now. He's amazed she got this far.

"No, I am not listening," he says. "That's why I just kept walking. Go home. Get away from here."

"Why is she here?" says Brad. His little feet stomp on the tiled floors. His heels squeak as he tries to stop in mid self-righteous march. "Why are you here?"

Lilith flips her hair and points at the kid. "Cute. He's the one pulling the shots now?"

Hermes feels a kick at his heels. He can tell from Lilith's eyes moving slowly upwards that Herakles has stepped up behind him.

Feeling smug, Hermes crosses his arms across his chest. "Answer the question."

"Because we need your help."

Hermes waves her off with a wave of his hand. "We were banned by the Lightbringer himself," says Hermes. "If you're not going to pay attention, then we don't want you here."

"Did you do it?" says Brad. He sniffles back some tears.

Hermes pulls Brad closer to him and rests his hands lovingly on Brad's shoulders.

Brad continues his stare at Lilith, who refuses to acknowledge his presence and questions.

"So you are not going to come get what is rightfully yours?" Lilith says with a smile and a not so subtle lick across her lips.

"I told you we are over," says Hermes. "Not that we were ever on, I guess."

"That's not what I'm talking about."

Herc grabs Lilith's hair and pulls forward. She stumbles

forward, barely catching herself from falling. Her chin smacks into her chest and she's left staring at Brad's feet in front of her.

"I think you forgot to answer a question," Herc says between clenched teeth.

Hermes smiles. While the rest of the hospital is left dealing with the wounded and the panic, he gets to watch his worst enemy— okay, one of his worst enemies—get tortured by his best friend. That loyal, loveable, big lug.

If only he could squeeze harder. Just a little bit.

"If you let go of me, maybe I can tell you," she says.

An orderly comes by the scuffle and pauses. His eyes search Brad's for some sign of problems. Stress? Trouble? Should he maybe go call for help?

Hermes shrugs and waves him away. "We're fine. Thanks."

The orderly walks away.

"Says you," mumbles Lilith. She fixes her breasts, shoving each one back into her tight, tight bra.

"As you were saying?" says Herc.

"As I was saying," Lilith takes a quick breath. "Hell is in chaos at the moment. That little stunt you pulled last year really ran a number on them."

"What stunt?" says Hermes.

"Taking the boy? Getting Ba'al killed? Now Lucifer has no generals and there is a rush to take his place. As a matter of fact, lots of people are not fighting to take that place. Lucifer is left to defend his tower against the general wannabes and their pathetic little armies."

"Is Lucifer going to be dethroned?" asks Herc.

Lilith answers with a cackling laughter that echoes in the hallway. She stops when she notices that no one else has bothered to laugh with her. "Trust me, honey, you wouldn't want that. None of us want that."

"Why not?" says Brad. His arms are crossed across his chest, just like Herc. He scowls at Lilith, lips pursed. Putting a front.

"Because," says Lilith, "the contenders—you know, hopeful

generals—could be worse than Lucifer. Any one of them could turn out to be a worse Prince of Hell.

"Who else is in the running?" says Hermes.

"Be'elzebub, Mam'mon."

"Mam'mon!" says Herc. He crunches his knuckles under his fingers. "I'd love to see that bastard one more time."

Lilith rolls her eyes. "With the army that he has, you'd be lucky to even get close to that bastard. He's untouchable. Probably the worst thing to happen to Lucifer since being cast out of Heaven."

"He's gotten that powerful?" says Herc. His grin hasn't disappeared. He looks hungry, eager to fight. Hermes had seen that look in his eyes before—right before he slew the Nemean Lion.

"Why do you think I'm here?" says Lilith. "If that asshole makes it to the throne, we're all fucked."

12

B rad almost steps on Lilith's obsidian black high heels, shiny, sharp, and deadly. "You still didn't answer my question," he says.

"For Christ's sake, kid, I didn't have anything to do with your mother."

"How do I know you're not lying?"

"Because sometimes life is that fucked up for you. That's why."

Hermes pulls Brad behind him.

"Be nice, Lilith. He's had a hard day."

"Who the hell hasn't?" she says. She waves her hands in the air to help prove her point. "Take a look out there," she says. "We have people praying to a group of glowing balls from the sky. Fucking morons."

"Balls from the sky?" says Herc.

"I was going to get to that part," says Hermes. He clears his throat. "I think we are going to have lots of problems."

Herc steps forward. "Like good problems or bad problems?"

Lilith raises an eyebrow, then the back of her hand. "Good problems?" she says. She lowers her hand, deciding that Herc's face isn't worth the pain it'll cause her.

Hermes shrugs off the stupid question. "It could be bad. Very, very bad."

"What about Hell?" says Brad. "Can they help?"

"I cannot get in," says Hermes. "It seems to be blocked."

"Like I was telling you," says Lilith.

"Blocked by these angels."

Brad loud-whispers, "Angels?"

Herc takes a set on the small metal bench that sits against the wall. "This is not good."

"Why isn't it good?" says Brad. "I thought the Angels were good people."

"That's just what they want you to believe," says Hermes. "Just like us, they can be good or they can be bad. If they're here on the Earth realm, then that can only mean—"

"That Heaven is making the first move," says Herc, "but why?

"Because of the infighting in Hell," says Lilith. She takes a seat next to Herc and rests her hand against her forehead as if this is the reason she's going to faint.

Not the fact that she's wrapped like an Italian sausage in that dress, not the fact that she nearly runs out of air she yells so much. The stress of knowing that Heaven could win, that is what makes it.

"If Hell can't get its shit together, then that means the world is out of balance."

"And what's so bad about that?" says Brad. "I thought Hell was a bad place."

"Who cares about Hell and Heaven right now? What about Sophie?" says Hermes. He points both of his hands, exasperated, at the back doors leading to surgery. "She's dying and we can't do anything about it. We have to rely on these human doctors. Those idiots who can only sit on their thumbs and tell us that she's in trouble."

The word human tastes like sour milk coming out of his mouth. The word human and the idea of fixing things seem counterintuitive. Humans have been trouble. Too much trouble since they were first put on this earth. By Zeus or God or a great big egg in the sky—whomever you want to believe.

"Dude," says Herc.

Hermes grits his teeth as he hears "dude" for the who knows how many millionth time just today.

"Dude," says Herc, "you need some relaxing time." Herc picks Hermes up by the waist and hoists him over his shoulder.

Hermes's arms drop down over Herc's strong back. His entire body sways back and forth with each of Herc's thunderous steps back into the waiting room, where the crowds panic and cry and pray like it's going to fix it all.

Cast it all away.

"Here," says Herc. He hauls Hermes off his shoulder and drops him into a seat.

The lights begin to flicker in the room and everyone peers upwards.

Those who were praying stick their hands tighter together. Close their eyes tighter. Pray harder.

The screams stop screaming and faint instead. Hermes's head silently thanks them.

"Want some coffee?" says Herc.

"Coffee will not help," says Hermes. He feels his underwear ride up underneath his pants. Only wearing underwear for a year, he's still not quite used to them.

The idea of underwear came from none other than Sophie, who insisted that if she had to live next to a bunch of barbarians, they could at least look like they were civilized.

Apparently civilized men wear underwear. Tight, white underwear.

Hermes adjusts his seating and picks at his crotch. "What now?" he says.

The crowd turns to the television and silences themselves. They hold still, captivated like a kitten by a laser pointer. With each word that passes by the bottom of the screen, each if their heads move right to left, reading.

"What's going on?" says Lilith. She kicks open the door with a subtle flick of her heels against the coffee brown door. Behind her Brad shuffles in.

His eyes look more open, not excited, but adjusting.

But there's something about him that stands out now. Something deep in his eyes—a lightning, a fire, something crackling—that reminds Hermes of his father, Zeus, during the war against the Titans.

The entire crowd turns to face Lilith. All of those sick, panicked faces and eyes blinking and quietly whispering to her telepathically, "Shut the hell up."

"What?" she says and shrugs.

Brad runs to Hermes's side and hangs on his shoulder. Herc rests a giant bear-paw hand on the boy's shoulder and they all turn their heads to the television.

The scene is outside. The clouds glow bright against a midnight blue sky. Each of them has a phosphorescent glow that you only see in Northern Lights, a sight that Hermes has only been able to see just a few times in his life.

As a messenger of the Gods, his job never required him to go much further than the Alps for the most part.

The reporter's hair nods back and forth, the forehead attached and moving quietly. His itty bitty eyes peer up and then a look of surprise. He nods and the camera pans away from him.

The words LIGHT GIANTS FROM THE SKY pan below.

"Oh shit," says Lilith.

Everyone turns to Lilith once again.

"What?" she says. "You were all thinking it."

13

Michael has watched this area before, deep within the clouds, as the little people of the earth gather on these black, tar-encrusted streets in tight packs. Together they would gawk at the man they whispered about, calling him "Papa."

Pope.

The black street is really more of a large circus, the Roman idea of an amphitheater where the masses come to be entertained.

Before today, they were entertained by the appearance of the Pope, the head father—this poor, poor, misguided man—who led a large population of Earth in the direction of what they called "Christianity."

Today, Michael stands atop a building shaped almost like a human boat. Sharp pointed end, a blunt base that looked over something of a key-hole shaped encirclement.

The buildings, however. The buildings were pretty. White columns against yellow and sand-colored walls in other attached buildings.

It was an attractive monument to a religion long past its prime. This, Michael had to believe.

If only they knew the truth.

Michael blinks, shakes his head, as the people come into the roundup of human cattle. The group had already existed. They had anticipated a visit by the Pope. After the bright lights, Michael had overheard earlier, they thought that maybe God wanted them to appear before the basilica.

These misguided souls.

"I believe they are almost ready for you," says Michael. He looks over his shoulder, pulling back his cape as it flutters in the evening lights.

As the humans gather, they begin to make a dull roar down below. White noise, but getting denser and denser as the night grows longer.

From here, Michael feels their apprehension, their worry. He feels the mothers crying, hugging their children. The fathers and older men clutching to their families. To their rosaries. To their last remnants of families long past.

All of this he hears, and his heart breaks. His heart tugs at his brain. It cries for them to make some sense out of all of this.

"Did you hear me, Gabriel?"

Gabriel emerges from his circle of angels that hover about him. His generals and right-hand men. These were the angels that Gabriel could lead into Hell itself and each and every one of them would thank him for the opportunity.

They were what Michael was supposed to be.

But somewhere, somehow, Gabriel changed his mind.

"Yes, yes," says Gabriel. He adjusts his white armor. The silver eagle that spans across his chest glows a pearly blue and pink in the moonlight. "Let us deliver our message unto the people."

Michael surveys the group again. Just at the moment he turned his back, the group had grown larger, more dense.

There had to be more than a hundred thousand people pressed together, tight and sweaty. Even from up atop this basilica—Saint Peter's Basilica—Michael felt the heat and stench of their gaping breaths and unwashed, fearful bodies.

At the far eastern corner of the square, a rounded entrance, the people poured into the parking lot, sharing the space with little white automobiles parked in confused and disoriented lines.

As if following the lines of traffic, the large group of people filters into the next three streets to the left, the right, and straight down into the Italian streets.

The streets, Michael had never seen them this busy before.

His eyes trace the lines of people, the huddled masses, from the edge of Saint Peter's Square to the Egyptian obelisk to the base of the white, etched building upon which he stood.

He spots a dark-haired man, laying low near the front. He ducks underneath the crowd for a split second and then comes back up. His hand looks clenched tight. He holds it out to his side, flexing it as if feeling something he holds in his palm.

A rock? A weapon?

The man pulls his shoulder back and launches the rock up into the air. It goes up near Michael's head and reaches its peak nearly a foot away from his nose.

Michael's eyes widen, He peers back down at the man while snatching the rock from its descent. It is sharp on the corners, black and glistening in the holy light emanating from Michael's aura-like halo.

Michael holds the rock out between his thumb and middle finger, examining it.

A common rock. Though not naturally made. Something derived from the streets. A piece of tar. Maybe what the humans had called asphalt.

"A weapon?" he says to himself. "At us?"

These humans, Michael watches as a small corner of the room becomes flooded with angry, fearful humans. They clench their teeth, yet their eyes and eyebrows turn upwards, afraid. Unsure.

"We mean you no harm," says Michael to the crowd.

The wave of white and brown faces all turn upwards to stare at Michael's voice.

"We are not here to harm you."

Gabriel growls behind him. "What are you doing?"

Gabriel approaches the edge of the building. He pushes Michael back away from the edge and extends his white feathered wings. The wingspan takes up nearly six feet on both sides. The feathers are so pure, so white like fresh snow that they almost appear to give off their own light in the dark evening.

The crowd hushes.

Gabriel takes his hand and opens it in Michael's direction.

"Give it to me."

Michael's hand drops the rock into Gabriel's.

"Some of you may know us by name. Some of you may know us by our reputations." Gabriel's voice is deep, official. He uses the gift bestowed upon him by Jehova himself after Lucifer was cast out of Heaven.

The Deus Vox. The Voice of God.

From what Gabriel is doing now, even Michael feels the hair on the back of his neck stand on end. His heart pulses quickly underneath his chest. His brow sweats.

All this, and yet Michael feels paralyzed. Compelled to listen.

"We are the ones you may call Angels. Messengers from God. We are not these Giants of Light, but rather Bringers of Light, of Freedom. Of Peace on Earth. We have come with a message that all of humanity shall be peace. That Evil has been vanquished. That we, the Archangels of Heaven, are now your protectors and saviors."

The crowd falls into a random, seemingly lifeless applause.

The crowd closest to the basilica claps in a furious fashion. The rest of the crowd lies motionless. Unsure.

From here, Michael feels their collective heartbeat, their pulse, drop and speed up at the same time.

They are unsure, he feels. Unaware of the truth.

Some of them don't believe their message.

Some just do not believe in angels.

"And the one who threw this," says Gabriel. He holds the rock in his hands. It glistens in the light from his aura-like halo.

Eyes near the front of the crowd turn to the dark-haired man.

His head twists left, then right. Frightened. He pushes through the crowd and forces himself backwards, out to the streets.

From this high up on the walls, Michael sees that Gabriel's only inching along on his tiptoes.

Gabriel holds out the rock for more people to witness. "This is just a weapon of fear," he announces to the crowd.

The dark-haired man pushes through the crowd at a snail's pace. The people in the crowd, once again, they are paralyzed from the Deus Vox.

"But you are forgiven, you poor, poor, misguided soul."

The dark-haired man pauses and turns around.

Gabriel drops the rock from his hand. It rolls downward, clinging to the damp skin of the palm of his hand.

Reaching the edge, it drops to the ground. Falling end over end the way Michael has seen satellites fly in orbit around the Earth.

Gabriel's own golden eyes follow the path of the rock as it drops down, down, down into the crowd.

At this speed, it has enough force to kill someone. Michael's wings twitch behind him.

If he has to save someone, to catch the rock, he will do it.

If the humans are to believe them, to let themselves be protected, they need to trust the angels.

The rock nears the street and a gust of wind, localized and just above the crowd's head blasts through and crashes the rock against the basilica's wall.

Gabriel extends his wings again and holds his hands up toward the moon.

"Praise God and His wisdom."

Some of the crowd—the elderly and the women mostly—bow their heads, joining silently in the prayer.

Gabriel continues, bowing his own head while extending his hands out to form a cross. "Praised be the God and Father of our Lord Jesus Christ, He who in His great mercy gave us new birth, a birth unto hope which draws its life from the resurrection of Jesus Christ from the dead."

More of the crowd bows their heads at the hearing of the word "Jesus Christ."

Deep in the back, Michael feels the pain of tears leaving a young child's body.

She cries not from fear, but from relief.

Gabriel continues, "A birth to an imperishable inheritance, incapable of fading or defilement, which is kept in heaven for you who are guarded with God's power through faith."

Gabriel pulls his arms even further apart, wider than his chest. He reaches back and his wings extend in full behind him. The moon's shadow cast a glowing silhouette of him over a small portion of the crowd.

He continues, his voice deeper, more impassioned, "a birth to a salvation which stands ready to be revealed in the last days.

Amen."

The crowd, together, chants, "Amen."

14

By now Hermes has lost count of how many people have been on the television. He thinks maybe four or five reporters, twenty different "eye witnesses," and more experts than he bothers to count.

The television's sound comes in through bouts of fuzz and blares of sound that come crashing through the speakers.

The electricity, he gathers, must not be well-manned. Everyone going to church or boarding themselves up in their homes.

The new Apocalypse, one woman told the crowd as she gathered her children and exited the hospital. Her clothing was a mint green color, her shoes white and looking comfortable. A nurse.

Hermes hates to grin. Of course a nurse would leave. Just when the people need them the most.

Some of the more devout Christians hold up inside a far corner of the waiting room. They sit in a half circle, praying and holding their hands together and talking to God or Jesus.

"If this is the second coming of Christ," says Brad. "Where's Christ?"

Hermes shrugs. "There's so much we have to tell you," he says. "For now, let's just say he's not coming any time soon."

Brad nods, but his eyebrows remain crunched together, confused.

"So the angels are laying claim to the Earth realm?" says Herc. He pulls Brad closer to himself while keeping an eye on something over Hermes's shoulder.

Hermes looks over his shoulder and searches for who or whatever Herc seems to be looking at, a twitchy patient who sits restless in a padded waiting room chair at the end of the row.

"You're worried about that guy?" Hermes says, interrupting the flow of conversation.

"Well, yeah. He just seems weird."

"Twitchy?" says Hermes.

Herc shrugs. "Sure," he says. He looks down to Brad. "What's that mean?" he whispers.

Brad shrugs.

"Yes, twitchy," says Herc. He smiles.

Hermes checks over his shoulder again and thinks he sees what he's supposed to see.

At the edge of the row. A man, balding. He wears a plaid shirt that fits more like a tent than a button down. His pants sag off his legs and drape over his dirty tennis shoes.

His eyes look deep-set, dark around the base of his eyeballs.

No, not deep-set. Sunken. Like the dead Hermes used to ferry down to Hades and back.

Hermes clicks the picture in his mind and turns to see Brad, clutching his stomach and grimacing.

"Are you hurt?" Hermes asks.

Brad shakes his head. "No," he says. "Hungry."

"We should probably get some food," says Hermes. "It's been a while, hasn't it?"

Brad nods his head and looks over his shoulder. "I don't think there's any food here."

"Nothing that you would want to eat," says Herc. His eyes stay fixed over Hermes's shoulder.

"Do we want to try to take him home?" says Hermes. The coffee brown doors have not moved quite a while.

"Is that going to help anyone? We'll just be wondering about Sophie if we leave."

Hermes nods. "Then one of us needs to leave and get food," he says.

Herc's focus grows more intense at the man behind Hermes's shoulder. "yeah, yeah," he says. "I'll go. What do you guys want?"

Hermes looks to Brad for an answer.

"I don't know. Taco Hell?"

Hermes nods. "That again?" A pause as he looks deep into Brad's tired eyes. "Sure, we can do that."

Herc pushes his giant bear paw of a hand into Hermes's face, palm-side up. "Got the wallet?"

Hermes checks his pockets. He peers upwards at Herc, who still isn't paying much attention. "Um, no?"

Herc shrugs. "Fine. Then first I go to the apartment. Then I go get your food. So there."

Herc stomps off in his pouty, feet-so-big-they-could-be-boats-kind of way.

"So no food for a while?" says Brad.

Hermes shakes his head, then rubs Brad's. "In a while, buddy. Maybe we can sneak something from a vending machine or something." He reaches out to grab the boy's small, shivering hand.

"Are you cold?" asks Hermes.

Brad shakes his head no.

"You're shaking." Hermes lets his eyes check every crevice of Brad's tiny white hands. Nothing stands out. Nothing so much as a mole or a scratch.

His skin, it's nearly picture perfect. Even after being attacked by Herakles earlier this morning at sparring practice.

"You healed up really well," says Hermes. As the words leave his mouth, he wishes he could be the God of No Communication, pulling in each syllable and smiling the thoughts away instead.

"Yeah," says Brad. "I know." His gaze drops to the floor.

"But that doesn't explain the blood on your shirt," says Hermes.

Brad's silent, picking at stray bits of thread that poke out from his frayed shirt.

Hermes nods. "Right, so let's go get food, shall we? Maybe they even have ice cream."

Of course the two can't take more than three steps before being stopped by the creeper that Herc had his eye on earlier.

The man stands up in front of them. His eyes shift from side to side as if checking the room. But not looking at Brad or Hermes, but through them. As if talking to thin air.

"You got any change?"

Brad's fist tightens in Hermes' light grip. For a moment, Hermes twists his hands around, trying to loosen the grip and regain some flow to his fingers.

He looks down at Brad, whose face has gone nearly white, his ears red. Hermes thinks he can see the edges of Brad's jaw stabbing out near his ears, pressing or grinding his teeth together.

"No," he says. "No change. Sorry. I sent my friend to go get my wallet." Hermes shrugs and smiles. "But good luck to you anyway."

"I said I need money," the man says. "And I don't like your face."

Hermes takes a step back, lets go of Brad's hand. "My face?" He strokes the sides of his cheeks, his chin. His perfectly shaped nose. "I think my face is perfectly fine?" Hermes nudges over at another woman sitting patiently in the room.

The woman's curly salt and pepper hair bounces as she turns to look at Hermes.

"I'm sorry, ma'am, but you look like you know a good man when you see him. Do I have a bad face?"

The elderly woman smiles. Though her skin looks soft, probably because of the peach fuzz, the sudden appearance of wrinkles on top of the wrinkles causes Hermes to divert his attention back at their would-be attacker.

"Listen, buddy, I don't have anything."

The man grabs his head and drops to his knees. He rips his flannel shirt open, exposing a white T-shirt stained with sweat and maybe some sauce from something he may have eaten earlier.

Ketchup or barbecue sauce, Hermes can't tell.

"Can we get this man some help?" says Hermes. He kneels down to check the man for some kind of pain, maybe a gash or growth, something different around his ear.

But the man refuses to be helped. By the time he can grab the chair nearest to him to pull himself up, the crazy man already has his eyes set on Brad.

"Stay behind me." Hermes pushes Bradley behind him, shielding him from the chaos that he's going to see again.

Something, somewhere, has to go wrong. It always does.

"Those aliens, man, they're telling me to do weird things," he says. The man stands up, clutching his head in both of his hands, except this time, his mouth is open, his teeth bared.

Hermes had seen this look before. Usually in Minotaurs or centaurs. Even Ares, on occasion. The more bestial, the more ferocious.

"Just calm down, will you?" says Hermes. He extends his arm between himself and the man, hoping that it will serve as some kind of barrier to protect the kid, his stepbrother. "If something goes wrong, go run for Herc. Do you understand me?"

Hermes hears Brad squeak something and only imagines his stepbrother nodding his head "yes."

"Can we get this man some help, please?"

By now the hospital waiting room has turned into a ring of people centered around Hermes, Brad, and the man in red and green flannel.

The waiting room is calm, though devoid of any medical personnel.

Hermes hopes that this means they're back in the surgery rooms. Finishing up stitching Sophie back up.

Now that would be a good reason to ignore his requests for help.

"Brad, do you understand me?" Hermes says. He reaches his arm back around to feel for Brad, to ensure that he is still there, still safe.

Except he isn't.

There, anyway.

And maybe not safe.

"Brad?" says Hermes. He does the only thing he's pretty sure is pretty stupid the moment he does it: he turns around. "Brad? Where are you?"

Something moves around him, to his left and just outside of his field of view.

It moves too quickly to be human, so he ducks and protects himself. Whatever it is, it's shiny and lightweight, and thin.

"Watch out," says Brad.

Hermes lets up from his ducked, hands over his head, kind of take cover and looks up. He feels something cold and hard hit the side of his face, throwing him to the floor.

Hermes's eyes close at the impact, so all he hears is clanging of metal against bone, a grunting sound, and then something bouncing on the carpet twice.

Then sobbing.

Hermes releases his head from the safety of his forearms and grabs Brad. He pulls him close, checking for scrapes and bruises.

He finds nothing more than a wet, red face surrounding these lightning blue eyes that blink. Confused, but content.

"Are you okay?" says Hermes.

Brad nods. His body still shivers.

It's adrenaline. His little body isn't ready for war, for the rush of the kill. The shaking, the sweating, it's the body's way of getting rid of the excess anger and energy.

He's becoming more of a warrior godling by the day. In the last year, it's almost a complete turnaround from the little, curious boy he had met in the hallways of his apartment building.

"Oh my shit."

Hermes looks up to see Lilith standing, frozen in place.

"What did you do to this guy?" she says.

Hermes raises an eyebrow. "What do you mean?" He looks up to see what Lilith's eyes are locked onto.

In the doorway, just barely standing on his own, the man in flannel stands still. His calm voice defies the wrecked, bloody look in his face.

"What?" says the man, calm as a—what was the phrase Sophie used all the time?—a cucumber.

"Wow," says Lilith. She drops a yellow and white snack bag of chips. "You have a metal pole in your head."

15

Michael follows Gabriel's lead, dropping down to the black asphalt of Saint Peter's Square.

The crowd pulls back. Not out of considering, but of fear. After the death of the man who threw the rock, they dare not do anything silly to anger these angels, or aliens.

Michael feels the frustration of the crowd, the confusion of what to call these beings.

As they fall, each of the Archangels extend their wings to slow their fall. Their white, fluffy, feathery wings flutter in the wind, but remain strong at their side, pulling them up in small drafts.

Down below Michael watches as all four of their shadows gets larger, larger, the closer they get to the crowd of people.

He bites his tongue and knows deep down, this could have gone differently.

No, not could have gone differently. Should have gone differently.

Michael's own stomach trembles deep inside his gut. His heart beats faster. These things he feels, these thoughts he knows, these feelings that pierce his being, fast and quick as a lightning strike, because the people around him feel it.

The messages, the emotional waves that pulse through his skin, are all too strong for him to ignore.

The curse of being an empath, a link to the humans from the celestial homes above.

The two Archangels are followed by two more soldiers, Galadriel and Jamaerah. Their feet hit the ground with a light tap rather than a heavy thud. In this realm, their gravity is lighter than what Michael is used to.

He hasn't visited the Earth realm in such a long time. In the lifespan of a celestial being, it is maybe two days' time. In the life span of a planet full of tiny, fleshy mortal beings, it's eons.

"They are afraid, Gabriel," says Michael. "Just approach with caution."

Gabriel looks back at Michael with a coy smile.

Michael knows he won't be taken seriously, but it never hurts to try.

Even if he needs to take matters into his own hands.

Michael steps forward from the group and takes the front of the group. "Ladies and gentlemen, boys and girls of the Earth Realm."

A rock flies in the air toward Michael, end over end, bouncing off his chest.

"What is this?" he says. He looks downward to find the rock. Or was it a rock? A weapon of some kind? Mankind had created bigger and bigger weapons. Each one more deadly than the next.

And then, just as the weapons started getting bigger, they suddenly got smaller. Harder to detect.

Was this one of them?

He kneels down and searches the ground, running his fingers in the darkness against the shiny obsidian of the streets.

"You're pathetic," says Gabriel.

He stands tall in front of the group, taking front and center. His wings come out, full expansion in front of the crowd.

He does this for dramatic effect. If anything, Gabriel knew how to make an entrance.

In this beautiful city, the yellows and whites and sandy pinks of the basilica and surrounding buildings, in all of this color, Gabriel knew how to demand attention.

It is what had always made him a leader the other Archangels wanted to follow. They never had to because of rank. No one felt obliged to follow.

Each and every Archangel has a gift they bring to the celestial table of Heaven's Armies.

Michael's is empathy, an ability he used with great finesse to solve problems and encourage compatibility.

Gabriel's as he willingly displayed to the rest of the world, was inspiration.

And like a switch of light, like the way God activated the world with a word, Gabriel could turn his ability on at will.

Michael not so secretly envied that about him.

Gabriel's arms remain folded across his chest. His broad shoulders stand bare, sleeveless, in the crowd. Gabriel drops his armor from his body and lets it clang against the stony floor.

"Who dares to attack the Heavenly Archangels, those who have known the love of Heaven, the warmth of the Lord himself?"

The crowd goes silent. Unlike before, they don't offer up a human to sacrifice.

They had seen what happens when they offer—even though subtle means—up the culprit. They've seen the death that it causes.

Michael's head pulses with the voices he cannot read. Just emotions. Tugs at his heart, his stomach.

Gabriel floats just a bit higher over the ground, enough to look over the collective sea of worried and fascinated people.

"None? That weapon came out of nowhere, then?"

The crowd grows still.

Michael's palms sweat.

"Gabriel," say Michael. He reaches out to the angel. "Let them be. They are afraid. They must learn to trust us, and we them."

"Alieni!" a woman shouts at them, pointing.

The once quiet crowd grows into a dull roar of whispers and gasps.

Gabriel turns to the Michael. "They think us aliens?" He smiles.

His wings stretch further out, casting a large, triangular shadow upon the group of humans. "Is that what you think us?"

Michael could swear he hears a chuckle escape from Gabriel's lips. This is not a part of their plan.

"Gabriel, what are you doing?" Michael rushes to Gabriel's side, but something shiny, loud, a collective echo of stomps.

"What is this?" Gabriel says to Michael.

Michael sees the blue berets and green and black camouflaged uniforms. A small battalion of yellow and red-striped uniforms of the Swiss Guard.

Almost a hundred shiny metal guns point at the Archangels. The commands come at them from afar, from quiet and shaky voices. Too unsure if they—the alieni—will understand them.

But the guns, they think, those are almost always a universal weapon. Shouting plus pointing equals threats in almost any language.

"Just remember," says Michael. "They are afraid."

Gabriel drops gently to the floor and lands on his tiptoes. His wings fold back up behind him. His arms extend out as if offering a hug to any particular takers.

"My friends," says Gabriel. He takes a small step forward—small because they are surrounded by horrified, fearful humans packed into the area by the thousands. "My friends. We are not here to harm you."

A localized explosion. Something travels at Gabriel's chest in a straight, rapid line.

Even Michael can feel the shockwave of the impact, the metal bullet landing, then crunching, against Gabriel's powerful archangel chest.

Michael swallows. He knows what will come next.

Gabriel, to Michael's surprise, keeps his smile. He only offers his arms wider, further apart. "I come to you with arms wide open, to show you the love and grace that the Lord has shared with each of us."

Gabriel takes another step forward.

The crowd steps backward in slow trickles.

Another shot fired. Again, it hits Gabriel in the chest. This stuns Gabriel, if only for half a second. "My friends?" he whispers, losing his patience, losing hope.

Another shot fired. This bullet rubs past Gabriel's shoulder, eventually flipping off into the air and landing God knows where.

A sudden change in Gabriel's mood. His shoulders raise up, his chest puffs out.

His wings twitch, the ends fluttering about, ready to expand at any moment.

"And this," says Gabriel. Again, he takes to the air, though he hovers only a few feet out of the humans' reach.

Another bullet, but this one seems to miss.

"This is why God has not spoken to you," he says. "I am the Deus Vox," he claims. "The Voice of the Lord, who, in six days, created all you see before you. And this is how you repay his creations, his brilliance. His wisdom."

There's a metal clicking across the square at the entrance to the parking lot.

But one of the generals, a soldier, or someone in charge holds out a hand, says something quick and jumbled together. Maybe in Italian. Maybe German.

The gun pauses and lowers it barrel to the ground.

"This is why we must come. To bring justice to your mistakes. To show you the glory of sacrifice for the good of yourselves. For the good of God's plan."

Gabriel hovers just over the crowd now. The flapping of his wings is the only thing anyone can hear in the short eight kilometers that surround them on either side.

"It was a mistake to create you ingrates," Gabriel shouts to the masses, "God has mercy upon your souls and sent his son to help you. And this," says Gabriel.

He pauses and surveys the crowd. He dusts off the spot on his chest where the bullet bounced.

"This is how you repay him."

Gabriel's golden eyes glow enough to light the first ten feet in front of him like an incandescent cone.

"This," he says. "This will just not work. You cannot be trusted," Gabriel says. "You were given free will and you have abused it. Taken advantage of the Lord's forgiveness and love for you all. Some of you have even turned from that love. And like responsible shepherds, we have come to take you back to the flock. Willingly or unwillingly."

16

L ilith takes a salty potato chip and slides it into her mouth. She makes sure that everyone is watching first as she does this.

After all, it's hard to be sexy without an audience.

Then it's the slow step and pause that she does so well. That little bit of movement to make sure that everyone—at least all the guys—are staring at her. Wanting her.

"How in Hell did this happen?" She slides another crunchy chip into her mouth.

Hermes stares at her. "How can you eat at a time like this?"

Brad coughs. "Where did you to those?" he asks.

Lilith drops the bag to Brad's level. "Want some?"

Brad dips his hand into the bag and pulls out three greasy chips barely hanging on between his fingers.

"I don't know," says Hermes. He extends his hands as if to display the man, who's already too obvious for everyone to ignore.

"What's happening, guys?" says the man. What used to be green on his flannel shirt is now a dark red, so dark it's almost black.

The lower half of his face shines from the blood dripping down his cheek. Or what's left of it.

"Shit like this," Lilith says, drawing a line from top to bottom with her sharpened black nails, "just doesn't happen because you don't know." She pops another chip into her mouth. The crunching fills the silence and bewilderment.

The patients, it seems, do not freak out at the accident. A few take a step back, in case it's contagious.

But the others, they turn away, not looking. Even in an emergency room this is just too weird for them.

Hermes approaches the man with his hands up. He extends them out, putting yet another barrier, just in case the guy gets angry again and starts to attack like a hungry hydra.

"Stay back," says Brad. "Don't get hurt."

"Relax," says Hermes. "We're not going to hurt you."

The man's personality has gone bland. A blank slate. Like a soul lost in Purgatory.

"My face itches," the man says. When he goes to scratch, the pole gets in the way of his fingers. He pauses, confused by the extra something sticking out where it shouldn't be.

Lilith cackles, crunches another chip, then cackles some more. "These are surprisingly tasty," she says.

Brad hides behind Hermes. "I'm sorry," he mutters.

"There's nothing to worry about," he says. "It's okay."

"Is it?" Lilith offers Brad another chip.

He declines.

Lilith scoffs. "I mean, he's got a freaking pole sticking out of his head."

The man gasps.

"Oh come on, like you can't feel that thing sticking out?" Lilith says. "You humans are much tougher than we were led to believe," she says. "Heaven is going to have a hard time exterminating you."

Hermes throws her onto the seat. The bag bounces in her lap.

"Be careful, you almost crunched my chips," she says.

"You will shut the fuck up, or I will make you shut up," says Hermes. He looks at the crowd, A nothing-to-see-here smile. "We don't need a panic, you bitch."

"Who's panicking?" she says. "These people seemed to have accepted their fate."

"Because they aren't out there, but it's worse, isn't it?" Hermes says.

He searches for Brad, who takes a seat behind them on the chairs. Still silent. Still depressed.

"Angels do not appear in warrior's armor unless they want to hurt something. Unless it's needed."

Lilith's deep blue, almost purple, eyes lock with Hermes.

Hermes averts his eyes, covering them with his hands. "Stop that, will you?"

Lilith crunches down on another chip. "You have no idea what you're up against."

"Why don't you go back to Hell if you can't help," he says. "You have nothing to contribute."

"And yet, you waited this long to tell me to disappear." Lilith takes both of Hermes's hands in hers. Her skin feels soft on his own. Like skimming the surface of water soft.

"Because I thought you might be useful."

Lilith's greasy fingers trace the surface of Hermes's forearms, then jump to his crotch. She traces just the outline of his groin before Hermes takes a step back.

"You whore," he whispers. "I am not interested. Period."

Lilith crosses her legs, raising one high enough to give him a sneak peek. "That's a tragic shame," she says.

"Then you misunderstand," he says. "I am not going with you, I cannot save Hell. And I sure as hell will not try to be Hell's new commander. Overthrow Lucifer? What's wrong with you?"

Lilith stands up and adjusts her dress. "So that's a no, then?"

Hermes pulls back his shoulders and lets loose a roar into the air. Unfortunately, it's nothing like Herc's, that confident lion's roar that demands attention.

Hermes's roar only demands snickers from the group.

"If you really want to stick around this group, then march your ass right back into that surgery room and help out Sophie."

Lilith sucks at her teeth. "Why don't you ask me to impale myself on the Spear of Destiny?"

"Because I don't know where it is," he says.

Lilith does a half-smile, half-scowl thing with her mouth. "I cannot do anything about this. There are forces at work here that we don't understand. You don't feel anything?"

Hermes stands tall. He begins to nod, but it's not convincing to either Lilith or himself. "No, I guess I don't."

"Then you're already too far gone," she says. "You're more human than you know."

"I am not a human," Hermes says. The words erupt out of his mouth faster than he could stop them. These weren't the words he meant to say. Were they?

Lilith cracks another smile. "So you've got some of that Hellfire in you yet?"

"I am not domesticated," he says. The term that celestial beings use to mean becoming more human. Procreating, cavorting, and socializing with humans.

"Oh, I believe you," Lilith says. She takes a step forward and places the palm of her hand gently on his chest. "But the boys downstairs. Well, they think you've gone soft." Lilith's eyes lower down Hermes's torso.

Hermes takes his fingers and lifts her chin so her eyes meet his. "Eyes up here, witch. And it is not going to work. I cannot allow myself to go backwards. I have a family up here that I must take care of."

"And a fine job of it you're doing," says Lilith. A brother who's so afraid of himself that he's a danger to others, a woman whose life hangs in the balance. And an idiot half-brother who can't find his own dick with both hands. Fine job you're doing."

Hermes grabs at Lilith's throat and takes her down to the ground.

Lilith's eyes begin to water, but her blood-red lips part in a sexy smile. "There's that fire I remember."

Hermes lets go and stands up tall. His chest puffs out, he feels his neck stretching straighter. More confident.

It felt good, choking this bitch.

But of course, as with anything he likes or loves, it doesn't last.

"What the hell happened to him?" says a familiar voice.

The electric doors open in the distance. Herc emerges with small white paperbacks with a red lettering on them. They remain tucked up underneath his arms.

"Does he have a pole stuck in his head?"

Lilith points over at Brad. "He did it."

Herc's mouth drops open. First time in a short while that Hermes has ever seen him speechless.

Then, his lips crack into a smile, to a full grin. Then his bearded chin spreads open wide to reveal a proud, toothy smile.

"Dude!" says Herc. He drops the bags and holds up his hand. "High five!"

Brad raises an eyebrow and smacks Herc's hand with a light tap.

17

Hermes rushes to the Herc's side to pick up the white paper bags. The bags smell of salt and juicy meat. Something sweet mixed in there.

"Hey," Hermes says to Brad, tossing one of the three bags over to him. "It's your favorite."

The bag lands at Brad's feet. He holds his hands out in front of him.

"You missed," Hermes says.

Brad crumples up into a little ball. His face goes buried deep in his hands, his arms cupped around him, trying to push out the rest of the world.

"Buddy," says Hermes. He rushes to his step-brother's side. "What's the matter?"

Hermes tries to lift Brad up from his crouched position, but Brad's legs say hauled up near his body.

"What's the matter?"

Just the act of hearing the words seems to break the dam that held Brad's emotions in place. He begins to bawl so hard even his ears turn a deep red.

"Is he always like this?" says Lilith.

Hermes shoots her a look that says "Don't you dare open your mouth again."

Hermes tries to reach around Brad to pick him up, but his small five-foot-six frame doesn't have the power behind it.

He peers over to Herc.

Herc nods. His soft steps take him to Brad's position where he picks him up and cradles him like one holds a baby human.

"It's fine," says Herc. "The food will be okay. It just touched the ground."

Hermes coughs to get Herc's attention.

When the big, stupid lug doesn't look up, Hermes says, "It's probably not that," he says. Hermes nods toward the doors in the back.

Herc makes a silent, "Oh," with his mouth and rocks Brad back and forth.

Hermes holds his hand up to correct Herc. Brad is, in fact, not a baby, but he decides to let it go. It's not important right now.

This food, however, is.

He opens up the food and lets it slide out into the magazine-occupied end table.

The greasy paper-wrapped burgers leak their juices and ketchup over the faces of popular, attractive celebrities.

The other hopeful patients sit at the edge of their respective seats, damn near drooling over the smells and colors of the brightly wrapped sandwiches.

Hermes takes the largest one and carries it over to where Herc rocks Brad in his arms.

"Maybe he should eat," says Hermes.

Brad buries his head in Herc's strong chest.

"Or not," says Hermes. "What's wrong?" he says to Brad.

Brad sobs again. A deep, heavy sob that pulls his shoulders up around his ears.

"Maybe he just needs to be alone," says Herc.

Brad stops sobbing long enough to shake his head up and down.

"Really?" says Hermes. "Is that what you want?"

Brad pulls his face away from Herc's chest. He rubs his eyes with the backs of his hands and then his electric blue eyes meet Hermes's. "Yes."

Hermes looks down the hallway. The hospital waiting room grows with people, each hour some new groups coming in.

The problem is, no one seems to be getting called into the back rooms. No sign of anyone getting help.

Hermes scratches his head. It couldn't hurt, he thinks. At least he knows he can defend himself.

Against something human, anyway.

"Fine," says Hermes, "but please don't wander too far and do not go outside. Do you hear me?"

Brad nods his head slowly. He crawls off of Herc's lap and takes small steps off to the far corner.

"Keep an eye on him, will you?" he says to Herc.

Herc nods, "Of course. I'm not a complete idiot."

"I know," he says. "But you never know. Things are strange enough as it is."

Hermes feels the sharp, pointed fingernail of Lilith's hand poke along his shoulder. "Hey guys, you might want to come see this."

18

_____

Michael's wings shield him from the loud onslaught of piercing rubber bullets. The Italian and Swiss guard fire shot after shot at the four Archangels.

Never in a million years was it supposed to happen this way. This is not the way God had intended it.

"We cannot keep this up," says Michael. "I fear our mission has failed."

"I have fought the gods of old," says Gabriel. He uses his snowy white wings to protect him from the rocks and bullets thrown his way.

The pressure of the struggle causes him to move slower, but with the humans running away, screaming, there is suddenly more foot room for them to march toward the army quicker than before.

"I will not back down so easily," says Gabriel. "Do they not understand that we are here to save them?"

Michael moves his wings from his eyes just long enough to see evidence of their misguided attempt to save humanity.

"I would say not," says Michael.

"Ever the optimist, Michael." Gabriel unfurls his wings wide open and lets the rest of the bullets and rocks hit and then bounce off his chest. "When will you figure out that your weapons cannot and will not harm us?" Gabriel says.

He lifts up a leather boot, strapped up the sides with straps laden with gold designs, and presses it against the side of the obelisk in the center of the square.

He kicks it over. The obelisk's shadow twirls from the morning position to just over Gabriel's intended the targets. The gunfire ceases just long enough for them to scatter like roaches.

The obelisk shatters into several pieces, taking out the cars and shielded riot gear of the Italian military.

"We should try to minimize the amount of force we use, Gabriel. We do not want to harm God's children."

"Do you really think they are concerned with the same thing?" Gabriel says. He marches toward the military at the end of the funnel that bottlenecks the military down a narrow street lined with pink and sand-colored buildings.

Michael knows that Gabriel meant the question to be rhetorical, but as always, he has an answer. One that he feels will be sufficient to bring the conversation and the struggle to an end.

But he dares not bring it up. It is not what Gabriel wants right now. And as the Deus Vox, Gabriel's will is God's will.

When Gabriel reaches the far end the street just before the narrow roads, the combined forces of the Italian military and the Swiss Guard pause and reconvene.

They keep a constant eye on Gabriel, however, as they discuss with each other just what they should do. Their previous courses of action, Michael has noted, has not proved to be very successful.

He had always thought humans cleverer than that.

Michael hopes that Gabriel is not truly paying attention to their inability to fight successfully.

Any sign of weakness and Gabriel is sure to exploit it. It's how he managed to finish Lucifer's army and complete God's expulsion of the Lightbringer after only a few short months.

Michael shouts down the alleyway. "Gabriel!"

Gabriel pauses his stomping toward the armies to listen.

"We have done enough damage for now, Gabriel. We should let

them tend to their wounded. Let them heal and reconvene. What good is saving a humanity that is extinct already?"

Gabriel nods and turns to face Michael. "Fine, you may have it your way," he says.

The other three Archangels follow Gabriel's lead as he flies upwards into the clouds. The angels, all of them with their wings extended, flapping in slow unison, they must look like true gods themselves in the eyes of the humans below.

Even from up here, Michael feels the wonderment and awe that they inspire. He hears words that he doesn't quite understand.

But their intent he does understand. They used to mean them no harm. The humans were frightened, fearing alone and defenseless when confronted by winged giants. These four, spouting off a philosophy that lay mostly understood.

The humans, they were only doing what humans do with their free will. They were only doing what Jehova intended.

Gabriel's eyes look as if fire has struck them from the inside out. He smiles at his fellow Archangels with a grin that reminds Michael of the ancient battles nearly two thousand years ago. The battle for the throne, the fight to protect the Throne of Heaven from the likes of Lucifer and his armies.

It had been that long since Gabriel could physically confront another being—human or celestial.

Michael watches as Gabriel cheers on his friends and congratulates them all for a successful first day of Heaven's rule.

Heaven's protection, he meant. Gabriel must have just slipped.

Not Heaven's rule, but Heaven's protection.

19

The man with the pole in his head walks up to the waist-high check-in counter. The nurse's expression stays still, frozen, in something between horror and amusement.

"So there's nothing you can do about this?" says the man. His wound will not stop bleeding. Blood drips down his flannel shirt, now red and black and sticky.

"Sir, we are trying to get you in, but we have no one who is ready to see you." The nurse's voice is calm as she can be, but her eyebrows turn upward where they meet, her brow furrowed.

"What is really going on?" Hermes asks Lilith.

She shrugs. "I would not know where to start looking," she says.

"I cannot see why a hospital would stop taking new patients," he says. "Not unless they were already filled up."

"Shut up, you idiots," says Lilith. "We need to see this."

The television screen stops flashing reruns of the lights falling from the sky, instead revealing four tall winged giants in the middle of a crowd-filled street.

"What is this?" says Hermes. "Turn it up."

"It is up," a woman with her wrist bandaged up tight in white gauze says. "Shit's just fucked up."

"Then shut up," he commands. "Maybe we can hear it then."

The woman looks off to the side, insulted.

Lilith snorts back some laughter.

On the television, the winged giants—angels, Hermes recognizes—cease their walking toward to the crowd to take to the air. As they fly upwards, one of them looks familiar to Hermes.

"That one," he says. He points to the screen. "That one right there. The little one with the brown hair. He is the one that I saw chasing me from the River Acheron."

Lilith squints at the TV.

"I don't see anything. Just these winged freaks on the television."

"Angels," Hermes says. "Those are angels. At least that is what they told me."

Lilith looks at Hermes with a look of concern. "You met them?"

"Well, not met met. Maybe just listened in on their conversations. I tried to get back into Hell to see about getting some magical help for Sophie when they blocked off the path."

His voice trails off and he stares at Lilith.

"You can't get back into Hell, can you?"

Lilith shakes her head. "And you thought about that all by yourself?"

"But that means you are stuck in the Earth Realm," says Hermes. "Why are you out here to begin with?"

Lilith crosses her arms and shifts her weight to her hips. The black dress that she's wrapped in pulls and tugs on her skin to bunch up at the top of her curved hip. "I told you already."

"But you would have been out for a while now," says Hermes. "At least a few hours. Maximum, maybe half a day."

Lilith doesn't say anything to incriminate—or not incriminate—herself.

"Were you following me?" he says.

She shakes her head. "No, why would you even ask that?"

"You said you wanted to get me to go back, but you knew you couldn't go back, didn't you?"

Lilith shrugs and looks away. "Maybe I did."

Hermes tries to study Lilith's eyes, but she looks away into the distance any time he gets close.

Herc pushes himself off the wall just underneath the television. From that location, he could keep an eye on Brad.

Brad had preferred to keep his distance and be alone for a while. For what reason, no one knows. But thanks to Herc's suggestion, he claims that he can handle himself, that he needs his space.

He's eight. He doesn't need space. He needs to go out and play.

But that's hard to do when your mother lies in a hospital surgery room being operated on by stressed out doctors for hours on end.

Should it even take this many hours? She was stabbed. Not blown apart. Hermes realizes he has a limited knowledge of human anatomy, but even this seemed a bit excessive.

Back on the TV, the winged soldiers march toward a group of armed humans, brightly dressed in yellow and red striped uniforms.

Did humans really dress like that in the Old World? That seemed a bit excessively weird.

The angels on the television finally fold up their wings, blocking the attacks of the soldiers on the screen. Though there are no closeups of the men, Hermes can see the scrunched up brows of fear. These men, they have no idea what's going on.

The bottom of the television flashes the words FIRST CONTACT WITH ALIENS.

An elderly bearded man with his arm in a splint and wearing pants that are two sizes too big for him shouts out, "No it ain't."

The crowd doesn't reply.

Hermes says to Lilith, "I think we are officially under attack."

Lilith shakes her head. "Not quite yet. They're playing with them right now."

Hermes lets the words run around in his head. She said "them", not "us."

His words used "we", not "them."

Reality kicks him in the face like a steel-toed boot. He is getting domesticated.

"Mom?" says Brad.

The door swings open wildly and slams against the check-in counter.

Sophie stands at the doorway. She's standing, not sitting in a wheelchair.

Wasn't that proper hospital protocol?

She takes a wobbly step forward. Her feet shake like she's just learned to walk and both of her hands stay fixed on her neck, holding a soggy, dark red rag against it.

Hermes is the first to rush to her side. He grabs her arm and pulls it around his neck. He helps her to the waiting room chairs and lets her sit down.

Walking along the carpet slowly, Hermes gets a whiff of the coppery smell of blood leak out of Sophie's mouth. Her entire shirt smells like wet metal. Her skin, like sweat and pheromones.

She doesn't want to, fighting him to bend her knees, to take it easy.

She has bruises and scrapes along her legs and neck. Some of the scrapes look deeper, enough to peer into the flesh and fat just underneath her skin.

"What happened?" says Hermes. "I thought they were working on you."

Sophie's head doesn't move when her eyes crawl up to meet Hermes's. She coughs first, then says, "I guess they stopped."

A doctor bursts through the door. "She cannot leave." The doctor—female—has her hair tied up behind a light green mask. Some bit of cloth hangs from her neck, held to her by strings tied around the back. "She's seriously injured and she's not to leave."

Sophie looks up to Hermes and lets a bubbly, coppery sigh escape her mouth. "Fuck them," she says. She takes in a deep, what sounds like a painful, breath. "Let's go."

The nurse and about two orderlies stand across the doorway. "I cannot let you take her out of here." The woman's eyes are wide open, afraid of the confrontation in front of her.

Herc stands before the woman and his friends. The large behemoth of a man stands about six-feet eight inches and has more muscles in his shoulder than most people have in their entire body.

He could bench press the Empire State Building for a warm up.

It's because Herc looks like he can do all of these things that the woman doctor's arms shake as she extends herself across the electric glass doors.

She's already shut off the automatic switch. The doors, they aren't triggered by the motion of people in front of them anymore.

Hermes feels the weight of Sophie's red slick body slip from underneath his arms.

"But she's checking herself out," says Hermes. "I am new to hospitals, but I am pretty sure you cannot just keep her here."

The doctor's face becomes suddenly still, even confident. Her shoulders relax and she drops her hands.

"Fine," the doctor says. She points to Sophie. "She's under a psychiatric eval. Seventy-two hours."

Hermes shrugs. "What is that?"

Brad slaps his cheeks. "Seventy-two hours?" he says. "What does that mean?"

The doctor walks away as the two other orderlies grab both sides of Sophie and turns her around. "It means that she is technically under arrest for the next three days."

Hermes feels something slip from behind him. The rustling of shorts and a light thumping.

"Brad?" says Herc.

"Where is he going?" says Hermes.

The orderlies keep their grip tight on Sophie, but they pause at the sudden outburst of attention.

Herc sighs. "I'll go after him."

20

M ichael surveys the smoking, destroyed building—the Saint Peter's Basilica, according to the human's thoughts. The building still stands, but walls of it are laden with holes, smoking and crumbling under the weight of its own construction.

Michael's heart feels squeezed somewhere in the bowels of Hell. Some humans along the edges of the street hide in the shadows, covering their heads and peeking out, unsure of the next attack.

A mother mourns the loss of her son, trampled to death by the stumbling humans. The mother holds her baby still in her lap. She cries, wipes the sides of his face and hugs him tight.

Michael turns away from the ravaged destruction. Though he knows that the chaos is out of sight, he will continue to feel it deep in his heart and his soul.

Gabriel allows the other angels to sit atop the basilica, but he prefers to stand over the wreckage.

"This is really what they want, isn't it?" Gabriel says.

Michael clears his throat. "Not really," he says. "If you had bothered to listen to me, we could have done this so very differently."

Gabriel rests a cold hand on Michael's shoulder. "But first we needed to see that those animals threw the first stone. They were the first to gather their militaries."

"They were afraid. Nothing more. Of course they reacted strongly."

"They reacted wrongly," says Gabriel. His lip curls a little bit into a smirk. He thinks himself clever.

That ass.

"That may be the case, but they reacted the way Jehova intended."

Gabriel removes his hand from Michael's shoulder and makes a tight fist. "You mean to tell me that you know the will of Jehova himself? That you are fit to tell me just what is in God's plan? I am the Deus Vox, I am the Voice of the Lord. As intelligent as you are, Michael, you know nothing of these matters."

Michael feels his shoulders pull upwards towards his ears with each punctuation mark of Gabriel's admonishment. He feels the pain of knowing that he's only digging himself deeper into a hole he's not entirely sure he can get out of.

"Just what do you think you can learn from these actions," says Michael.

"What do you mean?" Gabriel says. "We are finally taking the lands while Hell is in disarray. We are winning the War of the Souls."

"True, but according to the Bible, Heaven will reign when the Christ Child returns." Michael swallows his self-doubt. "He is not here."

Gabriel clearly crunches down on his own teeth. "We will deal with that as it comes," says Gabriel.

Something else scratches at the back of Gabriel's mind. "I fear that we were not fast enough to seal the gates to Hell."

Gabriel's pose stiffens. "What did you just say?"

"We have some escaped demons from Hell. They reside somewhere in the United States, I'm guessing. We followed on to the southeastern shores."

Gabriel grabs Michael's collar and pulls him to standing. "You had one job to do," he says between clenched teeth.

"Yes, I understand, Gabriel." Michael's words come out sounding hollow, airy. His throat tightens up in Gabriel's grip. "But they were out before we could close the gates."

Gabriel releases Michael, who collapses to the floor.

Still holding himself up from the ground, his wings laid out behind him like a white cape. "They were already out," he says. "There was nothing we could do."

"But you said you chased one of them?"

Michael nods.

"Then you will retrieve that demon and bring him here. We cannot allow them to wander the Earth. As long as they walk the Earth, we have a rebellion in our midst."

Michael nods and brings himself to stand up tall. His shoulders and neck feel tight, the skin stretched and bruised. "Yes, sir."

Gabriel turn to the other two Archangels. "Galadriel, You are to seek out all Gates of Hell and ensure that they remain protected. Nothing comes in our out. Am I understood? Succeed where Michael has failed us."

Galadriel nods and take flight. He disappear in a white flash of light in the Earth's atmosphere.

"Michael, I need for you to capture our little Hell spies. Take Jamaerah with you. You will apparently need help in the matter."

Michael nods, turns to take flight, but Gabriel's hand on his wings stops him from lifting into the air.

"And Michael," he says. His voice is dark and rocky. "If you fail me, do not come back."

21

Brad huddles next to the side of a vending machine. Being so small, it's easy for him to disappear like he wants to. Away from the adults. Away from everyone who knows who he is. What he is.

Everything in this hallway smells like sour lemons and wood. The same stuff mommy uses when cleaning out the bathroom and the kitchen floors.

Brad never seemed to like the smell before, but right now, in the middle of everything, he's happy to have the smell sitting right underneath him.

"Brad?"

Brad's feels his ears perk up. The humming of the machine disappears, replaced with the soft footsteps of his step-brother Herc, this giant man who is the real Herakles you learn about in school.

One day Brad hopes to be strong like him, but how can a little boy be so strong? He couldn't even protect mommy.

Why is it so hard to be a hero?

"Brad? Where are you?"

Brad pulls in his feet even further into himself. He tries to hold his breath, but it only lasts for maybe a minute, but probably less.

"Brad?"

His brother's shadow stretches out in front of him. Herc is standing in front of the vending machine. The glowing lights inside casts a bright light that makes Herc's shadow look like it has larger shoulders than he really has.

Brad grips the tiled floor with his hands and pulls himself backwards, even taking in a deep breath to make himself even flatter.

And it would have worked, if his palms didn't squeak as they slid out from underneath him.

"Brad?"

The vending machine slides over to the right like it was made out of paper.

"What are you doing here?" Herc says. He offers his hand, but Brad knocks it away. The hand is almost as big as Brad's head. In fact, if he wanted to, he could probably wrap his whole hand around Brad's head and pluck his head off like a grape.

And then eat it.

But that would be gross.

"I don't want to go over there," Brad says. Because Herc is here, he holds in his tears and tries to talk slowly. He feels the pressure and the coughs in his chest, trying to climb out of his throat. He knows he could cry at any moment.

But heroes don't cry.

They also don't let their mommies get stabbed by bad men.

"What happened back there?" says Herc. "Why did you run off?"

Brad wants to say something, but the words keep getting mixed up. He doesn't know which words to say first.

After standing there long enough, Herc decides to sit down next to Brad. He walks over to the wall, rests his big, gigantic shoulders against it, and then lets his feet slide out underneath him.

By the time Herc is sitting down on the ground next to Brad, his shirt is pulled up around his strong back.

"Are you going to tell me what happened back there?"

"I hurt him," says Brad.

Herc nods. "But there was nothing you could do about it," he says. "I promise."

"Not that," say Brad. "Not that man."

But now that Herc mentions that, Brad pulls his knees closer to his chest.

Brad feels that awkward silence between them. He waits for Herc to say something, but he doesn't. Brad wonders maybe if he's supposed to say something.

"I meant the other man," says Brad.

"What other man, Brad?" Herc's voice sounds weird to Brad. Maybe angry, but not angry. But he sounds calm.

"The man who hurt mom," says Brad. "He's the one I hurt."

Herc sits up. Brad can't tell if Herc is smiling or frowning. Maybe a bit of both.

"So you hurt him?" Herc says back to him, slowly.

Brad nods. "Sort of."

"Sort of?"

Brad wonders of Herc is going to repeat back all of his words back at him. "Yes, sort of," says Brad. "I hurt him, like killed him."

Brad pokes at the bits of dried blood on his shirt. As he jabs at it, they break into jagged, dark flecks.

"That's not Sophie's blood, is it?" says Herc.

"No."

"Wow," says Herc.

"Are you mad?"

Herc groans. Or something. "Why would you think that?" he says.

"Because I killed someone."

"And that's something to be angry about?"

The question shocks Brad. "It's not?" he says.

Herc's giant paw wraps around Brad and brings him in for a hug. "No. You were protecting your mom," he says with a smile. "You just need to control your strength a little. Trust me, you pack quite a wallop."

Brad looks at his hands. Some dried blood splatters over his knuckles and the soft back of his hand. "But mom says that I shouldn't hit anyone."

"You didn't hit anyone," says Herc. "You were protecting someone."

Brad pulls away from Herc. "But I did something bad," he says. "And I couldn't control it. I just kept hitting and hitting." Brad just gives in to the tears that now drip from his eyes. "And it was all so weird," he says.

Brad stands up and measures just how far he should back up. He takes three steps back, three big steps, and measures that he should be just out of Herc's reach.

"Dude. Brad, you're not a bad person," Herc says. "You're a proud warrior. You protected your mom. You brought her to safety, and you're the hero." Herc's smile is covered in a thick beard that makes Brad think about black bears.

"I am?"

"Of course you are. I'm so proud of how much you've grown up," says Herc. He flexes an arm out to the side. His bicep bounces up and down like a roller coaster. "And some day you'll be as big and strong as me."

Brad shakes his head. He feels a little smile come from his mouth. "I'm stronger."

Herc chuckles. "Oh are you now?" he says.

Brad nods and pulls his smile back into a frown. "Promise me you won't tell anyone."

Herc scratches his head. "About what you did?"

The way Herc phrases this, it feels evil to Brad. Herc didn't say "killed the man" or "protected his mother."

Instead, he said, "What you did."

Like Voldemort from his Harry Potter books his mom bought him when he was five. If you don't mention his name, then it cannot come back to haunt you.

"Yeah," says Brad. "About what I did."

Herc extends a bear paw out to Brad. "Deal," he says.

Brad feels his hand shaking a little, but he brings it out and shakes hands with Herc. "Deal."

22

Hermes and Lilith watch the television change from one location to another. Each one looks like it was touched by the apocalypse, vaguely reminding Hermes of the all out war that broke out in Sodom and Gomorra.

No one made it out alive in either of those wars.

If they are this close to reenacting that war, maybe no one will make it out of this one, too.

Next to Hermes, Lilith has her legs crossed at the knee, her left leg folded over her right. The left boot kicks up and down on the knee, bouncing and reflecting the light from the morning sun that creeps in through the front glass door.

"Stop it," says Hermes. "You're blinding me."

"No, I'm not and stop being a baby."

From across the room, Hermes can see the real focus of her attention: a youngish nurse sitting at the desk. He is speaking to another nurse at the station, his hands holding him up over the her, his shoulders and elbows wide and open.

Lilith hopes to get the poor guy's attention with her flashy leg wear and maybe a little reflected light.

So far, it seems, it's a bust.

"You're not going to get anywhere doing that," says Hermes. "You have to go up and talk to him."

"Since when do you care?" says Lilith.

This is meant to hurt, but it makes Hermes laugh. "The more you flirt with others, the more you leave me alone."

Lilith nods and stops kicking her legs. "Good point." She shifts her weight so she is sitting sideways in the chair, her legs almost kicked over Hermes's legs. She rests her elbows on the arm of the chair, then her head on her hands.

"So, how is your day?" she says.

Hermes stands up. As he does so, he watches Brad and Herc come around the corner of the hallway.

"Is everything better?" Hermes asks.

Herc holds his hand out and moves it back and forth. "Meh," he says.

"Brad," says Hermes. "What was that all about?"

"I know you said no last time," says Lilith, "but seriously, is he always like this?"

"Shut up," says Hermes.

Brad looks up to Herc and nods. "I'm okay."

It's not that Hermes doesn't believe Brad, but lying comes with the genes in his family. So he checks Herc for clarification.

What he receives is a nod and half-assed smile.

It's going to have to be close enough for Hermes.

"Good," Hermes says. "Now let's talk about how we're going to get Sophie home."

"You're kidding me," says Herc. "She's bleeding out. She will die if she isn't cared for. And I don't know about you, but I can't do it."

Lilith nods. "You're crazy."

"But she does not want to be here. And look at her! She was able to walk out on her own. She was still alive. And she was able to talk."

"But she's bleeding, dude. She can't stay like that. Not for long," says Herc.

Brad is surprisingly quiet about the whole thing.

"And what do you think?" says Hermes. His little brother, only nine years old today, seems to have no opinion. His eyes are red, puffy. His cheeks dried and chapped from the crying. Still, he holds his head high, staring directly at Hermes. "She should stay here. She needs a doctor."

Anger and frustration bubbles up into Hermes's lungs. He wants to let it all out, let loose a roar equal to whatever the humongously bestial Herakles could let out.

But he looks around the room. All of these scared people. Many who come in with the splints, sprains. Colds and sniffles. Headaches and rashes.

He'd be foolish to think that she doesn't want to be here, that she's taking all of the attention when these people here, they need attention too.

Hermes would be doing everyone a favor for sure.

"But she does not want to stay here," says Hermes. He resides himself to the floor. He crosses his legs and tucks them in tight on his lap.

"But that doesn't mean that she doesn't need help," Herc says.

Hermes looks to Brad for comfort. Surely he understands. He knows that she needs to leave.

But Brad's face remains still, stoic.

Even now, he's the hero when Hermes can't be.

He's gotten soft.

His own nine-year-old brother, a hardened god.

Fuck this. Fuck them. Fuck it all.

The man with the with the pole sticking out of his face approaches Hermes. His original skin color gone and painted red from his permanent bleeding problem.

"Hey," he says. "So what was wrong with your girl?"

The man wipes away the slick redness that trickles down his cheek.

"How are you still alive?" Hermes says.

"I don't know," says the man. His personality has gone completely. Only a few minutes ago, he was ready to freak out, rob people and flee.

Now he's a puppy. A blank slate with a vocabulary of a highschool drop out trucker.

The metal pole still reflects light with its silver paint, but only at the end. The rest of it drips with thick red blood that just won't stop pouring out of his head.

It extends about a full foot out of the front of his face. When he turns to look at Hermes, he pulls his head back, sometimes even extending his hand to keep the bar from slamming himself in the face.

"So seriously, you're just okay with that pole?"

The man shrugs. "Not really," he says. "It kind of hurts."

"Kind of hurts?" Hermes looks at where the pole sticks deep in the man's head. Part of his skull comes out in a small bump on the back of his head, smaller than a baseball but bigger than a bug bite.

His brain, Hermes realizes. Going through the front of his head and into his brain. It must be affecting him somehow.

"Here," says Hermes. "Come with me."

Hermes stands up and takes the man's hand in his. He leads him to the front desk yet again.

"Sir," the front desk guy says. "I told you, we are doing what we can, but right now we do not have the room to see new patients."

The man in plaid slaps the counter and looks at Hermes. Hermes pulls his head back and watches the pole swish past him.

"See?" the man in plaid says. "Can't get help. Where is the help when you fucking need it?" He turns around and stumbles back to his seat. As he walks away, he lets out a loud sigh as if let everyone hear his disdain.

Hermes leans in over the counter. "Tell me, seriously, why are you not letting anyone leave?"

The male nurse pushes his dark bangs back. Hermes feels the male nurse's eyes meet his own bright green eyes.

The nurse's irises grow full flower, a large black spot deep in the midst of hazel circles.

The male nurse likes what he sees.

And this is just what Hermes needs.

"You can tell me, can't you?"

The nurse looks from side to side. "I'm sorry," he says. He sounds like he really means it. "But I can't. It's really not my place to say. And I think it's illegal."

"I'm not a reporter or anything." In his year up here, Hermes has learned that for some reason, reporters are feared. Something about them makes people stop talking. Maybe start worrying.

"Um," the nurse says. His dark blue nurse's scrubs sit tight against his shoulders and flat on his chest. The man sits hunched over the keyboard. His hands sit over the keyboard's keys, but not typing. Just tapping lightly across the upper row of q, w, e, r, t, and y.

"So there's nothing going on back there?" says Hermes. "I mean, I saw my friend come out, and she was still bleeding. You mean to tell me that nothing is going on and your doctors cannot stitch up a single stab wound?"

The nurse pulls at his collar and looks around. "It wasn't just a single stab wound, sir."

The nurse now seems to have found the nerve to talk.

"It was stitched up," he says. "And I'm only telling you this because she's your friend. I can't, by law, speak about other people's situations." Hermes sees that the male nurse's shoulders perk up as if made lighter by his confession. "But if you wanted to know what's going on, the stitches came open again."

The nurse sits back. All along the waistline of his scrubs and his pants is a dark red patch. Blood, most likely.

"And why would a stitch just burst right open?" says Hermes.

The nurse shrugs. He looks nervous. "I don't know," he says.

Something knocks on the coffee brown doors. They once again swing open.

The entirety of the waiting room looks over, almost drooling for a chance to see a doctor.

At the same time, a few large vans stop just outside the glass sliding doors to the outside. The men in dark blue suits rush to the back and slam doors.

From here, Hermes sees two nurses, or maybe they are doctors, and three paramedics come into the waiting room. They push along a person on a wheeled table, the metal legs crossed at the middle.

The wheels twirl back and forth, unsteady, as the medics push them back into the room.

As the table flies past him, Hermes gets a good look at the new patient. His face is black, charred. His neck looks exposed and raw like leather.

The next person on a metal table has a white sheet over him. There is blood, so much blood, just leaking off the table. Whatever is under the cloth is still writhing, moving, though Hermes gets the impression from the nurses that it really shouldn't be.

"So you're just going to let them in? What about my friend? If you are not going to help her out, at least let her go home."

The nurse stands up and nods for the medics to just go into the back room. Then the nurse turns his head to Hermes and sighs.

"Listen," he says. He walks around the counter and adjusts his shirt, which sticks to his waist from the damp, sticky blood. "We would let your friend go home, but right now, she's supposed to be dead and she isn't."

A medic runs out of the room in the back, out the coffee brown doors and into the van outside.

"For some reason," says the nurse, "no one seems to be dying when they should be."

23

The glass sliding doors open wide and again more boys and girls and men and women come strolling in with serious injuries.

Not a single one of them should have gotten up and walked away, but here they are, waltzing into the building with wheelchairs and crutches.

The male nurse, the one with the cute hair and big hazel orbs for eyes, he hurries them back and then peers at Hermes through the corner of his eye. He winks at Hermes, a coy smile, and then he goes back to whatever he was doing on his computer.

"We're going back there," says Hermes.

He stands next to Herc, who with his arms crossed looks more like a bodyguard than an actual patient.

"Say what now?" says Herc.

Hermes nods to the coffee brown doors. "Back there," says Hermes again. "We're going back there. We retrieve Sophie and we get out of here."

"You're drunk," says Herc.

"I am not drunk," says Hermes. "Trust me, you would know if I were drunk," he says.

"Oh, I know," says Herc. He rests his hands on his friend's shoulders. "I know."

"You're an ass."

Herc smiles.

"An ass that's going to help me save her."

"She doesn't need saving," says Herc. "She needs medication."

Hermes just blinks, staring at this burly, hairy beast of a man. Why isn't he getting it? Why doesn't he understand.

"This isn't some old adventure. There is no dame who needs to be saved here, buddy. This is something completely different and we are so, so outclassed."

"So you're afraid," Hermes says. "Got it." He progresses toward the door, but feels the pull of Herc's grip against the tail of his blue shirt keeping him back.

Hermes stops walking. "Let go," he says calmly.

"No."

"I won't say this again," Hermes says. His heart wants to explode in his chest, but his voice doesn't show it. "Let. Go."

Herc says, "No," but he lets go anyway. Hermes shoots forward and lands on his hands and knees.

"Thank you," says Hermes. He doesn't look back. His focus relies on getting past those doors, on getting past whatever guards are back there and retrieving his friend, the mother of his stepbrother.

Hermes marches toward the door, unphased by the rest of the world around him. All of these times he's traveled to and from Hell. He's made it to Mount Olympus, he's chained up monsters to the rocks of Tartaros.

And yet this feat seems insurmountable. How do you save a princess that doesn't want to be saved?

The male nurse flashes him a smile as he walks by. Hermes returns the nurse's smile and pushes open the door with his shoulders.

The doors swing closed behind him. Back here is a different environment altogether. The nurses and doctors rush from one room to the next. They grab metal clipboards, and these headphone thingies that hang off their necks swinging from their necks.

Hermes smiles. This might just be easier than he thought.

He takes his first step and a female nurse looks at him. She says nothing, however. The hair bun on the back of her head bounces as she turns her head down the hallway.

Whatever her goal is, it has nothing to do with Hermes.

As Hermes takes his next step forward, he begins his transformation. With each step, each breath, he becomes more and more invisible until he feels the light pulse through him.

That is, until he becomes stopped by a woman in front of him.

"What are you doing?" she says. Her accent pulls Hermes's attention instantly. Her voice is deep, but with an accent. Something British, he thinks, like those actors he saw on the BBC.

Hermes looks from left, then to right, and then tries to walk around her.

"No," the woman says again. "You."

Hermes shouldn't, but he feels a finger poke him in the chest.

"Why are you acting so funny?" she says.

"You can see me?" says Hermes.

The woman cocks her head back. "What do you mean I can see you? Of course I can see you. Are you daft?"

Hermes doesn't know what daft means. "No, I don't think so."

"Then what are you doing back here?"

Hermes pulls himself together, looking down to see if he can see his own feet. He searches for his hands, holding them up in front of his eyes.

"Are you on drugs?" she says. "What have you been taking?" Her eyes stop from studying Hermes's face and instead focus on his eyes.

Hermes blinks and takes a step back. "N-no," he says. "No drugs."

"Then get back out there." The points her clipboard back at the coffee brown doors.

"I can't," says Hermes. "I need to see my friend."

The woman's eyes narrow. She's checking his face, his stature to see if he's lying. Hermes saw this before when watching television. The detectives do this same thing.

And they say that television isn't real life.

"I'm not lying," says Hermes. "The woman, with the stab wound in her neck," says Hermes. He motions toward his own neck, slicing downward. "She bleeds a lot. Tried to leave earlier."

The woman nods. "Right," she says. Hermes isn't sure why, but she points in a room in the back corner. "She's there."

The nurse walks away and leaves Hermes alone. With the other doctors and nurses and whoever else back here, the chances of him getting stopped, maybe might be higher than he'd like.

And she saw him. The nurse saw him when she shouldn't have.

Why? Is he that far gone already? It's only been a year.

His fingertips touch the door's handle and his wrist shakes from nerves, from anticipation.

He swings the door open and Sophie sits with her head on a pillow, her side bandaged up with miles and miles of gauze that now runs red, almost leaking down her sides.

Sophie's face is pale, her cheeks wet from perspiration.

"I'm here to take you home."

Sophie smiles. He thinks.

He unplugs a needle in the back of her wrist and unwraps her from the bed sheets.

She's light in his admittedly scrawny arms. Her legs dangle over his forearm like a doll's leg.

"Are you ready?" says Hermes.

Sophie nods.

With his foot, Hermes nudges the door open and takes a quick glance out to the hallway. The lights look brighter, the hospital staff more attention. Like they know he's here.

Like the lost souls of Hell, they wander as if they have no plans. Just being told to go here. Go there. Go over there again.

No, no, you need to go there.

Hermes watches with interest as his path clears up. If he goes now, there could be a straight shot out the coffee brown doors and out the glass doors.

If he's lucky.

And Hermes was a gambling god once upon a time.

He still feels lucky from time to time.

Maybe today is one of those days.

Hermes looks into Sophie's own green eyes and blond hair that drips with sweat.

She looks like Hell, but so beautiful at the same time. The red in her cheeks makes her look pale and weak.

And Hermes wants nothing more than to put her to bed—his bed—and help her get better. Bring her water. Bring her food. Wait on her. Hand and winged foot.

"Okay," he says. "Let's go."

The plan goes smooth out the front door.

It's not until he exits the flapping coffee brown doors out to the waiting room that he hears a voice command him to stop and two clicking sounds.

So, he does what he's told to do.

Stop.

Those clicking sounds. Hermes swears those sounded like guns from those television shows he watches.

"Are those guns?" he says.

Brad and Herc stand in front of Hermes, both of them nodding.

24

Hermes and Herc take turns carrying Sophie down the road and back to the apartment.

The hospital is just outside the outskirts of the city, which means miles of walking at a pace that seems slower than snails. They are surrounded by the mating calls of animals and brightly colored birds hiding in the trees around them. The grass is a bright emerald green, freshly cut this morning.

Hermes takes in the breath of air. This smells always reminded him of springtime. Of life.

The sidewalk goes all the way into town, though Hermes doesn't remember seeing anyone actually walk it all this past year he's been here.

"Can I carry her?" says Brad.

Hermes stops long enough to help Herc get a better grip on Sophie. "No, Brad," he says. He tucks Sophie's legs over Herc's large forearm. "You're just a little too small."

Brad sticks out his lower lip, but keeps on walking, not waiting for the rest of the party.

They continue to walk, not making any attempts at conversation. Even Hermes, who usually feels the need to break the silence with a little conversation of a casual "Did you know" says nothing.

His mind is otherwise preoccupied.

He wants to say he did the right thing. That she really will be better off at home. Because she wanted to go home.

And Sophie's an adult, right? She knows what she wants. She knows what's best for herself.

But all the blood. The blood keeps coming.

And then there's that thing that the male nurse told him.

No one is dying.

But why?

Herc shifts Sophie's weight a little bit. "She's dripping on me," he says.

"She's going to keep dripping for a while," Hermes says.

"Why?" says Lilith. "Don't humans just bleed out or something?" She looks to Herc. "You would know. You know, on the battlefield?"

Herc nods and then shrugs. "It sounds about right."

"She's not going to die because she can't die."

Brad's pace, up ahead of the pack, stops in mid-step. "She can't what?"

He turns around with a smile on his face. His red, tear-dried cheeks now rosy.

"It's not what you think," Hermes says. As the God of Communication and not the God of Honesty, he runs over the large amount of lies he could tell right now.

Could, but won't.

"It does not look like anyone can die just yet."

Brad's head cocks to the side. "What do you mean?"

Herc's steps catch up with Hermes and Brad. They continue walking down the hot sidewalk in the coming midday sun.

The school they have to walk past is just a half block away. The pace is impressive, Hermes thinks. Even though he could have made it faster flying.

But she's in no condition to fly. Not now. Not with all that blood.

Lilith covers her eyes for a moment and stops walking.

Not that Hermes minds much. She can stay there for all he cares.

"Who's that?" she says.

Things fly over them. Too large to be birds.

"Shit," Hermes says.

The things fly over them and into the forests that lay to their north.

"I think they are going to the entrance to Hell," says Hermes. He covers his eyes and follows their trajectory. "Yeah," he says.

He takes to the air and flies upwards.

"Where are you going?" says Brad.

"I have to go," Hermes shouts down to him. "I have to see what they want and make sure we are okay."

Brad doesn't seem to believe him. He pouts again and crosses his arms. "Fine," he says.

"Brad," says Hermes. "I promise I'll be back."

Brad nods. "Sure." He continues the walk alone down the street.

Herc shrugs and nods him off. "Just go and come back quickly," he says. "She will probably be awake soon."

Hermes nods and flies upwards.

This catches their attention, and the winged creatures land to the streets about a hundred feet behind them.

"Hey!" shouts Herc. He stops and turns around. "Thanks for not killing my friend here!"

The two angels, clad in white and gold armor, the same soldier armor that Hermes had seen earlier, shrug and look at each other.

Their hair is about shoulder-length. Both are white and pale, but their eyes remain a watery clear blue like the oceans. Their lips, pink, rosy.

"I think I've heard about this," says the one on the left. The cuter one, if Hermes had a take a guess. "This is what they call sarcasm."

Hermes bites his lips to keep from grinning.

"No," says Herc. "I don't know what you're talking about. Sarcasm? Pfft. Whatever."

The one on the right, the one with the soft cheeks and rounded nose looks to his soldier-at-arms. "See? Not sarcasm."

"No, that cannot be correct," the one on the right says. His cheeks are hardened, sharp. His jaw is strong like it was chiseled out of stone. "This is definitely sarcasm."

"Bully!" shouts Brad. He holds something in his hand. Something gray and white and just slightly bigger than the palm of his hand.

"Brad!" shouts Hermes. "Don't."

Hermes lands to the ground and runs to Brad's side, but he cannot stop Brad.

The rock goes flying, end over end, toward the left angel's face.

He could not stop it if he wanted to. And even that is in question.

The rock lands directly in the left angel's face and stays there, leaving a red mark.

The angel stops cold, his hand slaps his cheek.

A look of astonishment, his mouth wide open as if to say "Ow", but lacking the air to say it outright.

"That actually hurt," the angel says.

The other angel with the sharp, strong features grabs for his sword and pulls it out, brandishing it toward Brad. "Maybe we found them," he says. "A normal human cannot throw like that."

The soft-cheeked angel looks to the ground for the rock. "Are you sure it was a rock?"

"Azarel," the other angel says. "We do not have time for this." He holds his sword out and rotates targets. Brad. Herc. Hermes. Brad.

"We should take them to Gabriel. Now."

The soft-cheeked angel grabs his sword, too, and holds it out to the others.

For angels, they don't seem confident in their weaponry. The soft, pudgier one holds his like this may be the first time. The other is aggressive. Sloppy.

Hermes even thinks he sees his wrist shaking a little bit more.

Young? New? Or intimidated?

"Come attack Brad, Son of Zeus!" Brad throws another rock and this one pelts the sharp-jawed angel in the nose.

He drops his sword and covers his nose with his hand, checking for leakage. Maybe blood.

If angels bleed.

"Son of Zeus?" says Hermes.

The angel with the dented nose flies toward Brad, his sword bursts into white and blue flames as he raises it up into the air. "You will regret that," he says.

Brad shifts his weight to the back of his leg, his arms up around his face and chest.

It looks like a battle stance that Herc may have taught him.

The boy looks ready, remarkably confident.

But it doesn't look good for Brad.

The angel's sword comes down swiftly, but Brad's little hands seem to stop it, grabbing the angel's wrists.

The angel nearly drops the sword. The look of surprise on his face says it all.

Brad sits, struggling, gritting his teeth and pushing back. And all the while, he's smiling.

Herc gets a good look at Brad before turning to Hermes. "Did you see that?" says Herc. "That's my boy!"

25

Sophie raises her sweaty head in the balmy humidity and says, "No, that's my boy," she says. "Don't let them kill him."

But Hermes can only watch as the boy handles himself with more wisdom and ferocity than he's seen in ages.

Brad's hands tighten around the chubby angel's wrist. Azarel, is what the other one called him.

Why do these angels have to have such weird names?

"Brad!" Hermes calls out, "what are you doing?"

Brad doesn't seem to hear anything. His focus remains in the angel in front of him.

"We have to go save him," says Hermes. He looks to Herc, who keeps Sophie nestled in his arms. She looks comfortable, too comfortable, for Herc to put her down.

That would put her in danger.

So, Hermes acts.

His wings kick into a rapid flap, pushing him forward and into the other square-jawed angel's stomach.

The two go flying to the ground. Hermes tucks in his arms, rolls to the side.

The other angel rises to his feet before Hermes can stop himself from moving.

"Brad!" screams Hermes. "Get over here!"

Hermes reaches out for Brad. He starts from a crawl on the ground, gaining speed and pushing himself up to run on the currents of air.

As he gets to Brad, Azarel's sword comes down onto Brad's protecting forearm.

Brad drops to the ground, breathing in to soothe the pain.

"I have you," says Hermes. Brad feels heavier than Hermes remembered, but he keeps him tight in his arms. His legs flap on the ground, lose and uncontrolled.

Brad's body goes into a heavy limp. Dead weight.

"Brad?" says Hermes. He loses track of where he's flying. He looks down and sees his step-brother trying his best to keep a tough face, to not cry, but he can't.

All of his energy goes from his body to his face. To be tough.

"Brad? You're okay?" Hermes pulls them both up into the air, over the battle. He looks downward and sees that Brad is bleeding, but it doesn't look deep. At least not yet. Drips of blood rush to the surface of his arm. Fresh, bright red blood drips off his skin and drips onto the sidewalk down below.

The houses to the left and right of the struggle—in blue, orange, and white—seem empty of people. Even from up here, Hermes doesn't see a single soul wandering the streets. Not a peeping Tom peering from the windows.

The angels turn their attention toward Herc and Sophie.

Hermes represses the urge to swear while he holds Brad in his arms. "We need to go back down."

Brad nods.

When Hermes gets to the ground, he releases his grip and Brad lands on his knees. He holds his flesh wound in his hand, applying pressure like it's second nature.

Hermes, however, all five-foot-eight of him, stands before the angels. Their wings stretch out behind them, flapping to make them look bigger to Sophie and Herc.

From the look on Herc's face, it's not working.

"Herc!" Hermes cries out. "Give me Sophie!"

Herc nods.

Hermes flies over the angels' heads and plucks Sophie's fragile body from Herc's arms.

Sophie grunts at first. Pain? Did he grab her wrong?

He adjusts his grip to just below her shoulders and around her knees.

"Please be okay," Hermes repeats to himself.

Sophie turns her head to the sidewalk and watches as Brad watches Hermes watching her. The three locked in a circle of not paying attention to the rest of the world.

He doesn't know just how far to take Sophie to keep her out of harm's way.

"I can be okay," says Sophie. Her voice is hollow and weak. "Put me down."

Hermes shakes his head. "No, it is dangerous."

"He needs help," she says.

Hermes looks down. "Herc never needs help."

Sophie doesn't turn to watch the fight. Hermes is happy about this because if she looked, she'd see Herc held with his arms locked behind him while the other angel releases his frustration and anger into his stomach.

"Go," says Sophie.

And Hermes hates to admit it, but she's right. Herc needs help.

But Brad seems to get the message before Hermes can say anything.

Brad watches as Hermes lowers to the ground, slow like an elevator going to the ground floor.

Brad shakes his head and waves them back up. "No," he says. "I have this."

Hermes stops, confused. "He's crazy," Hermes says.

Sophie almost shakes her head.

"Brad!" Hermes says, but of course Brad ignores him. Naturally. Why would anyone listen to him?

Brad runs at full speed, his forearm is held high around his chest, but his other hand pulls back into a strong fist.

Even from up here, this little boy looks mighty and fierce.

And as Brad approaches the angels, the one with the sword, the one punching Herc in the stomach, flaps his wings together and holds Brad in place.

Hermes has never seen anything like this. His wings wouldn't be strong enough for this.

"Brad!"

The wings separate slowly, pushed apart from the inside.

Brad stands in the center of the wings, pushing them away from his body with both arms. His injured arm, still bleeding, wavers while pushing, but he keeps the wings still.

Hermes smiles. But not from happiness, but from fascination. From the fact that he's more and more like his brother every single day.

And nothing like him.

"Sophie," Hermes says, "he's going to be okay."

Sophie nods and rests her head in Hermes's armpit.

Using the angel's weight against himself, Brad pulls the wings in a clockwise direction, twisting him around and knocking him off balance.

The angel named Azarel lands on his ass and bounces. Twice.

"How did you manage?" he begins to say, but doesn't get to finish the sentence. Herc's fists land in the Azarel's face.

The angel flies backwards from the punch, scraping his wings on the rocky asphalt street and rolling backwards, flipping and flapping to stay still.

"Are you okay, buddy?" Herc says. Hermes knows that Herc is getting into the fight when he sees his best friend rip his shirt off and flex his shoulders and chest. "Now we have a fight, fellas."

Brad tries to flex, too, but strains his forearm and winces.

"I'm okay," he says.

Herc pushes him off to the sidewalk and points to the curb. "Sit down and watch how it's done."

And of course Herc is smiling like a human boy at Christmas.

He had just learned what that was a few months ago. It excited him to no end, though it made no sense to him.

All the gifts from a mysterious person who wasn't a god? But worked for elves? These humans, such creativity.

Herc's arms are wrist-deep into the other angel's face when everyone stops. The sound of flapping, slow, steady and methodical, demands everyone's attention.

"More?" says Herc. He holds his hands over his eyes to shield them from the piercing sun rays. "Please tell me there are more of you."

Hermes clutches Sophie tighter in his arms. He recognizes that angel. A woman. The one the angel general called Jamaerah.

"You," says Jamaerah. She touches down onto the ground in a soft, graceful tap. "You should really pick on someone your own size." She grabs a sword that bursts into a blue and white flame from her waist. She holds it high, pointing it at Herc's chest.

Herc drops the angel Azarel, and cracks his knuckles.

26

"Hello there, gorgeous." Herc cracks his knuckles, but then flourishes to a bow in the middle of the street. "To whom do I owe the pleasure of meeting you?"

"Whom!" shouts Hermes from across the street.

"You are Greek, are you not?" says Jamaerah. Her voice is strong as steel and yet feminine. Commanding, yet sexy. She does not crack a smile whatsoever to Herc's foolish advances.

She must know his type well, Hermes thinks. Someone who looks like that and can wield a sword? Chances are she gets hit on all the time.

If angels are allowed to do that.

"I have been blessed by the Gods to be born of Greece," says Herc. "Yes."

Jamaerah rolls her eyes. She brandishes her sword in the palm of her hand. The fire does not leave a mark on her skin.

Hermes raises an eyebrow. Is the fire fake? Controlled? Does Hermes even want to find out?

"A simple yes would suffice, beast."

Herc taps his chest as if offended. He's been watching too many Real Housewives episodes. "What did you just call me?" he says.

"Beast," says Jamaerah. Her eyes roll yet again. "You are Behemoth of Hell, are you not?"

"Who are you to call us by those names?" says Hermes. "We are not of Hell anymore."

Jamaerah holds her sword out to Hermes and he shuts up. The blade compels him to do what she commands.

Hermes holds his hands up into the air and steps backwards. From behind his heels, Hermes hears Sophie's stifled laughter.

"It's not funny."

"Gosh, you're pretty," says Herc. He flexes his chest while slow, confident steps allow him to strut his stuff in front of his new possible lady friend.

"You are to come with me, demons." She takes the sword's point and shoves it into the ground. The angel rests her hands on the pommel and holds her shoulders high, her neck straight. "Or else."

"Aw, man," says Herc. "She's beautiful and crazy."

"Just the way you prefer them," says Hermes. He cracks a smile.

Herc points over at Hermes's chuckles. "Listen here," he says. "They're not all crazy." He flashes his big white teeth and folds his arms over his chest.

And Hermes completely considers saying something, but he decides not to when the angel flies forward and lands her fist into Herc's face.

Herc stumbles backward, his hand grabs his cheek and nose, checking for blood.

"You bitch," he says. Except, as he says this, he has the greatest smile on his face. "Oh, I was hoping you'd throw the first punch."

And he throws the second.

The punches fly at each other faster than Hermes can keep track. Even with his trained eagle-eyes, he swears there are twice as many punches as he can keep count.

Herc ducks down low.

Jamaerah steps forward and swings her sword in a half circle. Misses.

Herc swings upwards with both fists locked together.

The punch lands square in the angel's jaw.

She flies upwards and backwards in a smooth arc. A crash later and there is now a giant angel sized crater in the asphalt.

"You've got to be kidding me," she says. "You're stronger than you look."

Herc looks down at his pecs and flexes his muscles.

"What's that supposed to mean?" Herc kisses his left bicep.

The angel lunges forward. With her wings, she flies faster than Herc can react.

Herc's face suffers the consequences.

First a foot. Then a boot. Then the pommel of her sword.

Herc drops to his feet.

Hermes steps forward, but Brad sits in the way, gripping his hands.

Brad looks at Hermes and shakes his head. "He can do this," he says.

Hermes shakes his head. "I don't think he can, Brad."

"No, he can," he mutters back. "He's a hero."

From behind his heels, Sophie coughs. The grass crumples underneath her as she falls backward from watching on her side.

Hermes feels the sting of knowing that he can't leave. She needs him near.

He can't abandon her.

Hermes kneels down and checks on Sophie's wound. The rag that once was white is now completely sopping wet and leaking blood. Her skin is pale, sweating, looking like wet rubber in the sunlight.

Brad stands up. He makes little fists with tight, white knuckles.

"Brad," shouts Hermes. "Don't you dare. I know what you're thinking."

Brad lunges forward into the fight and grabs hold of the woman's wings. He grimaces and mashes his eyes closed as he pulls backwards with all of his might. His face glows bright red as he pulls back.

But she's too strong for him.

Jamaerah flaps her wings—out, then in—and Brad goes flying into the air.

Hermes watches him spin in the air. One lesson that Herc never worked on with him: how to land from a throw.

Brad's hands and feet kick out in every which direction. His eyes widen.

And try as he might, Hermes has a hard time keeping track of this kid with the sun in his eyes.

The boy shouts something that Hermes can't understand. But it's enough. He can follow that.

"Keep shouting," says Hermes.

Brad—for once—follows orders and shouts at the top of his lungs.

Hermes's wings flutter to carry him upwards. He closes his eyes, following his instincts up into the air and readies his chest and arms for the full impact.

The force of Brad's landing is enough to knock both of them to the ground, but Hermes hangs on to Brad tight. The two slide along the grass and land in someone's yard. Someone's poor, distressed, basically destroyed yard.

"Sorry," says Hermes and he taps onto the living room window.

Brad grabs his elbow and pulls it in toward his chest.

"Are you hurt?"

Brad nods and sucks in some air. "It hurts a lot."

Hermes nods. "We need to go back," says Hermes. He shakes his head at the damnable irony of it all.

If he had just stayed there, none of this—no.

Just do. Don't worry about the consequences yet.

Sophie needs help. Brad needs help.

And judging by the way Jamaerah has Herc in a headlock, flipping him up over her shoulder, Herc needs help, too.

"Herc, let's go!" Hermes shouts.

Herc gets thrust into a group of trees in someone's yard about a block away.

"I think he's losing," says Brad.

"Don't tell him that," says Hermes. "Listen, we need to go back to the hospital."

"But Herc needs help."

"And so do you, and your mom." Hermes looks back at Sophie. She lays straight on her back, her head thrust back to allow her to cough. "We really need to go."

Brad nods. He pulls himself up by the panels on the house. He begins the trek back to the hospital, walking while watching the thundering punches from one celestial being to another.

"Herc!" Hermes shouts again.

Herc stands grappling with the female angel, both hand to hand and forehead to forehead. Trying to push each other off balance.

Herc turns the pairing so he can look around her shoulder and still see Herc. "What?" he says between grunts.

"We gotta go! Brad and Sophie. We need to leave."

Herc nods and pushes forward.

But Jamaerah's wings flap enough to carry her upwards.

"No fucking fair," says Herc. "I can't fly."

With Jamaerah still holding onto Herc's fists, she flies higher into the air and then drops him.

Herc lands head first into the asphalt. Smoke and dust curl out of the air like ancient fingers.

Herc pulls himself out, albeit slowly, and sits on his backend. "Fine," he says. "We can go."

The deep, chest-shaking bass of flapping wings suddenly stops in the air above them. Hermes looks up.

The angel begins a quick descent downward, her flaming sword held downward.

Hermes lowers his eyes. "Herc! Out of the way."

Herc looks upward and cups his eyes from the sun. He falls to the ground and rolls to the side.

When the angel's sword hits the ground, the dust settles, but the area is surrounded in a rapid halo of blue and white fire. As soon as it appeared it disappears and Hermes is left with an intense burning sensation on his chest.

"What was that?"

Herc stands up, but just barely.

Jamaerah lunges her sword at Herc once more.

He manages to dodge her attack and grabs her wrist.

Jamaerah's eyes widen. "You wouldn't dare," she says.

Herc grunts and pulls upward on her elbow, bending it up and out of joint.

She drops to the ground and Herc wobbles to the sidewalk.

"Let's go," he says.

Hermes picks up Sophie and follows Herc's tortured body down the street.

"The sad part is," says Herc, "she was so damn hot."

27

The dark evergreen trees that blow in the wind only remind him of his best friend's incessant pining over an angel.

A literal angel who just kicked his ass.

Literally.

"Shut up already," Hermes says.

"But she was hot," says Herc. He holds his hands out in front of his chest as if holding two watermelons. "And she was beautiful, you know what I mean?"

Brad shakes his head. "No," he says. "What?"

The smile on Herc's face disappears instantly. He coughs into his fist and looks to Hermes for help.

"It means she had great hair. You know, that came down to her shoulders," says Hermes.

Brad nods and keeps walking and wincing. "Oh," he says.

Hermes shoots Herc a look: Don't do that again.

Herc nods and mouths an apology. "I'm sorry."

Hermes holds his hand up to Herc to shush it. The sound of people talking—a lot of people—hushing each other and complaining hits Hermes's ears.

The hospital now has a line of people just sitting outside.

Literally sitting because the doors are closed and no one wants to move and lose their spot.

Though if a line isn't moving, is it really losing anything?

"What the hell is this?" says Herc. He marches to the lines and rests his hands on his hips. Speaking with his massive chest the way women on television speak with their breasts, he says, "Why are you standing outside?"

The patients who take up almost half the lawn look at each other as if he hasn't heard the news.

"Because they ain't letting no one inside," says a man with his wife. They hold their babies in their laps, bouncing them and shushing them to go to sleep.

"No one's getting inside?" says Herc. "I don't think so."

He waves for Brad and Hermes to follow him. He steps over people sleeping and watching television from their little cell phones. Some are playing games and others just plain watch Herc sidestep them all.

At the back of his mind, Hermes wants to remember to try to buy a cell phone. Or at least upgrade.

That's what real humans do, isn't it?

For the trip to the hospital, Sophie felt light and easy to carry.

Not that Hermes has to work to step over everyone, he suddenly wishes he could just fly over them. The bounce, step, bounce, of getting to the front door is taking its toll on his biceps.

"Herc," says Hermes. "Can you carry her?"

He hates himself for even asking this. Having to hand her over, he feels like he's failed already.

But the lighter load makes it easier to follow faster and not worry about dropping this woman he might just be in love with.

Herc carries her like a baby in one arm. Yes, her legs drape downwards like they are part of his cloak, but she looks comfortable.

And she's safer with him than with Hermes.

Because everyone else is having problems with blood and bruises, Hermes knocks on the door and forces his head against the glass.

Inside, there's no one visible.

Hiding in the back, no doubt. So the patients maybe think the place is out of order.

Wait. Is that the right phrase? Hermes thinks it must be out of order. Or maybe out of whack.

He'll have to ask Sophie later. When she gets better.

Not if. When.

"Hello?" he says.

"You think we ain't already try that?" a woman's voice says behind him.

Hermes looks over his shoulder and sticks his tongue out at a teenage boy and girl, holding hands and not waiting patiently in line. "Well, you're not me," he says. "Deal with it."

Hermes is sure he's leaving a greasy forehead print on the clean glass when he peers back inside.

"Hello?"

The teenage girl says, "Asshole."

Hermes knocks on the door again. "Hello?"

Herc steps forward and nudges the teenage couple. "May I?" he asks.

The boy's eyebrows disappear somewhere in his long brown bangs. He steps aside.

When his girlfriend elbows him in the stomach, the boyfriend shrugs. "What?" he mutters. "He's bigger than me."

Herc taps on the glass with his knuckle and forces his nose and forehead up against the glass. "Anyone home?"

Brad huffs. "I think we're out of luck," he says.

"We're not out of luck. We're just getting in luck," Herc says. He shifts Sophie's weight in his arms and pulls the doors open with his free hand.

Hermes hears something stretch, then pop. A sharp, scraping sound like Herc just cracked metal in half.

The building's air conditioning brushes past Hermes's face. They all enter the building.

Herc, for good measure, and to make sure the crowd

understands that he's in charge, closes the door behind him and waves at the upset crowd.

"Hello?" he says again. His deep voice echoes in the empty office, enough so that the someone sticks their head out of the coffee brown door.

"What are you doing here?" says the voice.

The semi-cute guy from before. The guy who gave the tips. "We aren't taking anyone else," he says. "We're closed."

Herc pulls back the cloth on Sophie's shoulder long enough for the man to follow his trained instincts.

"You again," says the man. He disappears behind the doors and then emerges with a wheelchair. "Here," he says.

Hermes holds Herc's elbow still. "Please," he says. "Do not do this."

Herc nods at Sophie's body, now resting in the wheelchair. "Look at her," the big human ox says. "She needs help. We don't know how to help her."

"But," Hermes begins to say, but doesn't finish. He's got nothing. "You're right."

Herc rests his arm around Hermes's shoulder and squeezes.

"One more," says Hermes. He nudges Brad forward.

The nurse snaps his fingers and holds out his hand.

As if well-trained, Brad holds out his arm for inspection.

"What did this?" the nurse says.

"He got in a fight," says Herc. "You should see the other girl," Herc says.

"Girl?" The nurse kneels down and looks at Brad. "Are you in trouble?" he says.

Brad's eyes lower to the ground. "No," he says. Slowly.

"Are you sure?" says the nurse. "We can talk alone, away from them if you want."

Brad's eyes narrow. "Take care of my mom," he says. "I'll be okay."

"Well come back anyway. We need to bandage that up."

Hermes follows the three back into the examination rooms.

Brad hops up on the table-slash-bed or whatever it's supposed to be. It doesn't look comfortable with the thin roll of paper towel as a blanket.

"Why are you turning people away?" Hermes says. He leans up against the door, listening to the commotion outside.

"We're getting too many injured people and they aren't healing."

"Not healing?"

The nurse shakes his head. He holds out a roll of gauze and a layer of white padding over Brad's forearm.

"Not healing, and so we can't discharge them. It's the strangest things. I think it has something to do with those aliens."

"Angels?" says Hermes.

"If you believe in that sort of thing," says the nurse. "Never made me too concerned, you know, who was in Heaven and Hell and all that."

He finishes up the roll and pins the edge of the wrap along Brad's wrist with a fingernail-sized piece of metal.

"How's that?"

Brad nods. "Good."

The nurse smiles. "Good."

"So you're just going to let them all stay out there?"

The nurse sighs. "Take a look around. We don't have the room, and the other hospitals are telling us the same thing. For better or for worse, no one is dying and no one is getting better."

28

The sounds of the bustling doctors and nurses and all-around sick people who refuse to die creep in from behind the door. Inside, the room is white and quiet. A baby blue curtain is pulled completely around Sophie's bed.

The way the doctors and nurses check on her, Hermes starts to think that maybe she really is dying. Maybe they just missed something.

The television, hanging from a metal pole from the wall, is off. Sophie says she doesn't want to hear about the news. "It's bad enough living it," she says.

The room is too quiet for Hermes, however. He needs the hustle and bustle from outside. It's the sound of movement that lets him know that life is still going on around him. That he's not just surrounded by death and injuries.

It's when the room gets too quiet that Hermes hears something catch his attention. Sitting in the metal chair, only barely padded with maybe a thick cloth, he turns his attention from the window outside to Sophie.

"Did you know the sky is turning orange outside?"

"That's what happens," she says, "when the sun sets."

Hermes checks the clock on the far side of the room. "I think it is two o'clock in the afternoon. The sun does not set that soon here."

Sophie wipes away at her eyes.

"You are crying," says Hermes. He sits up from his chair and watches her face try to hold still and keep from crying. She can't, however, hold it for long. "What's the matter?"

"Brad is going to die," she says. "If we figure this out, then I die, and Brad is going to get injured."

Her chest heaves up as she takes in a deep breath. Probably to calm her down.

"He's already hurt from the fight."

And the thought of that, it's enough to push her emotions down the hill. She begins to cry. Giant tears. Her face red and shoulders pulled up around her ears.

Hermes stares at her, then motions for her to lean in.

Since the admittance to the hospital—or re-admittance—Sophie has been placed under a constant watch. This is what happens, Hermes is quickly learning, when patients decide to check themselves out without doctor support.

Her clothing is now balled up on the floor. The doctors and nurses took no care to bag it up for her. Not enough time. Instead, she sits in one of those hospital gowns that looks like a paper curtain draped across her shoulders.

Hermes finds it unflattering for Sophie's perfect figure.

She can't bend over because she's too busy crying, so Hermes pulls her in and lets her sob on his chest.

He can already feel the warmth of her tears on his shirt. It's a small price to pay, he thinks, to keep this woman—this amazing woman—comforted and happy.

But he wants her to smile. To laugh.

How do you do that when her son has a flesh wound to the forearm and the rest of the world is perpetually dying?

"Everything will be okay. He will be fine," says Hermes. "He is a tough little boy."

He feels Sophie's head nod. He hopes because she agrees and not because she is wiping snot on his shirt.

Hermes takes the chance and kisses her forehead. "And we will protect him. I promise."

Sophie smiles, then nestles her head in the crook of his arm and chest.

Hermes, too, finds himself closing his eyes.

Until the door bursts open. Black high heels clip clop into the room. Lilith turns around and kicks the door closed.

"We need a little privacy," she says.

"I agree," says Hermes. "Now leave."

"You should really stop lying to the poor girl." Lilith still has another bag of potato chips in her hand. She crunches on a few and wipes her greasy hand on the hospital bed next to Sophie's.

"Nothing is a lie," says Hermes. He clutches Sophie's hand in his. "We will protect him."

"This shit you're talking about? About it all being okay?' says Lilith. She crunches on another potato chip. She uses the silence to savor the flavor. "We have never seen this before," she says. "And Hell is scared to," she pauses. Hermes can see her fighting for the right word. "Well," Lilith shrugs, "to Hell. And if Hell is scared, then you know shit is going to go down."

"Get out," says Hermes. He feels the blood just under his cheeks begin to boil.

"Not until you admit that you've been lying to her all the time."

"Get out."

"No," says Lilith. Another crunch of a chip. "This has never happened in human history. No celestial power has just come down and taken over."

She crunches a chip and sits down on the bed. Lilith makes sure that everyone is watching when she takes one leg and crosses it over her knee.

She smiles, her red lipstick, like flaming rubies, sparkles in the sunlight that cuts through the vertical blinds.

"Face it," she says. "If they want everyone dead, they can make everyone dead."

Hermes stands up. He looks calm, tries to keep his eyes straight ahead, no emotion.

He snatches the demoness's neck and takes her outside. Her heels drag behind her, though she doesn't struggle.

Once outside, Hermes closes the door behind him. He slams her against the wall.

"What the hell was all of that about?"

Both of Lilith's hands grab each of Hermes's ears and pulls him in with a kiss.

Hermes feels the little bite of sharpened fang on his lower lip.

He pulls away and tosses her down.

"You are crazy, you know that?" Hermes wipes the blood away from his lip.

"And you're deluded," says Lilith. She rises to her feet and adjusts her black dress. Happy with her appearance once again, she points a sharpened index fingernail at Hermes. "You're the one that needs saving. You're a god, a powerful one at that, and you're wasting your time with these mortals."

Lilith swings the door to Sophie's room open.

Hermes reaches to close it, but it falls out of reach.

"Do you use that in there?" she shouts at him. "That's going to be her whether she survives this or not. She will die. Because she's mortal. Is now. Always will be."

Hermes reaches for the door and tries to smile at Sophie. "This'll be over in a minute," he tells Sophie.

Her smile back to him is jagged, confused.

The door clicks shut.

"I never said anything about this being forever," says Hermes. His hands grab hold of her neck and he squeezes just a little to let this bitch know he's serious. "But I like her. A lot. And if you do anything else to mess it up, I swear I will destroy you."

Lilith squirms under the tight grip. She moans, liking the pressure.

"You sick whore," says Hermes. He takes a step back, collecting himself. "You sick, stupid bitch. When will you get it through your dyed little head that we are through." He lets out a laughter of realization. "Fuck, Lilith! We never were to begin with!"

"You say that like it's a bad thing," Lilith mutters.

"And you just do not get it," says Hermes.

Lilith holds out and grabs his shirt. "No, you do not get it, asswipe. You say you love her, but she has no idea. She thinks you are all friends. Just little playmates to keep her little brat happy and babysat while she did whatever the fuck she does." Lilith's eyes meet Hermes.

He feels the need to look away.

"And while you two dumb asses are busy babysitting that runt, the rest of the world falls apart. And you're too weak, too stupid, and too domesticated to do anything about it."

Hermes lets go and backs up away from her. But the hallway is too dark, too small, to escape.

His back meets the cold paint of the wall. It shocks him awake. His legs weaken and he begins to fall down, slowly.

"You know, just because you want me to go so bad, I think I'll stay," says Lilith. Her slick, gray-purple tongue rubs over her red lipstick. "I'll be here to watch that bitch bleed out and die. And when she does, I'll be the first voice you hear laughing her ass off."

29

Seeing it as the most magnificent palace on Earth—and because Gabriel always had an eye for expensive things—the archangels decided to take up the Vatican as their new home.

Michael paces the hallways of the building the Italians called Basilica di San Pietro.

Though he much preferred the ancient tongue used to describe the building: Basilica Sancti Petri.

Now that was a language that sounded official and warlike in the same sentence.

Michael paces into the giant room of the basilica, the center of the church itself. This room is golden and massive, even to his giant angelic body. The over one hundred meters of space between the top of his head and the roof of the basilica was impressively painted with white images of knights and saints against a deep royal red background.

Each image was framed in white and black, decorated in the styles he used to see nearly six hundred years ago. The area he walks through is supported by white, square columns that come together in a beautifully carved flower-like design.

He never saw such plants or animals here or in the celestial heavens. Still, it is breathtakingly beautiful to now behold.

Michael nods in approval. The mighty things these creatures of Jehova can do.

Michael walks slowly through the blue rays of light that shoot down like Heaven-sent halos through the ceiling. Three of them cover his head and each of his shoulders.

Even down here, he can see why the humans would come to worship.

At the end of the building sits an ornate statue of four figures, each rising up to the central piece: a golden sun. Or halo. It was not Michael's skill to detect the true intention of art. Art was a human skill. A divine inspiration that skipped the angels upon their creation.

To avoid the envy, Michael decided to just stop caring.

At the front of the statue, he kneels before it and bows his head. The figures, Michael believes, must be someone important, and it is important to offer his respects.

Footsteps come from behind him. Michael stands up, but does not turn around. Let the mysterious guest—angel, judging by the power of the footsteps—come and introduce itself.

"Ser," says the voice.

"Jamaerah," Michael says with a smile. "You have found the demon."

"Demons," she says. Michael can hear her heartbeat speed up. Her emotions remain tense, and taste like metal in his mouth.

"Demons?" Michael turns around and holds his hands behind his back. "There are more of them?"

"I count three," she says. "A boy, a small one, and one as strong as an ox."

"A boy?" says Michael. His voice echoes in the vast emptiness of the space around them. Michael lets his words hang out in the dome above him. They sound like a type of music to his ears.

Or maybe Gabriel had been correct all this time: He does enjoy the sound of his own voice.

"Yes, ser," Jamaerah says. Now that Michael has turned around, she bows and takes a knee. "He called himself 'Brad, Son of Zeus'. He is a mighty one, but untrained."

"Son of Zeus?" says Michael. He belts out a laugh. "My Lord, that man is setting up little Olympians all over the place, is he not?"

"Yes, ser."

"And you return without them. What happened?" Michael motions for Jamaerah to stand up.

She rises and bows her head in gratitude. "They fought hard. The ox," she says. "He will be one to watch. He may even be dangerous."

Michael's eyebrow raises. He pauses, searching her face for signs of truth. "There is more," he says.

Jamaerah lets out a loud sigh. "Yes, ser," she says. "He defeated me."

"Pride cometh before the fall," says Michael.

Jamaerah nods. "Yes, ser. Thank you, ser. But he will be dangerous. I am one of the strongest of the Chorus, and yet he took me down with some difficulty."

"With some?" Michael smiles. It's not often he gets to see her this humbled.

"Some," she agrees. "Well, maybe more than some, but the fact remains: they will be a threat if allowed to go untamed."

"You know , Gabriel will be angry if we show up without them."

"Gabriel will be even angrier if we admit defeat," says Jamaerah.

Michael nods. She was right.

"But one is bad enough," says Michael. "Three will force Gabriel to run an entire army to their location. Where are they?"

"A small town called Saraday. In the United States."

"And that poor town will be subjugated until the demons are surrendered."

"I doubt the town even knows of the demons' existence. That would be a costly move."

"And it would go against the workings of Jehova," says Michael. "Then we will shield this knowledge from him. Keep that town secret. Spare the people, but keep a look for the demons."

"Yes, ser."

"And always, keep with you that we are not in the business of taking prisoners. We are only here to spread God's Word."

Jamaerah presses her closed fist against her chest and salutes. "Aye, ser."

Her footsteps echo in the halls, until replaced by the flapping of wings.

A light gust of wind blows in through the halls and pushes Michael's wings closer to his body.

Michael looks to the golden statue of the sun, reflecting light as if it possessed the brilliance of the Heavens itself. He kneels again, bowing his head.

"Lord," he says quietly, "I await your further commands. Allow me the gift of vision, to see your plan, to live your Word."

He crosses himself, forehead to stomach, shoulder to shoulder.

"Amen."

30

Sophie pats Hermes on the back of his hand. "You should go," she says.

The machines in the room are off. No blips or beeps. Just silence and unplugged. The doctors claim there's not much to do about this. "An act of God," one of the doctors called it.

It was close enough, Hermes guesses.

"I cannot just leave you," he says.

Dozens of people gather into tight vigils on the lawn just outside the window. They hold up candle lights and paper signs that read "God is wonderful," and "Peace and Love."

Sophie coughs. "What are you going to do? Watch me sit here and breath?"

Hermes wants to tell her, is that so bad?

"Well, why not?"

"Because you deserve more. Find out what's happening. Go save the world," she says with a smile. A wonderful, still cheerful smile in spite of all of this.

"Do not be ridiculous," says Hermes. "I will stay."

"No, you won't."

Just in the hall, despite his wounds, Brad rams his head into Herc's chest.

Herc's belts out a burst of air and then falls to the ground, clutching Brad, laughing, close to his chest.

"I want some time," says Sophie. She takes in a deep breath, "with him."

Hermes follows her eyes.

"With Herakles?" He feels the indignance rising in his shoulders.

Sophie coughs. "Don't make me laugh," she says. "With Brad."

Hermes nods. "Yes, of course."

"If you go," she says. "Just be careful, okay?"

Hermes nods. He leans in and hesitates. Is now a good time to do this? Should he?

Before Hermes can finish the thought, Sophie rests a finger on Hermes's lips. "I know," she says.

"You," he says. His lungs hesitate to push the rest of the words out of his mouth. "You know?"

Sophie nods, smiles. "Yes," she says. She rests back on her pillow, the white sheets and light blue blanket keep her legs from moving anywhere. Still, she seems to pull her legs to the side, bending them at the knees and then extending them again. Like a frog, Hermes thinks. A little frog in the water.

"Are you uncomfortable?" Hermes says. "Can I get you anything?"

Sophie shakes her head. "I'm okay."

"Sure?"

Sophie nods. "I promise. Just a little tired again."

Hermes stands up and steps away. He does so watching over her.

Step. Checks on her cheeks, her forehead for color.

Step. Check for sweat on her brow.

Step. Look for spasms or jerking from pain.

"Stop looking at me like that," she says. "I'm fine." She puts on a smile that Hermes knows is not real.

She doesn't want him to worry.

"I know," he says and hopes that he means it.

Herc and Brad run around the hospital, thundering down the hallways and bumping against the soft white walls.

"Herc!" Hermes shouts down the walls. "Herc! Wait up! We need to go."

Sophie smiles and lays her head on the pillow. The soft white pillowcase wraps itself around her cheek and forehead.

Hermes watches, not making a sound, watching her fall fast asleep.

31

Hermes and Herc stand just outside the hospital. The sun begins its last half of the day's journey across the sky.

The line outside the hospital doesn't get much shorter. If anything, it has grown almost three times the size this morning.

"I'm thinking Vatican," says Herc. "That's where the bad guys are at, right?"

"We do not know that they are bad yet."

"Do you not remember them trying to kick our asses a few hours ago?" Herc rubs his lower back and stretches backwards. Hermes hears ten, maybe fifteen, cracking sounds. "Because I know I do."

"And you survived, did you not?"

"That is not the point," says Herc with a laugh. "And you know it."

"Then what is the point?"

"The point is that we stop this nonsense, save Sophie, and keep one more celestial being from taking over the Earth Realm."

Hermes scoffs. "Again, we cannot be sure they are out to conquer the realm."

Herc looks the sky, peering west near the end of the sun's path.

"East is that way," says Hermes.

"Yes, I know," he says. "Just looking."

"But we should just look around. We can gather enough intelligence and ensure that the everyone is safe."

"And kick some ass."

Hermes looks at Herc, shakes his head. "Just reconnaissance."

"Then kick some ass."

"No."

"You watch too much spy television shows," says Herc. "And then we kick some ass."

"That doesn't even make any sense." Hermes takes flight and flies around Herc's shoulders. "Do me a favor and do not laugh this time."

"But your dainty little hands tickle."

"Do you want to be dropped?"

THE TWO FLY over the Atlantic Ocean. The vast blues and greens stretch as far as their eyes can take in. Herc, not used to seeing this sight from this advantage point, holds his breath.

Hermes feels Herc's chest expand and stay there.

"You can breathe," Hermes says.

Herc's feet twitch as he shakes his head.

"Don't tell me you're afraid," says Hermes.

The first streak of land--the shores of Italy if Hermes's sense of direction is spot on--comes into view.

Herc's feet twitch again, as if trying to walk.

"At least let me get us on dry land first," he says.

The two touch ground and Herc hits the ground sprinting, then slowing down to gather his composure. He grabs his knees and bends over, coughing.

"You okay there?"

Herc tries to say something about "sea", but that's all Hermes can gather before he rants all over the emerald green grass.

In the distance lies a small village by European standards, maybe larger than Saraday.

"We can be there soon," says Hermes. "Can you hang in there."

Herc stands up and wipes his mouth. He nods first and tries to catch his breath. "Yeah, yeah." He checks the corners of his mouth for spit or vomit. "I'm good."

Herc sniffs his fingers and his face curls into a twisted, sour mess.

"And it's on my shirt?" says Herc.

He takes his shirt off and tosses it into the ocean.

"That's not very kind of you," says Hermes. "Poseidon would be pissed."

"He would be if he were still alive," says Herc.

Hermes gathers right behind him, clutching at his giant friend's shoulders.

"No, no." says Herc. When Hermes goes for another grab at Herc's armpits, he slaps him away. "I said hell no. I'll walk this shit out."

Hermes erupts into laughter and flutters next to Herc.

Wandering through the small European town, Hermes takes note that the roads are cobblestone, small and light gray with black and streaks of blue in the rocks.

The only thing that keeps Hermes from thinking about his old residence in Hell is the fresh air. The briny winds and the smell of firewood.

The sun sets over the hills to the east. Being eight hours later by normal human time, this part of the earth is already snuggled in bed.

Perfect spying weather.

Hermes and Herc are careful to keep away from any of the open windows. Herc, preferring to stay in the ground, runs from wall to solid wall, trying to stay away from any human eyes.

Hermes, tired of hiding, just flies over the rooftops playfully tapping one chimney with one foot, the next with the other.

"Do you notice anything different?" Herc whispers.

"This is Italy," says Hermes. "Since you were here last? Yeah, a lot of things have changed."

Herc rolls his eyes and shrugs. "Yeah, well, ask a stupid question, get a stupid answer."

Hermes sighs. "Fine. I'm sorry."

Herc looks off to the side, pretending that he's hurt. But Hermes spots the protruding cheekbones, the ones that flex whenever he laughs.

"So," Herc snaps back. "I mean the skies. Listen."

The skies are silent. No chirps. No fluttering of bugs. Nothing even rustling in the streets.

"It's dead here, too."

By too, Herc means Saraday, of course. The skies had turned a funny color. Orange. Green. Blue. In no discernible order, it seemed.

"Where is everyone?" Hermes says.

Herc shrugs, but keeps walking. The silence and darkness never feared him before, but this time, his steps are lighter. More careful.

"We need to hurry," says Hermes. His feet tap on the rooftops. Maybe he can get a stir from the people inside.

When nothing happens, he stomps on the ground.

Nothing.

"These people are either gone or comatose," says Hermes.

"Let's knock," says Herc.

"Let us not," says Hermes. "We have a job to do."

"This is close enough, isn't it?" Herc leans against the building with his shoulder. His head leans over, resting along the wall. "I mean, this is a long way from home."

"Would you rather we fly away home?"

Herc's face goes white. "Right, so onward to the Vatican."

Herc prefers to run along the countryside to the Vatican. They enter the outskirts of Rome first, the streets much the same as the village before.

Dark, silent. Nothing creeping about except for two lost gods.

"This is crazy," says Herc.

Hermes points over into the distance. A series of lights flashing across the sky, their source coming from an open area near a giant church.

"I think that is our new target."

"Target?"

"Ground zero?"

"I don't think that's how you use that phrase."

"That is where we are supposed to be." Hermes pauses for Herc's asshole comment. But the silence between them rides for a few seconds. "Better?"

"Better."

Hermes and Herc take to the roofs. Herc, refusing to fly, digs his fingers and toes into the sandy yellow walls and up the building.

Hermes decides to watch from one of the surrounding terraces, but not on the building itself. Too close to the action.

Their job is to watch, not participate.

Herc finally hauls his fat ass up the walls and rests next to Hermes.

"I think I'm getting out of shape," he says with a smirk. He kisses his biceps and finally shuts off long enough for Hermes to pay attention.

"This is some party," says Hermes. "Maybe a rave," he says.

Herc slaps Hermes upside the back of his head. "You haven't seen a rave, and you have no idea what a party really is, do you?"

"I've heard of raves."

"From television," says Herc. He slaps Hermes yet again. "Stop watching too much TV."

Hermes tries to count the people in the square, but loses count after a two hundred. The lines move too quickly for him to keep track, so he gives up trying.

They all remain quiet, however, although huddled in such mass numbers. But willingly. Not enslaved or held captive.

"What are they doing?" says Herc.

Hermes flies upwards just enough to see the end of the line that pours out into the streets of Rome.

"I think they are trying to get into the square."

"But isn't that more of a circle?"

It was true. Saint Peter's Square, which Hermes had only briefly visited, was more of a circle than a square. But he shouldn't have to explain this to Herc.

"Yes, dumb dumb."

"No name calling."

"I swear I will make you fly with me if you do not shut up."

Herc folds his arms across his chest and huffs. "Fine."

The lines in the square end just before the entrance to basilica itself. In front of the doors, four giant winged creatures, about twice as tall as the humans in front of them, stand in a row.

The mass bows and nods. Genuflecting, Hermes thinks it's called.

"What do you see?"

Hermes shushes Herc and squints as an old woman approaches the first of the angels and bows her head. In her hands, she offers up a human child.

32

Herc snatches the perfect viewing spot from Hermes. They sit perched on the edge of a roof, one of the walkways between the entrance to the Square and the road that separates the Vatican from the rest of the Italian country.

From the sky, the Vatican is just a pin drop of buildings and land kept tight together and surrounded by thin roads that serve as the borders between the two countries.

Like a moat. But with asphalt.

Thin wispy clouds roll in from the north, and from what Hermes can see, all of Italy has gone dark.

All of it, except for the Vatican. Specifically, this mass gathering in Saint Peter's Square. The group of people gathers in large herds, rather than a huddled mass. Together, they make almost no sound.

Hermes can feel the tension in the air. The people, they look down, whisper amongst themselves, but none dare say anything that might anger the four angels who stand in front of them. Hermes recognizes two of them from struggles in the past. The female warrior and the one who chased him to South Carolina.

Jamaerah, he thinks the name is for the girl. The man, Hermes doesn't remember.

But it's only in front of those who knows how many thousands of people that he can see just how much power they seem to have.

In the middle of the arena-shaped open area, just before the entrance to the building, the angels stand in line. Side by side, as if taking offerings.

And it's this new offering that takes Hermes's sudden attention.

"Dude, that baby is so cute," says Herc. The big guy makes some gaga noises and mumbles something else under his breath.

Hermes stops listening. It's too hard to hear what's going on if he's hitting Herc in the shoulder.

"I cannot hear. Shut up."

"Is he going to eat that baby?" says Herc.

Hermes looks up. "Seriously?"

"Hey, if they'd cut a little kid, they'd probably eat a baby."

"I doubt they would bother to eat a baby in front of all of those people."

"But that lady just gave up the baby like that. You saw her."

"Shush."

"Fine."

Hermes leans in closer to listen to the gasps and whispers in the crowd.

But the crowd goes silent as the tallest angel, the one with sandy blond hair, the one that chased him across the Atlantic, takes the baby and looks upon him with a smile.

This is what most humans think happened when Jesus was born.

And here in this center, with these thousands of eyes watching, the angel smiles upon the baby and nods at the mother. Though she seems old to be the baby's mother. Her face begins to wrinkle at the edges of her mouth, her hair turning white.

The angel brings the baby closer to his face.

"See, told you. He's going to eat the baby."

"Shut up," Hermes says. "I'm trying to listen."

If Herc were any smarter, he would ask, "Listen to what?" The entire square goes silent. No words. No tapping of feet. Nothing.

Silent, except for a gasp from the mother.

The angel brings the baby's head to his lips and kisses the forehead.

When he presents the baby back to the mother, she checks its cheeks and feels its forehead.

Then, she looks upset. Pissed, even.

"What's she saying?"

"I do not know," says Hermes.

The mother clutches the baby in one arm and raises the other to the angel. She sounds as if she's swearing at it, cussing it out for something it did, or did not, do.

Herc chuckles. "She's so angry."

"They think it was a blessing, not an offering," Hermes says. "They wanted the angels to bless the baby."

"Didn't work, huh?"

Hermes shakes his head. "Does not look like it."

The woman goes into hysterics. Her face red, her hands dig into her baby's side to keep it close.

Then, she bends down to grab a rock. She throws it at the angel, though it only goes as high as his knees.

The angel does not flinch. He allows the rocks to come at him. And to Hermes, the face is an honest to goodness sympathetic. If Hermes did not know any better, he would say that the angel may have even been crying.

"Do angels cry?" says Hermes.

"Doves do," says Herc. "Prince says so."

"Birds cannot cry," says Hermes.

"But Prince says they can. It sounds like music, I guess."

Hermes shrugs. "Right. Well, this angel is crying, I think."

Herc leans forward on the roof, jutting his head out over the ledge. "He is crying. That's weird, right? That's weird."

""That is indeed weird."

Hermes pulls himself back on the roof and kneels down.

"Why are they asking for blessings? Why is everyone here to see them?"

"They look like angels," says Herc. "Maybe they think they are being saved."

"Humans have been thinking they're being saved for the past two thousand years. Why is now so different?"

"Isn't Jesus supposed to be coming or something?"

Hermes nods. "Supposedly. Or the anti-Christ."

"That's for real?"

"You helped to kill a thousand-headed snake. What do you think?"

Herc shrugs. "Right."

Still holding the baby close, she kicks at the angel's foot and spits on his boots.

The one angel with dark hair, he nods at the female angel, Jamaerah, and she nods back.

"Come," says Jamaerah. She takes the woman's shoulder in between her fingers and hauls her through the crowd.

The woman kicks, screams, but holds on to her baby tight against her chest.

"What are they doing to do with her?"

Hermes shrugs. "Just watch."

Jamaerah drags the woman to the edge of the city. The rest of the people take to one side or the other, creating a straight line path for the giant woman to walk down.

The woman is panicking and screaming.

But Hermes notices something that seems to escape the angel. A small dot, a kicking and moving dot, on the cobblestone road.

"Oh no," says Hermes. "The baby."

Jamaerah, reaching the city, lets go of the old woman.

"The baby?" says Herc.

"She's lost in the streets."

The woman stands up and flips her off, taking her fingers and sliding them up along the underside of her chin.

"That's not good," says Herc.

Jamaerah, tilts her head at this gesture. Confused. She repeats it back to the woman and stomps back to the rest of the angels.

"What just happened?"

Hermes doesn't even bother to repeat anymore. He just watches, in silence.

When Jamaerah gets back to her friends, she folds her arm, but gives a worried look to the tall, sandy haired one.

"Should we not do something for that child?" the tall one says.

The angel with dark hair shakes his head slowly. "Not a chance." His voice is dark, raspy. "They must know what it is like to live without God in their hearts," he says. "Let them see that they need God. "They will ask for him to come back to them."

"Is that what we are doing, Gabriel?" says the sandy haired one.

"Do not question the Deus Vox," Gabriel says. "They need to know the truth of suffering if they are to love and turn to God."

33

Hermes feels the air escaping his lungs. Arms that are too strong to be human remain wrapped around his chest. The little bit of breath he can take in gets smaller and smaller.

"I'm not letting you go until you calm down," says Herc. "You're such a human sometimes."

Hermes beats at Herc's ear. "You take that back."

"Not until you calm down, you little human girl."

Hermes forces himself to stop hitting. His arms and legs go motionless. Limp.

"Better?" says Herc.

Hermes nods. His face is still flush red, his heart feels as if it wants to explode. "Yes. I'm better."

"You're lying," says Herc. "I can tell. But since you're calm, I'll let you down."

Hermes's wings begin to flutter, but Herc grabs Hermes's legs from underneath him. "You're not going anywhere."

"But they need to be taught a lesson," Hermes says. He shows Herc his fists, as if they could really do anything.

"And you're being stupid about this," Herc says. "We said we would check things out. Be spies. Remember? Spies don't go blowing shit up."

Hermes pauses. "James Bond?"

"Who?"

"Some white guy with different faces," says Hermes. "I saw some movies on TV."

"When we get home, I'm selling the television," says Herc.

"You wouldn't dare." Hermes shows his fists in Herc's face. He doesn't look impressed.

"Calm."

Hermes takes in a deep breath. "Fine," he says. "Calm."

Herc smiles. "Good." Herc stands up and lets the go of his friend's ankle. "So now what?"

Hermes kneels down on the roof and looks down over the group of humans. As Herc tries to copy Hermes's stance, a roof panel slides off.

Hermes holds his breath and flutters down to catch it, but misses it.

The panel shatters on the black concrete like it was terra cotta or a light brick.

"What are you doing?" Hermes says. It begins as a whisper, but doesn't remain so for long. "Are you trying to get us caught?" he says.

"No more than you were just a minute ago."

"That was different," says Hermes.

"And how?"

Hermes, the labeled God of Communication, falls silent for a moment. "I hate you."

He sits back down and eyes the child in the center of the road.

"We have to help that kid," says Herc.

"That is what I was trying to do," says Hermes. "I want to help the child."

But when Hermes looks over to see Herc, he notices that his eyes aren't fixed on the baby on the streets—a baby that no one in the crowd bothers to touch.

Instead, Herc's eyes appear glued to the female angel. "You like Jamaerah, don't you?"

"It's that obvious?" says Herc.

"Oh no, not at all. I was just guessing, you know. Out of the blue."

Herc nods. "Good guess."

"Did I already say that I hate you?"

Herc nods. "Yup."

"Good."

Herc drops from the roof and cracks his knuckles. Hermes knows the sign.

"But you just told me that we are not to go in," says Hermes.

"I lied to you." Herc smiles. "I just wanted to be the first one in."

"Typical." Hermes lands on the ground next to Herc. "So, would you like to do the honors?"

Herc bows with a huge shit-eating grin. His feet dig into the stone floor and he kneels forward like a sprinter at the Olympics.

"Ready?" says Herc.

"When you are."

Herc doesn't wait for a "go." He sprints off into the crowd. His strong legs allow him to leap over the first half of the crowd and make a perfect landing in the alley left by Jamaerah's return trip to her fellow angels' side.

"We're back!" shouts Herc.

Hermes shakes his head. "We need a catchphrase," says Hermes.

Herc shrugs. "No we don't. I got this."

Herc points a thick sausage finger at Jamearah and shouts, "I'm here for you, toots."

Hermes shrugs and tries to keep from laughing. While Herc confuses the angels with his speech and threats, Hermes hovers over the ground and picks up the baby.

His wiggles in his arms, but the blanket it's bundled in—white with Disney characters dancing to some hidden music—keeps it tight and safe. "I have you, little guy."

The baby wails at the sight of Hermes's face.

"Gee, thanks."

The baby's mother remains seated where she was left off, just outside the building's walls next to a white funny-looking car. The vehicle looks like a hatchback, but smaller and with no decals on it. The kind of small white vehicle that might have candy in it. Candy for children.

Hermes flutters to the end of the street and nods at the mother. "Is this yours?" he asks.

The woman nods. Her hair is held up tight in a bun at the back of her head. As she smiles, her wrinkles become more pronounced around her nose, her lips, and her cheeks. But she appears happy and grateful.

"Si," she says.

Hermes nods. "Good." A voice beckons at Hermes from around the corner.

"Exa-cusa me," the voice says in broken English.

Hermes turns his head. Two men, one holding a giant camera on his shoulder, approach Hermes. But slowly, as if trying to pet a wild tiger.

"Can-a you, uh, talk toa us?"

Hermes shakes his head. "Is that a television camera?"

The man whips out a microphone. His hair is slicked back and shiny in the light. His clothes look pressed and business attire professional.

These Europeans, always knowing how to dress to impress.

"TV?" the man says. "Yes, this is TV."

Hermes runs his fingers through his short brown hair. "Oh wow," he says.

As Hermes is ready to agree to an interview, however, something from within the square makes the crowd scream and go running.

"Damn it," says Hermes. He holds up an index finger. "One minute, please?"

The man nods. He looks to his cameraman, an overweight fellow who moves slow and wiggles his hips when he walks. They both agree. "Yes, yes," they say. "Later."

Hermes smiles and flies into the square.

The people come rushing at him like a tidal wave. The flood of people rushes toward Hermes head-on.

He flies upwards and lets the rush of people funnel through the doorway below him. Heat rises from their fear and frustration. The heat waves meet Hermes's feet and ankles, making him actually sweat.

At the source of the flood near the church's doorway, Herc and the female angel Jamaerah wrestle in hand-to-hand grappling moves that Hermes has seen a few times on TV again.

Their heads next to each other, their arms locked in a configuration that only confuses Hermes from this high up. And their legs both hold still, trying to push each other forward.

The dark haired angel, however, flies upward.

Hermes flies to catch up with the winged creature.

But the dark haired one, the one they called Gabriel, he is fast in the air, flying against the natural air currents with his wings as long as two Hermes head to foot.

The size, however, means to Hermes that he can keep his eyes on him easier. Even in the dark sky.

The crowd begins to disappear beneath him, filtering out through the entrance and into the Italian city streets.

Flashing lights—blue and red—flicker down below him. From up here, it looks like a play land or theme park gone horribly wrong. The fights, the screaming, the lights. All of it would be playful if it weren't for the threatening angels.

Gabriel appears to pick up speed, a speed that Hermes isn't sure he can match.

But he tries, pointing himself forward and keeping his hands and legs close together to minimize air resistance.

They fly over the northern half of Italy and the skies get darker, a midnight blue with thick, gray clouds.

But Gabriel only seems to disappear up in front of him. A small, flapping white dot in front of him.

But Hermes bites down and tries to fly faster, but there seems to be no point. The angel flies faster than Hermes's wings can keep up.

So he hovers over the land, looking down below and seeing that the people have disappeared in their houses here, too.

Each building has dimmed lights. Shades drawn. The streets overrun with pigeons and doves.

No humans anywhere.

With nowhere else to go, Hermes turns back to the Vatican.

Another one of the angels flies up to meet him. His armor is white with a silver eagle stretched across his chest. His pants, boots, everything is white and pristine in the moonlight. "You were a fool to come here." He crosses his arms and hovers, wings flapping in place, in front of Hermes.

"So were you," says Hermes.

The angel does not argue. "I could protect you," says the angel.

"Protect us? From what?"

"You should take your friend and leave. Leave us and I will protect you. Those are the terms."

"I cannot just let you do whatever you want. You cannot have Earth."

"That is not your decision," says the angel.

"I will make it my decision."

The angel charges toward Hermes. His strong wings flap like thunder in the skies, gaining speed until the angel's shoulder slams into Hermes's stomach and then flies away.

Hermes flips around in the air. His wings flap out of control, trying to stop the twirling in the middle of the air.

But his strength leaves him and soon, Hermes feels the wind rushing through his hair, flapping at his clothes.

The wind is gravity, pulling him downward.

34

Brad could always tell when his mom hid something. She did this thing with her nose, wrinkled it up so her two front teeth would show. It was funny, Brad used to think, like she was a cartoon bunny.

But now, it's not so funny.

"Of course, more angels on television," says Sophie. She presses hard on the white—well, it used to be white—cloth on her shoulder. She coughs once, but tries to hide the second one because she knows her son is paying attention.

Someone knocks on the room's door. "Hi," says a nurse's head, popping in from around the corner. She wheels someone in—a little old man. Not injured, but with a metal tube next to him. Like a fire extinguisher, but in silver, not red.

"No," says Brad. "You cannot come in here." Brad stands between the nurse and the bed. He rests his hands on his hips and holds out his chest. "No."

Sophie coughs. "Let them through, Brad. Sick people need the hospital, too."

"But, mom. You're sicker." Brad runs to his mother's side and rests his head in her arms. "I don't want anyone in here."

The nurse hesitates and then pulls back on the wheelchair. "Should I just come back?"

Sophie shakes her head. "If you need the room, the no, please. Come right in."

The nurse smiles. She's a young looking nurse. And pretty with her hair hanging just onto her shoulders. She's not wearing white like what they tell you they wear in all of those hospital shows. Instead, her scrubs are pink with a light blue line along the edges of them.

"Thank you," says the nurse. She helps the man onto the bed and tucks him in.

The man's breathing thing hangs at his side. Using it makes him sound like Darth Vader, the deep inhales and exhales that sound like they are all air.

"Brad, don't stare," says Sophie.

Brad closes the curtain between the old man and his mother. He wants privacy, but the world doesn't want to give it to them.

It's not fair. Never fair.

"Mom," says Brad. The words push at his throat.

"I love you," she says. With her wet, sweaty palm, she pushes the hair back on his head. It flops back over his forehead again and she smiles.

The hair tickles his eyebrows and he blinks to get them out of the way.

But the smiles. He loved it when she smiled.

"Mom," he says again. "I love you, too."

Sophie strokes his head and plays with his bangs. "I know, sweetheart."

When she stops, he looks up. "Mom, are you okay?"

Sophie gasps. "Hermes is on television."

"Huh?" Brad turns to look at the TV. All day the shows just kept talking about the bright lights that fell from the sky. Then they talked about the end of days, whatever that meant, and then these tall winged people that made everyone come and see them in this place in Rome.

But Brad new the secret. It might be the end of days. It might be the end of the world, even.

But the angels. They weren't like storybook angels. Or Bible angels.

Brad scratches at the scar on his forearm, left there from the flaming sword of an angel guardian. He thought it was okay to hit a little child.

That's how he got the scar.

"Brad, stop scratching at that," says Sophie. "You need to let it heal."

"Yes, Mom."

Brad climbs up onto the bed and cuddles next to his mom. The camera looks shaky. Like the man was maybe nervous or something.

Then on the screen, is Hermes. He's helping some woman get her baby back. But she looks too old to have a baby. Maybe a grandbaby?

Hermes smiles as the camera and flies off.

"Mom, is it a bad thing that people are watching Hermes fly?"

Sophie takes a second to answer. "Maybe," she says. "I don't know."

"Are they going to think he is a bad guy because he has wings on his feet?"

Sophie grins. "No, honey. I don't think so."

"Mom," says Brad.

"Yes, honey?"

Brad feels his throat choke up and get tight. "Are you going to die?"

Sophie pulls him closer to her body. "I don't know," she says. "I do not want to lie to you. But I don't know."

Brad cries.

"Hermes says he can fix this," Sophie says. "And I believe him. We just have to have a little bit of faith in them, okay?"

"I hate those angels," says Brad. "I hate them all."

"You don't mean that," she says.

Brad nods. "Yes, I do. They hurt me. They hurt you."

"What do you mean?"

Brad takes in a deep breath. "The angels are keeping people from dying," he says. "It makes sense, and it's what Hermes thinks."

Sophie coughs.

Brad continues, "So I hate them."

Sophie rubs Brad's back. "No you don't."

Brad lets the argument die. Now is not the time to argue with his mom. It's not how he wants to remember her.

He wants to remember her smile. He wants to remember having no regrets.

"Mom?" he says again.

She nods. "Yes?"

"I have something to tell you."

Sophie sits up as best as she can. Despite all of this pain, she still smiles and Brad takes in every minute. Every line on her face, the shape her of cheeks. Brad commits it all to memory.

"Mom," he says. "I killed the man who hurt you."

Sophie nods. "I know," she says quietly.

"Are you mad at me?" he says. Tears well up in his eyes.

"No, honey." She pats the back of his head and hugs him. "I could never be mad at you."

"Do you promise?" he says. "Because I'm afraid."

"What are you afraid of?"

"Myself."

35

Hermes tries not to think about the stiff landing and the probable dent he left in the cement after falling from twenty feet in the air.

He rests his hands on his back, rubbing the sore bruises he knows he's going to get tomorrow and follows the sound of destruction and screaming.

The Italian police have arrived, but they keep their cars at a distance that can hardly be called responsible. It seems they are more afraid of being hurt than doing some hurting.

Not that they could hurt Herc or Jamaerah. Good luck on that one.

Hermes comes to the street just outside the Vatican's Saint Peter's Basilica. From the outside, the angels can be seen just standing above the fighting. All except for the one who got away: Gabriel.

Hermes flies to the top of the roof of a nearby building and watches as Herc and Jamaerah trade blows. Herc grabs Jamaerah's ponytail and pulls it forward, kneeing her in the face and then tossing her off to the side.

Jamaerah stands, stunned, and wipes the pink spit from the

edges of her mouth.

If something doesn't happen soon, they're going to destroy this whole church.

"Herc!" Hermes shouts.

Herc's feet twitch as he stumbles for only a split moment. He heard him. This is good. Maybe Hermes can be the voice of reason.

"Herc! Don't destroy the building."

Herc nods and flexes once again. He stands, his arms apart, his hands held like claws, ready to shred the angel into pieces.

And in keeping with the violent efforts, Jamaerah rushes into Herc headfirst into the building.

Amidst the debris and dust, Herc pulls his arms up over his head and digs in.

"No! Not destroy. Not destroy!" Hermes shouts.

Herc's eyes widen. He realizes his mistake too soon.

Herc draws his hands down and pulls the sand yellow wall down with him.

The entire wing, part of the Saint Peter's Square, comes crashing down onto Jamaerah and Herc.

Herc, however, appears prepared, jumping through the debris and getting just behind the angel's reach.

"There you are, toots. I win."

Jamaerah's wings twitch as if paralyzed.

"Shit, no," says Hermes. "This isn't good." He looks up to the roof of the basilica.

Two more angels—the sandy-haired one and another one who looks to be a soldier—stand watch over the battle.

As the building comes crashing down, however, the soldier reaches for a spear and points it at Herc.

Except the sandy-haired angel extends a hand out in front of the soldier. He shakes his head and mouths the words "No."

All good television shows have narrators, so he does what any good, self-respecting detective would do. He announces his thoughts out loud. "No?" he says. He strokes his chin as if the camera were on him. "What does he mean? No?"

Herc looks over the rubble and leans over to where he thinks

Jamaerah's head would be. "So, if you're free sometime, you know after slaving humanity and all, would you like to go out sometime? Get something to eat?"

"Herc!" cries Hermes. "Let's go."

"But she didn't say yes yet."

The angel's feet twitch again. Rubble begins trickling down the sides of the pile of rocks and mortar that covers her.

"She's going to get up," says Hermes. "Let's go before he changes his mind."

"Before who changes whose mind?" says Herc.

"Oh, for fucking out loud," says Hermes. He launches himself off the roof and flies toward Herc's shoulders. Coming near them, he extends his arms out to grab the god's armpits.

"No," says Herc. He drops down into a ball.

Hermes flies just over him, almost hitting the wall in front of him.

"You idiot," Hermes says. Hermes keeps his eyes on the angel in charge and the soldier just beside him.

The soldier angel looks twitchy. His spear changes hands and he shuffles his weight back and forth on his feet. Itching to come down and do some damage.

"So you're saying we have to go?"

Hermes begins the flight back home, keeping low to the ground in hopes that Herc will soon follow.

He hears the beginnings of flapping. A deep, chest-thumping flap coming from the basilica.

The soldier angel comes down from the roof and rushes to the female angel's aid.

Herc, seeing the soldier coming his way, begins his run to catch up with Hermes. But even up here, Hermes can hear Herc's winded attempts to catch his breath. With each step, he can hear the pain that Herc must be in.

"She hits pretty hard, huh?"

Herc cracks his jaw. "You could say that." He grins, however, leaping over cars and fences. "But I hit harder."

36

B rad expected more of a struggle from his mother when he told her he was afraid of himself.

Instead, he gets to sit in silence with her while she decides to walk away into the afternoon.

Brad has nothing else to do. Through the dirty window, he can watch front lawn packed full of wannabe patients and picketers marching and stepping in unison to a beat that Brad rather finds catchy.

The room smells like the stuff his mother uses to clean the bathroom. Not lemony, but something bitter. And maybe a hint of sweetness. Only pictures of flowers and pastel boxes hang on the walls. Nothing exciting or interesting for a nine-year-old, almost ten-year-old boy.

So he listens to his mom's roommate snore.

And snore, he does. Brad bites his lower lip to keep from smiling and maybe laughing because the guy smiles so hard.

It's the way his snores sound that makes him want to laugh. The man's intense, deep breathing that sounds like someone is buzzing through a tree with a chainsaw. Then he smacks his lips twice after each snore. And only twice.

Brad counted each time.

This type of stuff Brad has only seen in a cartoon while watching TV with his buddy Hermes.

Were they okay? Why hadn't they said anything yet? Where even were they?

And Brad eyes the room's door. Was she supposed to be out there alone?

"Mom?" he says. He stands up and walks to the door. As his hand rests on the door, the figure of his mother comes into view. "Mom!"

Brad jumps backwards.

Sophie grabs her stomach and hops backward as well.

The two are left staring at each other, unsure if they should laugh or scream.

So Brad laughs first.

Then Sophie.

"Oh, I needed that," she says.

Brad looks down at his feet. He kicks the pack of cards. "Are these yours?"

Sophie nods. "Could you pick them up for me, please?"

Brad takes them and reads the package. Poker cards.

"We're playing poker?"

These weren't the cards that he was used to seeing in school, with the big numbers and bigger symbols. Diamonds. Hearts. He couldn't remember the other ones.

But he knew they were black. But that's all.

"No, honey. I was never good at poker."

She sits down and pats the side of the bed for Brad to join her. "Come here."

Brad's steps are narrow, uncomfortable. He fumbles the pack of cards between his hands. Left. Right. Left. In line with his steps.

"Have you ever played spades?" she says.

Brad shakes his head and hands the package of cards on the table.

"We're supposed to play with more people, but I don't think anyone wants to join us."

"I don't want anyone to join us," says Brad.

Sophie frowns. Brad does, too, feeling the stabbing heart pain of disappointing his mother.

"Here," says Sophie. She takes the cards out of the box and sets the box to the side. The cards slide apart in his mother's weak hands.

He reaches over and gathers the cards and puts them back in a straight stack. "Let me help." He smiles to hide the fear that his mother is getting weaker. That some day he might lose her. "How do we start?"

Sophie sticks out her tongue out of the corner of her mouth. This is how she thinks. Brad sometimes catches himself doing the same thing when he thinks really, really hard. "I'm not sure, honey. Just go ahead and pass everything out."

"Everything?" he says.

"Everything."

Brad comes up with a plan. He splits the cards in half almost perfectly and hands his mother the bottom half. "Here you go."

Sophie laughs. "No, honey. That's not going to work for now."

"Why not?"

Sophie flips the cards over. "Because they are still in order. There's no way we could play like this." She laughs and it becomes a kind of music to his ears. "Make sure you shuffle them first."

Brad shuffles slowly so he doesn't have to mess up the moment. He wants his mother to keep laughing.

Maybe by holding the cards, he can keep the moment alive forever? Maybe he can just not let her die because she still have to finis the game?

"Brad, honey. Are you going to pass out the cards?"

"How?"

"I get one. Then you get one."

"Oh," he says. Of course Brad knows how to pass out cards. He's played cards at school with the other kids. Sometimes they would play poker with jellybeans or sometimes they would play Go Fish.

He learned to pass out cards when he was five. He just turned nine yesterday. He's not that little.

Brad's hands shake as he hands out the first card. He nudges the top card off the stack and drops it on his lap. Then he takes the next and hands it to his mother.

"Honey," she says. Her voice is calm and fake happy. This was the voice she used when she told Brad that she lost her job and needed to look for a new one.

"Brad, honey. I want you to listen to Hermes."

Brad's eyes begin to tear up. "Yes, mom."

"And I know you always do, but I think he's the best one to listen to. You know how Herakles is."

Brad wipes away a tear and hands out another three cards.

"And remember, that if he tells you to eat your vegetables or not stay out at night, you had better do as he says."

Brad nods. He can't look up at her or he'll lose it. And he might wake up the old man next to him. That would be embarrassing.

"And keep practicing with Herc, okay?" Sophie takes the cards with one hand and holds out the other one to touch the back of Brad's hand. "I think you're going to be a strong, strong boy and a very handsome man."

"I will, Mom. I promise."

"And always do your best in school. No matter how strong you get, you will always need to be smart."

Brad feels the burning of his eyes. He doesn't want to let go. He needs to be a man. A hero like Herc. But soon, his eyes turn into a full-fledged torrent of tears. "Yes, Mom. I know."

"And you know I'll always love you."

Brad puts his hand of cards down and stares at her. He feels bad because he made his mother cry.

But these are good tears, right? Good tears because of a bad situation?

Brad scoots along the bed until he can bring his arms around her completely. She takes in a deep breath, but Brad doesn't let his hug go soft on her.

"And I'll always love you," he says. He closes her eyes. And even with them closed, the bright fluorescent lights burn through his eyelids. He smells his mother through all of the bandages and creams and alcohol wipes that were used to clean her up.

Through it all, he smells her scent. Like soft, subtle flowers. The way you smell when you're happy.

Brad closes his eyes and takes in the moment. Like a camera, he lets his mind snap the different feelings. Her soft hair around his hands. The smell of her body against his nose. Her cheek caressing the top of his head.

All of this builds into his mind and he closes it for safe keeping.

"I'm so sorry," he says. "For everything."

From behind him, Brad hears the man on the television. He speaks with a deep voice that makes him sound believable and maybe a bit like someone's grandfather.

He says something like a Vatican is falling apart because of fighting.

When Brad is just about to let go and let the moment swim around in his head, he hears his mother gasp.

"What the hell is wrong with those two?" she says.

37

The rocks begin trickling down the sides of the small mound of bricks, mortar, and lots and lots of dust. The mound rumbles. Dust explodes from the sides and then a hand--Jamaerah's hand-- bursts through the mound's peak.

The skies begin showing thin streams of yellow light across the Italian buildings, though the air smells of stale dust and debris. Nearly half of the city known as simply The Vatican lies in remnants below Michael's feet.

From a freestanding wall, the only piece of Saint Peter's Basilica still stands after Herakles and his prized soldier went to pound on each other in public.

It was not one of his most favored moments, that was to be sure. However the message sent. Or Gabriel's message, that is.

Angels will not back down from saving Humanity.

By force if necessary.

One of the archangel's strongest soldiers, the most powerful of the Chorus, erupts from the mound. Her wings extend across the square. Jamaerah stretches her arms out, reaching for the skies. No doubt the battle wore her down.

Michael counts almost three cracks that pop off like the guns of the humans. Crack. Pop. Crack.

Then Jamaerah roars. Her voice echoes across the walls and into the hallways of the square itself.

"Where is he?" she screams again.

Micheal's ears catch the sounds of feet scuffling down the streets out of the Vatican and into the city of Rome. One of the escapees holds a large black camera on his shoulder.

"We are done," says Michael. "We need to return to Gabriel. There has been enough destruction here." Michael's eyes roam over the destroyed buildings and the puffs of dust that billow out of the collapsing buildings around them.

So much destruction. So much pain. He feels deep in his chest the breaking hearts. The pain and suffocation of those caught in the rubble of the walls.

Each breath becomes more difficult to take, so he does what he's always done.

"We must go back." Michael waves his arms up at the massively built Saint Peter's Basilica.

Winged soldiers march out of the building in slow, ominous steps. Their spears at their side, held up parallel with their arms. The soldier angels' eyes look directly in front of them.

Nothing leads them astray from their commands.

Michael whispers the word halt and the angels all stop on command.

Jamaerah is the first to take flight over the city. What seems to be midway between the Earth realm and the sun, Jamaerah stops, her wings flapping loud as rolling thunder deep within Michael's own chest.

He can feel her pain, her frustrations, as well. She grinds her teeth and wants revenge. Though she doesn't know why.

She wants to see and feel pain.

Michael knows this because every sensation Jamaerah feels deep in the muscles of her body also resonates with him.

Because of this, he knows he must go. This is too much for an empath like him.

The other soldier angels follow Michael's lead. He leaves into the air, his wings carrying him high up over the city.

The angels take to the skies in a horde. One after the other, they fly up and toward the sun rising in the east.

Jamaerah waves her hand. "Follow me," she shouts to her soldiers.

And follow they do. The skies begin to darken. Gently at first.

And Michael is struck with the pains of fear. The headaches of screams and chest-clenching pressure in his lungs.

The people down below fear them.

And when the angels fly so thick, so tight together that they block out the sun, Michael catches a glimpse of the irony of their situation.

The sun, blocking out the earth, a metaphor.

For while the earth has darkened from the angel's large numbers, so too, as their message.

And with a heavy heart, Michael himself takes to the skies and follows just behind them as they make their way to the clouds of Heaven.

38

Michael is the first to walk through the Gates to Heaven. The gates appear reflective, almost smooth as liquid, as they shine in the haunting blue light that radiates through Heaven. The halls feel empty and his own footsteps echo louder the deeper he gets into the building.

There is a warmth that radiates from the walls. Never as hot as the peninsular sun of the Earth Realm, and surely not as warm as the human-packed Saint Peter's Basilica. The warmth was comforting in most times.

But today, there was very little anyone—even God's creations— could do to calm his nerves.

The soldier angels and Jamaerah remain just behind him. Maybe a step or two by Michael's accounts.

It's not out of fear that they tread slowly behind him. As the primary General of the Archangels' Chorus, Michael was responsible for the success or failure of this mission.

A thought, he believed, was completely unfair.

Michael was an angel of mercy, of compassion. It was his job to seek compassion in others, to pull it out of those who feel none.

He was not a fight. Certainly not a warrior. He had no desire to kill. No desire to rule over anyone. As far as beings were concerned, he wished to be as pure as the flawless white building in which he now stood.

The walls had small bits of human-esque designs in them. Columns built into the walls in a liquid smooth white that mimicked the Earth realm's alabaster. A white marble-like ceiling that sparkled despite an obvious light source.

The light, this ethereal glow, did not give off any heat in and of itself, and the walls did not hang on to any particular smells, giving the hallways a purity and blandness that made Michael almost yearn a return to Earth.

The colors, the sensations. It was proof positive of God's glorious will and his compassion. Everything was a sign of life.

Here, things turned cold and white. Blank and devoid of emotion and life.

Human spirits lucky enough to have seen this side of Heaven remark on its beauty and its simplicity.

Typical of humans, to not know what they have when they have it.

This is one of the reasons why Michael feels compelled to speak to Gabriel to begin with.

The room that holds Gabriel's brooding self feels expansive compared to the beautifully ornate Saint Peter's Basilica. The eternally pure white gives Michael the impression of it lasting forever.

Not like the streets of Italy, the winding roads that themselves appear to go into the distance. Lasting eternal. It is easy for Michael to believe that maybe those roads connected all around the world.

In the middle of the room is a large rectangular table, also a pure white made of a substance that most humans would never comprehend. The edges of the table are beveled, giving the table a slight three dimensional shadow that contrasts greatly with the lack of gray and black present in the room.

"Failure," says Gabriel. The de-facto leader of the Archangels of the First Order, the strongest Chorus of Heaven, wears the silver and gold warrior's armor he earned. The breastplate fastens near his shoulders in thick straps not of the earth, but made of a material far stronger than what can be made by human smiths. The way Gabriel has his arms folded behind him, the Silver Eagle that spreads across his chest appears to want to jump free and take flight.

Gabriel stands at the edge of the table, peering downward at the white table. On it, etchings of earth, of major cities, that glimmer with a multicolored light. Essences of the ethereal glow that pervades the entirety of Heaven.

"We did what we could, Gabriel, but we had to regroup."

"You did not have to do anything." Gabriel turns around from facing the desk. His warm hazel eyes meet Michael's. "You had simple orders."

"I had orders to make our presence known and to convince them of our supremacy and our compassion."

Gabriel appears to roll his eyes at the word compassion.

The words feel awkward coming out of his mouth. As if speaking a different tongue.

"And yet here you are. With my army."

"The humans rebelled. We have several ex-demons roaming about. One of them gave Jamaerah quite a difficult time." Michael opens his mouth, but then closes it. He must choose his words wisely.

"Then the humans have made their decision. They are not worthy of being Jehova's favorite. They deny him by denying us."

Michael raises a finger to speak, but Gabriel ignores him and turns around as he speaks.

"The rocks. The attacks. These are acts of war. Acts that cannot and shall now go unpunished."

"Do you not think this is a bit drastic? Punishment? They just do not understand. They are fearful of us being harbingers of death."

"Then they do not understand the meanings of Heaven, of Angels. They are not worthy of our blessings."

"You are not saying what I think you are saying."

"War?" says Gabriel. Michael swears he sees the corners of his mouth curl upwards into a coy smile. "Not war. We must allow them the chance to learn what it's like to live without God."

"He would not want this. Not for his subjects."

"He has already turned his backs on us," says Gabriel. "And on them. Look at them. They fight. They abandon their children. They gamble and go against the very same commandments laid down upon them. Give me one good reason why they should be allowed to continue this pathetic existence."

Michael holds his tongue. He shifts his leg behind the other, ready to spin around when Gabriel coughs to get his attention.

"I sense that you are not with me on this, Michael." Michael turns his head to see Gabriel's eyes, now looking almost golden in this pale light, piercing into his own. "I would not want to wage war divided as we are," he says. "You are not a warrior," he says. "I know this. This is why you must trust me on these things."

Michael nods and turns around. He hears another cough as he approaches the door. He freezes.

"And Michael?"

Michael nods. "Yes, sir?"

"Ready the troops for battle."

"As you wish, sir."

39

The door to Sophie's room slides open. Snoring rattles in the air behind a curtain that surrounds the bed next to Sophie's.

While Hermes feels blessed—all things considered—that he can walk through the door, his best friend Herakles limps.

"You look like Hell," Sophie says with a smile.

Hermes nods and bites his tongue. A sound comes from the curtains next to Sophie's bed. Hermes nods at it.

"We have a neighbor," Brad says, grimacing.

Hermes nods. "Another won't die person?" he says.

Sophie and Brad shakes their heads.

"I don't think so," Brad speaks up. "He looks like he's going to die any minute."

Herc rests his body in the padded chair at the foot of Sophie's bed. A thick plastic rail separates Sophie's foot from touching Herc's gigantic, muscled knees.

"That's not very nice," says Sophie.

Brad looks downwards, but Hermes senses the futility of making a pissed off boy very sorry about anything. He's been handed a shitty hand. It wouldn't be fair to expect a nine-year-old boy to understand much of anything.

"We had another fight," says Herc. He jerks his head first to the right, then quickly to the left. Three loud snap-crackle-pops follow afterwards.

Hermes scoots his thin ass at the foot of Sophie's bed. The soft pastel blue blanket feels good against his hands when compared to the thick, sweaty skin of his best friend. The same best friend who fought down an angel and barely walked away from it alive.

The room smells like Bacitrin, or some crème that humans put on their wounds when they get cut.

It happens to Brad nearly three times a week, especially when he insists on trying to help his mother cook.

The little boy tries to do anything and everything he can get his hands on. A precocious little thing, he could read magazines at the age of nine and was able to tell Herc how to drive a car before they got caught by Sophie.

In his two thousand years on and off the Earth realm, Hermes had seen plenty of death and destruction. From the fall of Troy to the destruction of the Twin Towers in New York City, these moments only served to feed Hermes's thoughts that the humans were playthings to be tempted with power and authority over the others.

But when family is attached, the little godling finds himself in a position of anger, fueled by rage and sadness he had not dared to experience before. Now, he wants the rage. He needs the sadness. These are the things that are going to get his Sophie back up and well again.

"So no luck?" says Sophie.

Herc shakes his head.

Hermes pats Sophie on the foot. "We may need to have a different approach. They are too strong, and now they are daring to attack us."

Herc nods. "Yeah, they are attacking humans everywhere."

"They're dangerous. For some reason, they want us to suffer," says Hermes.

Herc shakes his dumb-looking head. The bruises on his cheeks begin to turn purple from the red scrapes they looked like before.

"Right," says Herc. "Humans. To suffer."

"Then let's go kick some ass," says Brad. He sits up from the chair at the foot of his mother's bed. His cheeks glow a bright red with excitement. His eyes perk up, glowing for the first time since before the accident.

"Out of the question," says Hermes. "You will get hurt again. And this time it will not be as easy."

"But I'm a good healer," says Brad. He wiggles his hand around, but bites his tongue behind closed lips. Hermes can see all of this, but he smiles anyway.

"And you are also going to scare your mother if you go into battle with us," says Hermes. "You stay here."

"But he can fight as well as all of us," says Herc. "Look at the way he wrestled with Jamaerah."

"Who's Jamaerah?" Sophie sits up from her bed. "Who's that?"

Brad looks to Hermes who looks to Herc. "She's this chick I met," he says. "She's pretty hot."

"She is an angel. A general," says Hermes. "One of the bad guys," he says, raising his voice.

The sound of the snoring dies down. Hermes hears Sophie's labored breathing in the emptiness of the room. The conversation has gone quiet. As if nothing is happening outside. The entire world exists in this room and this room only.

Hermes studies Sophie's eyes. They appear dark in this brightly lit room. The fluorescent light above them, that humming, makes Sophie appear less and less alive by the minute. Washing out the life that she has left.

But she coughs and holds up a hand. It wobbles in the air. "Let him go," she says.

"You cannot be serious," says Hermes. "It is my job to protect him and you and I will not let him go and fight on our behalf. He is just a child."

"No one said you have to protect us," says Sophie.

"Yeah," says Brad. He crosses his arms the way he's seen Herc do when he gets indignant. That man will be the death of Brad. "Who says you have to protect us?"

"I said I have to protect you," says Hermes. He stands up from the edge of the bed and watches all three of them stand closer together. "I said it because I mean it. Who else is going to look after you?"

"No one has to look after anyone," says Herc. "We can all do it."

"You cannot be serious," says Hermes. "You cannot even make a peanut butter sandwich without destroying the refrigerator." He points to Herc. "And you," Hermes points to Brad, "you are way too eager to grow up," he says. "You should be a child and do child things. I do not know what those things are," he says, "but you should try. Because it would kill me to see your mother see you get hurt."

Hermes feels the tears choke him in the back of his throat.

The man on the other end of the curtains calls out, "Will you guys just pipe down? Jesus Christ, I can't even die in fucking peace."

"I'm the one who needs to protect Mom," says Brad. "Not you, not anyone." A tear slides down his rounded cheeks. "You think you know about protecting someone? I've already seen my mom hurt because of me." More tears shower down his cheeks. His lower lips quivers as he tries to keep himself together. "And it's my fault and I need to be the one to fix it."

Brad looks at his mother and runs over to her side, gripping her shoulder sand hugging hard.

"I'm so sorry, mom. I'm sorry."

Sophie closes her eyes and reaches over for Brad's elbow. The first of many tears drips a thin trail down her face. "I know," she whispers in an airy breath. "I know you are."

Hermes wipes his own eyes with the back of his hand and walks out of the door.

The hallway is quieter than he remembered. No one running up or down. The doors to the different rooms shut.

He looks to the left. Then the right. Something crunches behind him.

"If the boy wants to go," says Lilith, "and the woman wants him to go, then let the boy fucking go." She pops a few more potato chips in her mouth and smiles a greasy grin.

"Those are going to make you fat, you know. I saw it on TV once." Hermes pushes past her in the hallway and walks to the waiting room. Having been barred inside and not allowed to leave, the several people have set up blankets and rolled up jackets like sleeping bags around the floor. The children sit around the television showing cartoons—not the new channel like before.

These people have had enough news. All of it bad. Now they just sit around a hospital, the place where people go to get better, to wait out the upcoming apocalypse and pray for the best.

Hermes wishes he had been in the habit to pray. To do something other than just sit still and watch the world fall around him at his feet.

Brad's small but powerful feet stomp down the hallway behind him. "I'm coming with you whether you like it or not," he says.

Hermes sighs. "You sound like your father," he says. Hermes turns to see Brad standing at the sign in desk. His arms and legs stretched out straight, his arms at his side, his legs shoulder-length apart. And his eyes—Brad's eyes glow electric blue, as if an electric storm lay somewhere inside.

But something catches Brad's attention. Hermes notices that Brad is no longer looking at him, but just past his shoulder.

Hermes turns around. Outside, a large shadow looms over the skies, like a blanket darkening the sky.

40

B rad rushes to the front door. His hands slap the glass and he pushes his head as far against the glass as it will let him go. "What the hell is that?" he says.

Hermes taps the back of Brad's head. "Language."

But the boy was right. What was that?

Hermes squints and peers upwards. The shadow appears to wave in the sky. As if someone is shaking the blanket.

No, the blanket isn't waving. It's flapping.

"Those are the angels?" says Brad. He turns his head against the glass, causing a greasy smear across the face of the door.

Hermes nods and rubs Brad's hair. "Yes," he says. "I think it is."

"Wow," says Brad.

The rest of the emergency room's waiting area comes to the windows to watch the sun get blocked out by the dark wings of angels. Hordes and hordes of angels going to who knows where.

Then from deep in the flock, somewhere someone blows a trumpet horn that rattles the walls of the building.

"What was that?" says Brad.

Hermes can only shake his head. He looks at the ceiling. No signs of cracks. No structural damage. The building won't fall.

"Not an earthquake," he says.

"Why would it be an earthquake?" says Brad. "Earthquakes don't sound like trumpets."

Hermes pats the boy on the head again and pulls him from the door. "Go get Herc."

Brad nods and pushes through the groups of humans that push themselves against the door.

Amazingly, no one pushes and shoves. No one forces themselves to the windows. Rather they come to the door and gaze at the looming shadow.

When they've reached their fill, and they realize that their doom may be closer than they'd like to admit, they turn away and let the next poor onlooker lose hope just the same.

All except Hermes, who refuses to give up his side of the door. The glass of the window feels cold underneath his palms. He thinks about putting his own head against the glass, but is afraid of the grease mark he might leave along the glass.

As much as he would like to see what's going on, the mark would be embarrassing.

Though that doesn't stop the children as tall as his knee hobble over to the window and look outside. The girl, with pig tails and almost up to his waist, rests her nose against he window and rubs it, looking left and right without really knowing what she's looking for.

A line of thin mucous traces her nose's path.

"That is disgusting," says Hermes. He lowers down and rubs the glass with the sleeve of his elbow.

Hermes feels the crowd open up behind him. Feet stomp and the doors begin to rattle under Hermes's palms.

Herc's voice roars over the hushed whispers of the crowd. "What's this?" He rests his head against the glass windows. "Whoa."

Hermes feels tugs on his pants from behind.

Brad pushes himself between Hermes and Herc. "Did you find out what the horn was?"

Hermes shakes his head. He looks up and sees the smears of his greasy forehead against the glass though his peripheral vision.

"No, I have not."

Brad slaps his hands and forehead up against the glass. The door wobbles.

"Careful there, buddy," says Herc. He steadies the glass door by gently pushing on it. "You don't want to break the door down."

Brad nods. "Right. Sorry."

Hermes hears the faint blowing the horn again. It's somewhere over them, heading north. "They're moving north," he says. "What's north of us?"

Brad says, "Washington."

"What's a Washington?" says Hermes.

"The capital. Of the United States."

Hermes nods. "Right. I thought that was Washington, D.C."

Brad sighs. "It is."

To save himself from further confusion, Hermes just mutters, "Oh, okay," and drops the subject.

Hermes pushes off of the door, but the crowd of humans behind him keeps him still. "Excuse me," he roars.

Brad turns around and begins shoving people off. One of his little thoughtless shoves tosses an old woman onto the floor. She slides back ten or twelve feet. Her hair lays flipped over her eyes, her mouth wide open.

"I'm so sorry," says Brad to Hermes. Hermes nods and hovers over to the woman to help her up.

She slaps his hand away. "What'd you do that for?" her teeth click when she talks.

"I didn't do anything," says Hermes. From here, Hermes can see the tops of her stockings, dark skin tone that looks like she hasn't stopped wearing them since she was a young adult. Runs and stretch marks line the sides and upper band. "That was my friend here." Hermes points to Brad.

Brad waves and smiles. "Sorry."

The woman's mouth moves forward, in and out, like she's chewing on something. Finally she says, "You boys need to learn your manners."

"Yes, ma'am," says Hermes. His forehead feels hot from keeping those thoughts contained just short of his mouth. "I understand."

Herc stands at the doors, his back to the glass, and his mouth lies wide open. "What was that?" he says.

"An accident," says Hermes. He waves for Herc to follow.

"No, I mean." Herc points at the woman. She wobbles over to a side table to keep her balance. "You just apologized."

Hermes shrugs it off. He must be tyring to be funny again. "Yeah, and so?"

"Nothing, then, I guess." Herc follows just shy of stepping onto Hermes's feet. He can feel the close calls as each of Herc's feet barely touch the backs of his sandals.

The television's cartoon program shuts off and is replaced with a blue screen with a computerized earth spinning on its access.

"We interrupt your regularly scheduled shows to bring you important news," says a faceless voice.

The camera on the television switches to a cloudy sky, then shifts downward to the faces of three beautiful angels smiling out at an open crowd.

Okay, only two of the angels were smiling. One of them anxiously, putting on a show. Hermes recognizes the smile because it's the same one that Sophie puts on whenever he tries to take a selfie with her.

The faceless voice announces. "We have here three winged creatures—angels, if you will—about to give a speech on the lawn of the White House. They had come earlier, asking for someone to record this speech and to broadcast us here. I know, folks, says the male voice. We were just as surprised as you are."

A young black boy walks up to the television and switches the channel, but the image is the same on all channels.

On the television screen, the black-haired angel steps forward and offers a wave to the cameras. A grimace and a wave.

This must be what Hermes looks like when he doesn't have coffee in the morning, he thinks to himself.

"Man, this television is broken," says the little black boy. His blue basketball shirt has the symbol named for the Roman goddess of victory. Nike.

A swoop, the kids call it.

To Hermes, it looks like a big checkmark. Something to have to do with basketball, he thinks, though he's never tried to really study the sport.

He was more into running.

"What are they going to say?" says Brad.

The skies darken behind the dark-haired angel—the one they called Gabriel. Some of the angels that had been in the sky earlier, the flapping blanket, land behind them wielding spears and swords.

"I don't know," says Herc, "but I think that's their army."

41

The order that Gabriel gave Michael was to stand strong. Stand firm.

In other words, "Do not be you."

But Michael cannot help but feel the waves of tension that caress every muscle in his body. The sinews of his skin feel tortured, as if pulled apart and compressed and set afire. He feels what he thinks the humans call "exhausted."

This is a new sensation to Michael. Even the slight breeze that kisses the lawn, the sun from God's light above, none of this helps to keep Michael's mind focused at the task at hand.

The white building, a white house, stands behind him. Michael finds it a majestic building, with the columns and many windows reminding him of the Parthenon just a millennia or two before. The Greek architecture and its smooth white marble-like skin, these humans have shared a sense of artistry and appreciation that even he has found amazing considering that he is as old as the earth itself.

The grass rustles in waves as the breeze kisses over it. Amidst the confusion and the hustle of ensuring that they wait for the human media, the angel contemplates taking his boots off and letting the blade of grass tickle the bottom of his feet.

While they have clouds in Heaven, he does not remember the last time he had ever played on grass. Not grass this green. It looks soft. Almost ticklish.

And has he looks out amongst the crowd, Michael watches as little sausage-like feet dance on the green blades of grass. The grass looks slick and makes the bottoms of the little girl's feet shiny, slippery.

Michael takes his own big toe and rubs it against the next little toe. It slides past as if it, too, is wet.

The source of his amazement, of his child-like wants and needs.

Michael smiles. For all of the frustrations and pain, there is always something good. Something better, to look forward to.

The group of people—mostly men and women dressed in tight gray and black suits—look on with gaping mouths and watery eyes.

All of this Michael feels as well. He swallows and feels the slow crawl of fire up his throat. His chest tingles, his legs twitch nervously.

These humans, at least a few of them must have gone to eat spicy foods, filled with fat and some thick, sweet and salty sauce. A hamburger, he thinks. The taste, the burps fill his mouth and he streams it out in a light and steady gust so the other angels cannot trace his discomfort.

All of this he knows of the humans because he feels it, too.

Gabriel steps to the front and center of the lawn. His golden armor appears to have a halo effect in the brightness of the sun. It glows enough that the front row of the crowd has to clench their eyes shut or risk a poking pain and a headache to end all headaches.

Michael squints in response, rubs the tension from his forehead.

"Humans," says Gabriel. The moment the bass of his voice hits the crowd, they fall silent. Gabriel lets his words resonate with the crowd before he begins again.

"Humans, we came here to bring with us the love of God and a message unto you. You were to now be free from pain. Free from Evil. With Graciousness and Love of Him, you would be able to live as Adam and Eve lived in the Garden of Eden. The chosen ones to receive Him and His message."

Michael feels sweat trickling down his forehead. His chest constructs around his heart. He feels thrilled and tense at the same time. The pain of a hundred birds fluttering in his chest and throat.

"That was our original intent, however."

The crowd's mood falls flat. Michael feels something pulling on his heart, trying to drag it into his stomach, drowning. Drowning.

Michael gasps for breath and reaches for his throat as if someone or something was tugging on his neck.

Gabriel stops his speech and turns to his friend. He raises and eyebrow and Michael lowers his head.

Turning, he coughs, and then looks away.

Gabriel clears his throat and his voice booms over the crowd.

Michael doesn't have to use his empathy to see the emotion in their eyes. The water that gathers along their tear ducts, the pale cheeks, the sweat gathering at their brow.

Gabriel peers over the crowd. His shoulders flex upwards, as if shrugging, but his wings come up and wrap around him like the Shroud of Turin. "Many of you are confused," he says. "You are confused about what happens. You have placed your faith in a book, a book written by humans. For humans."

"There will be no Jesus Christ," he says.

The crowd gasps. Michael's ears begin to cry for help with pain and screeches. All of their confusion floods his brain. As he turns to gather himself, he feels the eyes of Jamaerah on his shoulder.

Michael nods and whispers, "I'm okay."

"You have turned your backs when you should have opened your heart. You have become faithless and cynical. It is now that you will be tested. For Jehova demands that we honor the first commandment. I—He—is your one true god and you shall have no other gods above him."

Michael raises an eyebrow at Jamaerah. Had she heard the slip?

"And like Job before you, it is not time for you to be tested. You have committed gross acts of vanity, of sloth. You have lusted, you have lingered in wrath and envy. You have warred for greed and for gluttony. And this ends now."

The men and women in suits that stand in front of Gabriel,

some ten or twenty of them, it's too hard to tell just who is a reporter and who is just an onlooker with a recording device, they raise their hands and their voices to ask questions.

Gabriel looks at the crowd and they stop, frozen.

Michael expected him to use the Deus Vox much sooner. Why this long?

"There's no antichrist. No Rapture. Just death, everywhere."

Gabriel does not wait for questions. He lets the crowd just speak to him while he looks to the sky.

It's a drama thing, Michael realizes. Gabriel loves the drama of the departure. He leaves with a magnificence that inspires others to gawk and point.

He's been like this since the days of the Old Testament, Michael realizes. He won't change now.

Jamaerah looks out to the crowd but follows Gabriel's lead. There really is no other path when the humans have so many questions.

But their minds, they are not designed for God's understand or the logic of angels.

And as much as Michael wishes he could explain it all away, he knows that all of this just beyond their reach.

For even the truth shames Michael.

With him as the last angel standing before them, the crowd crosses the pretend barriers that held them back. Those last bits of respect and barriers that they had, it all disappears as fast as Michael and unravel his wings behind him.

The flex backwards so he doesn't hit anyone.

But the crowd rushes toward him and he takes a step back.

The closer they get, the more Michael feels his own pulse driving up his wrists and neck like motorized vehicles. He feels the heat in his forehead, the slick sweat along his brow.

Michael extends a white hand out to the crowd. They pause. Michael is aware that they aren't stopping because they are afraid, they are stopping because they can't see past Michael.

He lets the reflections of his own skin freeze the humans in place because it's the safest thing for them.

Michael stretches his wings out by his sides and lets the crowd watch as he lifts himself into the air.

He peers downward at the crowd as his wings pull him closer to the sky.

The humans take pictures, throw question at him like spears aimed at nothing in particular. Michael feels their pain, their questions and can do nothing about it.

Or maybe he can. Is war really the answer?

42

G abriel stands in his golden armor, arms crossed across his
   chest and he surveys the groups of humans who try to walk,
no ramble, up to him.

The sun glints off the golden shoulders of his armor. The skies
above are cloudless, but over the horizon to the east, thick gray
clouds roll in.

These clouds, like thick puffs of cotton and black like factory
smoke, they roll slow and gently in the heavens above them and
threaten to drop rain.

These clouds come from a force far more dangerous than
Mother Nature. No, these are clouds of wrath. Of supernatural
forces beyond human control.

Michael recognizes them well. He remembers the cold rain and
the intense, tree-breaking winds of the Great Flood two thousand
years ago.

Jamaerah stands before the both of them, Gabriel and Michael.
Her wings extended and her flaming sword out and flaring tongues
of fire out at the crowd of agitated and incessant reporters. Her
sword and its threatening flames are the only things keeping the
humans at bay.

And Michael stands just behind Gabriel's strong shoulders, speechless, as the humans look upon the angels with mixed fear and awe and amazement.

Michael's stomach churns acid, burning the bottom of his belly.

"You cannot be serious," says Michael. "If this is a joke, it is not funny."

"I am not the joking kind, Michael." Gabriel looks over his shoulder and his golden eyes meet Michael's. They appear to reflect the light of the sun, almost shining with joy and wrath.

"You are enjoying this," says Michael. "I thought you were the Deus Vox. You must show compassion, not disdain."

"Do you think they have shown compassion toward each other?" Gabriel grabs Michael's shoulder and jerks him in front to watch the human news merchants scatter forward, then back as Jamaerah threatens them with her flaming sword.

Michael coughs, but tries not to move. Gabriel's nails pull at his neck, pinching his pale white skin together in a tight crease. Any movement and the pain only hurts more.

He takes a long breath and tries to focus away from the pain.

Pain from the pinching, pain from the human's fear. The pain of not know just how much damage Gabriel is willing to deal to God's children.

"They were blessed with the gift of free will, and look how they use it." Gabriel's voice echoes off the white stone buildings in the far distance.

The first few reporters in the front retreat from Jamaerah's sword. They flee without looking backwards, scrambling and kicking up green and brown sod into their from their sharp high heels and shiny, steel-toed boots.

"You think I make jokes when I threaten to destroy these pathetic cowards? Look at them, Michael. Look at them and do not pity them. They do not deserve God's pity because they, Michael, they are the jokes."

Michael's neck vibrates from the tension in Gabriel's hands and fingers. This talk about destroying humans, it brings about a sense of joy and frustration in Gabriel.

And Michael doubts that Gabriel even notices it in himself.

Michael wiggles his neck, looking upwards while bent over and held still by Gabriel's tight hold. At last he is released and Michael falls to the ground, the cool wet grass meeting his cheek.

He welcomes it and rolls over for the same feeling to caress his neck, which feels warm and throbbing.

"This is madness, Gabriel."

Jamaerah sheaths her sword and turns to face Gabriel and Michael.

Her eyebrows rise as she looks at Michael. He shrugs it off and nods.

He prays she does not do anything stupid, anything that could get her and him in more trouble than they already are.

Gabriel steps over Michael's still body and takes Jamaerah's hand as he looks over the green grass, the white monuments to human history, and the fleeing, fearful humans.

"You are a devoted angel of Jehova, are you not?" Gabriel's voice demands an answer, but Michael's throat swells with a choked up answer.

Michael nods instead.

"Then you will do me one thing that will prove your dedication to the cause."

Michael feels a rumble in his chest. His breathing slows, feels thin. He wonders if this is what the humans call a heart attack.

"You will seek out the demons that escaped from Hell. The ones that attacked while we allowed the humans to honor God with tributes," Gabriel says. He smirks, sending a shudder through Michael's shoulders and down his spine. "You will seek them out and destroy them. There is a little boy. He is too strong to live, a threat to our cause. Bring him to me so that he may know the sound of the Deus Vox."

Michael bites hard onto the tasteless flesh of his tongue. To hold his words, he bites down harder and nods.

The silence of the air is filled with the humidity of water sprinkling from the ground from little black spouts. His skin feels sticky as the tiny water droplets evaporate on his bare forearms and fingers.

"As you wish," says Michael. He offers a shallow bow and takes flight into the air.

As he takes off, Michael's chest and head are overcome with pressure and amazement. He can hear the humans pointing and whispering to each other.

They had never seen one of them in flight.

For a moment, Michael smiles and feels a sliver of pride in his wings and his being.

The humans, he thinks, they can still be reasoned with. They still admire the wonder and the beauty of the wings.

Maybe this war can be won over without bloodshed.

As Michael turns his body south, he glances downward.

As he had hoped, he is alone. The thunderous bass of Jamaerah's wings don't echo behind him.

For a moment, he is alone.

And he much prefers it this way.

43

The skies begin to darken and at first, Brad thinks that maybe there is a storm coming.

When he shoves his greasy forehead against the glass doors of the Saraday Emergency Room, he notices that the clouds are moving. But not across the sky.But inside itself.

Brad considers propping the door open for a moment, but Herc coughs behind him.

"Fine," he says.

His hands slap against the door and he pushes further out. Brad pretends not to notice that the doorframe is giving way to him right now. His pressure and strength, he's still getting used to all of it.

If he's not careful, he'll bring this whole place down.

The clouds go from grayish dark to black in small patches. Like birds flying in a tight cloud above the hospital.

It's a weirdly different mood outside than inside. From the insides of the hospital, its light brown rooms that remind him of his mom's coffee with about half a gallon of milk and creamer poured in. But outside, the wind blows, the clouds—those birdlike clouds—move and the rest of the world seems to be bright and shiny.

"Brad, come away from there, buddy," Herc says.

Brad shakes his head and points at the sky. "Look."

Herc comes closer to the window and then jumps back.

A male giant with big light blue wings lands onto the lawn and peers upward. His knees bent on the ground, his hand holding him up like an offensive football player.

"More angels," says Brad.

Herc grabs at Brad's shirt and pulls him away. "Dammit all to Hell," he says.

"Let's go kick their asses," says Brad. He swings his hands upwards like he's boxing. Protect the face. Block the punches.

He could do it. He knows he can.

He just has to get out there.

The winged giant is soon joined by three, four, then five more angels. All of them landing in quick succession like a rolling earthquake.

The glass and metal doors of the emergency room rumble. The glass cracks.

Then the angels begin walking toward the emergency room.

The first one takes his sword from a holster on his side and swings it at the doors.

Brad covers his head. He knows what's going to happen next.

People scream and Brad can feel the people pushing past him and Herc as they scamper away from the doors. The screams get louder, high-pitched, mostly women.

Brad clenches his eyes shut and forces his palms over his ears.

Maybe this was all a mistake. Trying to fight anyone.

"Boy, are you stupid," says Herc. He lowers Brad to the ground and cracks his knuckles.

Brad smiles, trying not to laugh. Someone's getting a beating. And it ain't him.

The angel stands in his white armor—now looking stained orange in the fluorescent lighting of the emergency room—and points the blade of his sword at Herc. "You are one of the ones we seek."

Herc shrugs and smirks. "Go to Hell."

Brad hides behind Herc's massive legs and peers around his

hips. The angel's sword bursts into a bright blue flame and that consumes the blade, stopping just above the hilt.

The angel looks unimpressed by Herc's brave attitude problem. Brad has seen Herc do this to him during their sparring matches. They size each other up. Poke their chests out. Draw their shoulders out and back. Their muscles tense up and flex.

They each grimace at each other.

The angel twirls the sword around in one hand and slams the tip into the orange and yellow striped carpet. The sword swings back and forth like the pendulum of a clock. Except upside down.

"You and your friends are to come with me. Gabriel would like to speak with you."

"Did all of you angels trade your wings for ears?" says Herc. "Go. To. Hell." He crosses his arms. His chest pokes out from his forearms, making him look like he's built solid like a truck.

The angels' white hair is cut short to his head, tiny bangs drape over his forehead like a picture of Julius Caesar or a Roman emperor Brad had read about in his mythology books. Underneath his armor pokes out bits of white cloth, like a toga Brad thinks they are called.

Brad considers for a moment, he could take on that one female angel, how difficult could it be to take this one out, too?

Brad steps out from behind Herc. "He said leave us alone."

The angel looks downward and his golden eyes meet Brad's. He looks unimpressed by the boy's stature and bravery.

"And there is the other one." The angel's eyes roam over the groups of people huddled in the corners. Shivering like scared dogs in a kennel. "I just need two more and I'll leave you be."

A second and third angel march into building and peer around the room. They say nothing, waiting for orders.

Herc steps forward, but his path is cut off by Brad.

"Leave us alone, I said." Brad crosses his arms to do his best Herc impression.

The angel lets out a chuckle. The other two keep silent, watching the sides of the room.

A fourth and fifth angel stand by the entrances of the emergency room. Their armors glisten in the sun's light outside, giving them a whole body halo effect.

They must have heard about the fight. How they fought off three other angels and walked away to tell about it.

Someone is mad at them for winning.

But Brad is madder.

"I won't say it again."

The angel's soft face snarls, looking unnatural on a face so beautiful. "Come with me, and we'll be more than happy to leave you be, boy."

Brad's feet dig into the ground. His heart beats in his ears.

Enough is enough.

He runs toward the angel in hospital and leaps.

The angel looks unprepared for any action.

Brad tucks his head into his chest and his shoulder burns with fire as it crunches into the angel's armor.

Sounds of swords being drawn echo into the air, like sharp piercing bolts of thunder.

Brad falls to the ground, landing on top of the angel's hardened stomach.

"You brat," the angel snarls. His hands reach out to grab Brad, but the boy catches the angel's hand and tosses it aside.

Brad stands up and kicks the angel's hip. The sound of cracking reminds Brad of Pop Rocks candy in his mouth.

Brad finds himself biting his lower lip as he kicks harder. And harder.And harder.

A trace of sweat drips down his forehead and down his cheek. He feels the fresh cold wind of the air conditioning against his wet skin. And it's the only thing that cools him down.

Deep inside, Brad feels hot. Boiling acid and blood.

He sees pain. Wants to dole out more and more kicks.

Brad drops to his knees and rips off the angel's armor.

The angel reaches out for the carpet to dig his nails into the ground. Pull himself up and away.

But it's no use. Brad has snappedth e armor off the angel and tossed it aside. His fists go wrist-deep into the angel's fabric-covered stomach. Like pistons in a car.

Slam. Slam. Slam.

Herc pulls him off the angel and holds him up into the air. Brad's fists shake from tension and fear. The thrill of battle.

"Whoa there, buddy," says Herc.

The other four angels line up by the fallen angel's bruised and battered body.

The grounded angel stands up and shivers from pain. He staggers backwards. An angel grabs his arms and steadies him.

"You will pay for that," he says in airy breaths. He reaches out for a sword.

An angel surrenders his and steps back.

Brad yanks himself from Herc's tight grip and lands on the ground.

He doesn't think. Only acts.

And with strong, confident steps, he approaches the five angels, one battered and four cautious. Maybe scared to death.

Brad doesn't hint at warnings. He's done talking. He only acts.

With a quick blow to the angel's knees, Brad brings the lead angel's face down to his level. Brad grabs his chin and punches him in the forehead.

The bruised angel's body flips backward and lands on his chest. His arms flail then slap on his chest.

Herc launches himself over Brad's tiny body and tackles the other four angels with his arms extended. Clotheslining them down into the ground in a collective clinking of their celestial armors.

Seeing the poor angel lying on the floor, Brad presses his foot along the angel's spine.

The angel's wings flap, pinching Brad's head between the strong muscles along the edge of the wing.

Brad seizes the wings with each hand.

The angel lets out a cry in pain.

Brad's fingers turn white as he grips the wings harder. Tighter.

"No," says the angel. "Don't."

Herc holds one angel in a headlock, the other two either pressed to the ground with his foot or held tight in his gigantic fists.

"Don't do it," says the angel. "Please."

Brad presses into the angel's spine and jerks back on the wings.

Blood splatters from the angel's back and the halls of the emergency room echo with ear-shattering cries for help.

44

The angel's screams rattle the wood and plaster walls. Hermes has seen these rumbles before. Earthquakes.

He takes Sophie into his arms and clutches her chest next to his. "It is okay," he whispers.

The walls rattle and begin to crumble. Frightened screams from just outside the door echo down the hallways and through the other patient's room.

This is what mass hysteria feels like, Hermes thinks.

He had seen this in a movie somewhere. Lots of people crying, running.Screaming.Zombies. They were running from zombies.

Hermes's grip on Sophie loosens as he peers out the window.

The grass blows in the light wind outside, but the skies are patchy with dark clouds that flutter by like flocks of birds.

"Damn it," says Hermes.

Sophie pulls away, coughs pitifully. "What?"

"The angels are at it again. This time, they've come here." Hermes tries to pull Sophie closer again, but she refuses.

"What happened? You look scared."

"I think I led them here," he says.

Sophie's lip quivers like Brad's does when he gets in trouble. Big trouble.

45

Hermes wakes to the shaking and pulling against his shoulder. "Hermes?"

He pulls open one eye lid, then other. It's not dark, but visibility is left to almost nothing. Dust and debris float along in the air. Only thin rays of light poke through the rubble above them. His nose and mouth feel covered with dust and a thin film of dirt. A thick piece of rubble rests against his cheek and his lower eyelid on his right side.

Everything smells like he jus shoved his nose in the bag of a vacuum cleaner. Stuffy and gray. Hermes breathes through his mouth to keep from feeling like he has to suffocate.

In this moment, with Sophie at his side, Hermes begins to forget that he's not human.

But to his left he feels the warmth and movement of Sophie's body. She moves slowly, sliding her arms up and down his back, whispering to close to Hermes's ears he can feel the wetness of her breath against his neck.

"Hermes?"

Hermes pulls back but his range is limited. Rocks and rubble surround them. The room has closed in on them, forced them together in a small square that surrounds the bed.

Sounds from the outside world are muffled through the debris. What's going on out there, Hermes can't tell.

Even Hell was never this close to inducing claustrophobia.

"Are you okay?" Hermes whispers.

He feels her head nod against his cheek.

Hermes smiles. "Good. What happened?"

He feels her cheeks flex and rub against the faint stubble of his chin and jaw as she speaks. "The fighting. Outside. I think. The angels. They came and. Destroyed the hospital." Her words wobble in the air, almost as much as Hermes's chest.

"But you're not hurt?" he says.

She shakes her head.

Hermes gives a quick, subtle nod and then pulls back to look around.

His movement is limited behind him. When the wall blew in, his back must have stopped most of it.

By the grace of Zeus, neither of them were seriously hurt, though Hermes feels a slight twinge in his back. Beyond that, his muscles feel fine if not a bit sore.

He can move his shoulders, his back, and he flexes his ass. Spinal vertebrae pop up his back in quick succession. His shoulders drop a little bit more.

He needed that.

"Can we get out of here?" she says.

Hermes looks to his left. The rest of the room has been caved in. Only the wall to the front of the hospital managed to stay intact. Everything else has exploded into the room, leaving them shielded and covered in dust and debris.

From the curve of the thin spikes of lighting that cut through the walls, it looks as if they are in a protective bubble. A solid dome of bricks and wood to protect them from the fighting.

"I don't know," says Hermes. An explosion of this size would only weaken the walls.

Sure he could cut through, but at what cost? Could he move any of the rocks and keep her safe? What if everything falls apart?

"Maybe not," he says after a moment.

"But Bradley," she says.

Hermes sighs and pats her on the back of the head. "I know. But he's fine. He's got Herc to protect him."

The biggest and strongest of all of them.

Hermes's eyes survey the rest of the room. He says, "Herc's proven that he may not be the brightest, but he doesn't go down without a fight. Trust me, Brad is in fine hands."

He looks into Sophie's eyes and for the first time sees true terror in them. Her lips pull inward and her eyes are wide open. In this kind of darkness, she appears to have bags under her eyes.

Like death warmed over.

No. Not Death. No thinking about Death.

"I can try to get us out of here, but I don't know how strong this dome is," says Hermes. "I don't want to risk hurting you."

"It's my fault," she says.

Hermes stares. Are they having the same conversation?

"Brad's out there. I'm in here. This hospital. I shouldn't have taken him with me. I should have let him keep choosing his cake. If I were just a little more patient."

Her words disappear behind heavy, chest heaving sobs.

Hermes feels the pull of his own tears. His chest twitches as he hides his own temptation to cry.

Be strong. Don't let her see.

The silence of their closed-in bubble disappears as the room's walls rattle. Something from the outside creaks.

Hermes prays that it isn't the walls around them, but maybe somewhere outside.

The way the walls roar and crack, Hermes prays that their friends are outside helping them.

He considers shouting for help at first. But the dust. Coating the insides of his mouth, the back of his throat.

There was a time when he had tried chocolate powder all by himself, instead of adding it into milk like the instructions—and

Sophie—had told him to. At first it stuck to his tongue. Then he made the mistake of trying to breathe through his mouth and he found himself in a coughing fit that destroyed any dream he had of doing this ever, ever again.

Hermes's tongue rubs up against the insides of his teeth and cheeks. The grit from the dirt scratches at them. He can feel the scrapes along his teeth through his jaw and into his skull, giving him a pulsing headache.

"We will get out of here," says Hermes.

The rubble shakes a brief, split second. Bits and pieces of drywall and wood fall from the couple's blockade, the thick walls that used to be the hospital, now a dome to protect them from the destruction and fighting outside.

For a moment, Hermes feels like a complete moron for not going out there, for not braving the tension and the darkness and calling for help. But his lungs feel too heavy and too full of gray dusty powder to do anything productive.

He doesn't feel the need to cough. Just thick. Warm and filled up inside.

But if he feels this bad, Sophie must be in so much pain. So much worry.

"I just wanted more time," she says. "With Brad."

Hermes's heart feels like it's swimming in his stomach. Bobbing up and down like a boat at sea.

"You will," says Hermes.

Sophie shakes her head.

Hermes's hands grab both sides of her head to keep it from shaking. He smiles at her. "Stop it," he says. "You will." His words come out as airy whispers. Everything so dark, so weak.

"I wanted him to be happy," she says. "I just wanted him to be happy."

Hermes nods and pushes her head onto his shoulder. She resists and pulls it back up.

Her eyes lock on with his. Her green eyes almost glowing in the little light they have left. Everything looking gray and dull and muted like a cartoon from the 1940s.

Everything except her emerald eyes. Seas of green just floating in the whites of her eyes.

"Shh," says Hermes.

He tries to stand up, but the walls are too close. The half circle of broken, cracking walls around them not giving enough room for them to even move.

Just how much could he do if he decided to try? How much of this is even possible?

The beams of light grow dimmer through the cracks. The light growing less and less bright and yellow. Less rays of the sun and more blue sparks of destroyed electrical equipment lying just outside.

At one point, his eyelids grow heavy. He rests them closed with his chin rested closely in the nook of Sophie's neck and shoulder. His feels soft and welcoming, and even in this dust and chaos, she smells sweet and soft like the flowery perfume she put in that morning.

But something rumbles in their intimate space. The walls crack and roar like tired statues. Hermes lifts his head.

Sophie shows no signs of movement, but the pulse in her neck beat-beats slowly.

She's sleeping, Hermes tells himself.

She's only sleeping.

He rests his hands on the sides of the bed and he pulls himself away from Sophie's resting body. Her arms entwined around his, her body still.

Everything about it makes him feel warm inside, forgetting just how much trouble they might be in.

The rumbling from outside stretches out across the entire side of the room.

The ceiling creaks from shifting its weight.

Hermes waits for a sound of something metal or angry from the outside, but there's only silence.

A muffled sound manages to come in from outside.

"Mmmlo."

Hermes sits up, though his hands never leave Sophie's side or legs.

"Hello?" Hermes whispers.

The rumbling stops.

Then shouting.

Hermes cannot make out the words.

Hermes tries to stand up but is forced into his knees from the lowered dome around them.

"Who is out there?" Hermes shouts.

The rocks pull out, one by one and the thin beam of light that tunneled in from the hallways grows larger, like a puddle of light.

Then, like the rays of Apollo's chariot, the light glares into Hermes's eyes and he's forced to cover them.

Sophie grunts from the light, and her body weight shifts on the bed. Turning away from the light.

"Who?" she says.

The voice from the light, it's female and says, "There you are."

46

Even from up in the air, Michael can see the full extent of the destruction. He does not have to be down on the ground, peering into the humans' eyes as they cower in fear amidst the destruction that his winged brethren have wrought upon the Earth Realm.

The green grass has turned gray and black from the charred remnants of destruction of the hospital's walls.

This place, a place of healing, now barely standing upright. Walls crumbling, falling down and caving inwards.

Michael's heart feels swollen in his chest, burning with pain. Everything in his body aches as he watches the angels move slowly and into the building.

Part of the ceiling looks to have fallen in completely, a part near the door. Here, a little boy with golden blond hair and a large man barely wearing what's left of a shirt stand tall against the three or four angels that stand before them.

Michael knows he should not condone this, but he smiles anyway.

Maybe there is hope.

He lands to the ground and a thin trace of gray, wispy smoke twirls around in the light wind that caresses the building. An electrical fire. Sheets on fire.

The smells and fear. It feels too close to home. Too familiar.

"What are you doing here?" Michael shouts to an angel.

The strong angel pulls his sword from its scabbard and holds it at the broken glass doorway. "We must seize the hospital and take the demons," he shouts.

He sounds too proud for Michael's taste.

After all, Pride cometh before the Fall.

"Who gave you these orders?" Michael says.

"You did." The angel looks confused. His wings are gray, flapping with excitement behind him. They are smaller than Michael's to be sure. He's not quite an archangel, but one of the lower choruses of angels.

He's but a grunt, in human terms.

"I gave no such orders," says Michael. He approaches the angel. Each of his steps thunders into the ground. "Who told you these orders you claim to follow?"

Michael seizes the boy-angel's cloth sleeve and pulls him closer. He drops his flaming sword.

"Tell me! Now!" Michael's throat hurts from the screaming, only three inches from the angel's face. The first time he had allowed himself to feel this angry, this vengeful.

"I did."

Thunderous flapping and then silence as metal boots click onto the walkway into the hospital.

"Jamaerah, why would you lie to them?"

She taps onto Michael's shoulder. He pulls away from the young angel and turns to face his general.

"Because you were incapable of making such decisions for yourself. It is God's will that we take these demons and save humanity from them."

Michael lets out a burst of nervous laughter. "God's will? Jehova had nothing to do with this." His arms stretch out, drawing a line from his chest to the picture of the boy and tall, strong man fending off two angels from reaching a group of young parents and their young.

"What makes you think that this is what the Lord intended?"

Jamaerah's eyes dart back and forth between the destruction and her general before her.

Michael turns Jamaerah to confront the entrance of the hospital entirely. "This is a place of healing, woman. Why would Jehova order us to destroy a place of healing? Is it not our job to protect the weak and innocent?"

"But it was ordered."

"It was ordered from Gabriel. Not from God."

"He is the Deus Vox, the—"

"The Voice of God, yes, but he is not God himself. He only delivers messages. He is not supposed to create them himself."

"So what do we do?" says Jamaerah.

"We pray, sister, that we have not gone too far."

Jamaerah grabs for her sword and draws it, pointing it at the group of angels that stand at an impasse with the boy and giant bearded man.

"You again?" says the bearded man.

"Kick her ass, Herc!" the boy says, his voice screeching his excitement.

The bearded man the little boy called Herc smiles and pats him on the head. He then stands tall, flexing his shoulders and chest as if it's meant to impress Jamaerah.

Even from behind, Michael can see Jamaerah's back shift as she tries to hide her chuckles.

Jamaerah holds her sword out, pointing its tip to the boy and Herc.

Then, as everyone watches to see what the great general will do, she drops the sword. The blade's fire fizzles out and it clangs against the cement sidewalk.

"What are you doing, general?" An angel rushes to her side and sweeps low to grab the sword. "You dropped this."

Jamaerah's boot stomps onto the angel's hand as he grips the sword.

"Leave it," she says.

Herc pounds one fist into the open palm of his other hand. "Oh, good. No weapons this time. Sounds like you want a beating."

"I am not here to fight, demon."

Herc stops midstep and jerks his head up. "Demon?" He turns to face the boy. "Did she call me a demon, Brad?"

"Sure did," he says. He, too, crosses his arms in cool mimicry of the bearded braggart.

"I see now reason for name-calling," Herc says. "Now you apologize or I'll hae to put you over my lap."

"I will do no such thing," she says.

Her eyes roll over to survey the extent of the damage. Bodies of angels and humans like lie on the floor. Strewn about in the room, bent in every which way.

The angels lying o their ground, one of the corpses n olonger has wings. The other only has half a wing left attached to his body.

Jamaerah's hand reaches for her face.

Michael comes to her side and rests his hands around her shoulder. "There has been too much bloodshed here, Jamaearah. Jehova would not want this. Not like this."

Jamaerah's hand reaches for her mouth, and then slowly lowers down to her sides. It shakes as she stands still.

The golden blood of the angels mixes with the red saturated pools of the human blood to create a sparkly, sticky puddle that coats the boy's shoes.

"What?" says Brad. "You started it."

Jamaerah reaches down for her sword. Michael can see the sides of her mouth clenching, biting and gnashing her teeth together.

"Jamaerah, think about what you are doing," he says calmly. "We have waged enough war."

"They have destroyed our brethren," she says. The sword's white blade bursts into a blue and white flame.

"You are not accomplishing anything by doing this," says Micahel. He begins to shout. "He is but a boy."

"Can a normal boy do this?" she shouts. Her blade points to the bloody angel laying on the floor of the hospital.

"Should goodly angels do this?" says Michael. He flaps over Jamaerah's head and points at the charred holes and burnt fabrics of the hospital's walls and insides. "Is it truly fair?"

Jamaerah's hand shakes, twitchy. Her fingers tighten around the sword's grip.

A light wind blows across Michael's cheeks. He watches as her hair blows lightly in the wind.

Then she releases her grip on the sword.

It clangs against the hard sidewalk and the flame goes out.

Her strong hands take Michael's shoulder and gently pushes him to the side. She marches boldly forward, her eyes resting on the little boy's stance.

As she gets closer, the boy's fists rise to his face, protecting himself. Ready to fight.

Jamaerah walks directly past him and into the hospital. She ducks her head so that she may fit, her wings wrap around her as she looks around.

A tear gathers at the corner of her eye and she looks at Michael and nods. "We must help," she says.

The other angels back away from the boy and giant, bearded man. They look at each other, then to Michael.

Michael can feel their confusion, the dozens of questions invading their mind, scratching around to make some sense out of their general's actions?

Turncoat?

Confused?

New tactic?

Traitor?

Jamaerah reaches down to pick up a woman from the ground and she carries her with both hands. The human woman's legs bleed red blood onto the floor. A trail of thick, red drops follow them to the flipped over couch.

The woman's expression is that of terror. Her eyes wide and mouth gaping open wide. After all of this destruction, she fears death, Michael knows.

He feels her pain, the extra beatings of her heart in her chest.

Feeling as if she needs to run, but cannot. She fears that this will be the last time she sees the skies. She worries that her children won't miss her.

Jamaerah looks over to a confused soldier angel. "Please?"

The angel nods and rushes to flip the couch over.

Jamaerah lays the woman down onto the couch's soft cushions and smiles.

The other angels grab their flaming weapons, spears and swords, and point them toward their general, this helper of humans.

"You are in direct violation of the Voice of God," the bravest one says. Even his sword wavers in the air.

Michael presses the angel's sword downward and shakes his head. "We have been misled," he says. "There is no Voice of God," he says.

47

The boy drops to his knees, collapsing upon himself like the walls of the once standing hospital around them. His shoulders heave up and down in quick strokes.

Crying.

Michael feels the sting of tears in his eyes as well, the pain in his chest. His hands shake so he hides them behind him.

The strong man, Herc, rushes to his side and scoops him up with one hand, cradling him against his bicep and chest.

"Is the boy okay?" says Michael.

Herc looks over the boy and nods. His bristly beard stretches across his face. Michael is reminded of God's beard, the thick cloud of white that hangs off his face.

Except this man, he is no Jehova. No proper God. He's too young, too brash. Too violent.

Ones like them, they belong in Hell where they can not harm anyone else.

"He's fine," says Herc. He cradles him further, rocking him back and forth.

The boy peers at Michael and scowls.

"I mean you no harm," says Michael.

Jamaerah rushes to the insides of the hospital and begins moving rock with her bare hands. The rocks of this realm are light compared to the white stone of the Heavens. The celestial stones and mountains of the Heaven and beyond are made of stronger things.

How these humans managed to make anything standing has always amazed Michael. One of the things he found respectful about Jehova's creations. Their art, their structures, and their determination.

"We will help you rebuild," says Michael.

"We don't need your damn help."

"But you may need our help, demon. We were responsible for much of this. Please. I insist."

"You can go back to wherever you are from and rot." His strong hands rock the boy, whose sobbing rests into a light murmuring.

"You do not understand, we are not here to harm you."

"But you sure did harm a lot of other people in there didn't you?"

Michael resists the temptation to look further into the room. He can already feel their pain. Their broken limbs. Their heartbreaks.

"This is true, but—"

Herc steps into Michael's face. His eyes are only a finger's width away from the angel. "What did you mean, there is no Voice of God?"

Jamaerah lifts half a wall from the side of the hospital, but freezes when she overhears their conversation. She rests it down to the ground. It would never stand up in its current condition.

"The voice of God has disappeared."

"Disappeared? Like he lost his voice?"

"Like he stopped speaking."

Herc bursts into laughter. "So he's mute?"

"He stopped speaking to use because we were no longer worthy," say Jamaerah.

"I doubt that's true," says Herc.

Michael sighs. "I fear that it may well be."

Herc's eyes scan the rubble over Michael's shoulder. He nods.

"So maybe you are right, and your God has stopped talking to you, has anyone tried to go speak to him and find out why?"

Jamaerah nods. "We have thought about that, but we do not know how."

"You angels must be really, really nervous about talking to him," he says.

"It is not so much that we are nervous," says Michael. "We just do not know how to find him."

"Did you check under the couch? Maybe he's hiding."

"Stupid demon," says Jamaerah. "Do not mock us. We are not here to be your enemy no longer. We are here to be your friend, to lend a helping hand. You asked a simple question and we answered. What more do you want?"

"Go knock on this God guy's door and see what his problem is. That's what I want."

Brad's head peeks out from Herc's arm. "What about mom?" he says.

"We have to find Sophie," says Herc. "And my friend Hermes. They're in there somewhere."

Michael closes his eyes and turns his focus inward. His feelings scan his body from his head downward, searching for pain, for answers.

"If they are in there," says Michael, "then they are unharmed."

"I guess that's good," says Herc.

Michael observes a few of the angels gathering together. They huddle, whispering amongst themselves.

When Michael considers breaking up the conversation, one oldest of the angels steps forward. "We cannot do this," he says.

"Cannot do what?"

"What you speak is blasphemy. God is not silent," he says.

Michael nods. "I think I understand."

The first of the angels jumps into the air and his wings catch him in midflight. He looks to Michael and nods, then peers upwards into the skies and flaps away.

The others, nervous but determined to join their friend, also leap into the air but wave nervously at Michael.

"I am sorry, sir," says the last angel in sight.

Michael waves them off. "Do as you must."

When the angels have disappeared into the thin clouds and light blue of the sky, his face turns serious, scowling.

"Jamaerah!" he shouts.

The walls rumble around them.

Michael takes a step out of the hospital for fear of tearing it apart accidentally. "Jamaerah, we are in trouble."

"Trouble?" her voice says. She steps to the side and her head become visible from behind a jagged wall, almost ready to crumble. "Trouble for what?"

"I fear that word of the Silence has broken out."

Jamaerah sighs. "Of course it has." She lifts another rock and attempts to place it on a pile of rocks, as if forming another wall. The rock, however tips forward and slides down the wall.

Architects, Archangels are not. Those were a role for the higher, eight-winged seraphim.

"Shall I hunt them down?" she says.

"I will not condone more pain and suffering."

"Who said anything about suffering? They will be dealt with swiftly," says Jamaerah, smiling.

"You speak of this like it's a game."

"I like your style, girly," Herc says and winks.

Jamaerah flashes a brief smile back at him and turns to enter the hospital. "Then I shall go after the two humans," she says.

"Uh, one human. One Greek god," he says.

Jamaerah pauses. "You wish me to go save a demon?"

"Well, you can go get the girl, that'd be fantastic. But if you do find Hermes, could you call him a runt for me?"

48

And the more the light comes into the dome, the more Hermes wishes it didn't have to.

The rocks rustle around them. More light trickles in like rainfall in the spring. Strands poke in from the outside, piercing the darkness that keeps Hermes and Sophie sitting still in their rocky cocoon.

Hermes pulls away from Sophie's tight grip around his wrist. Her nails scratch into his skin. Hermes like the pain. He deserves it.

For this and for everything.

He came from Hell to spend time with his new family, to protect them from evils. And yet here Sophie lies, the mother of his step-brother, the potential love of his life—if he had anything to say about it—and she's lying in a pool of her own blood.

The stitches and patches around her injured shoulder and neck leak blood through the crevices.

Her entire side is a slick, glossy red that smells like the iron and dust in around them. From inside this cocoon, he feels like he's watching her die drip by drip.

And for all the powers he has left, just remnants of being a Greek Olympian, he can do nothing but hope that Herc can punch and kick a little bit faster.

"Are they. Friend?" Sophie asks.

Hermes nods. He lies. "Yes, I think so." His hands make tight fists. If it's angel on the other side, he's going to get an ass whipping like he's never had. He's a caged animal, shoved into a corner.

And no body puts baby in a corner. Or so he's heard.

He must protect his love. Save the princess.

He is the knight in shining armor.

The features of Sophie's face sink into dark circles around her nose and nose. Her skin shines with sweat, like wet rubber.

Sophie closes her eyes as the light floods into the area.

Hermes's chest feels tight.

This could be the only time he can do this, the last chance before things get worse. Or deadly.

Hermes takes a gentle seat next to Sophie and watches her inhale and exhale. A thin strand of hair traces the sides of her face and her cheek, circling around her chin.

He wipes it away.

Sophie moans.

"Shh," says Hermes. "It's just me."

She smiles, eyes closed. And looks away.

Hermes leans in. His lips are too tight to do this.

He knows this.

Just like on TV.

Just lean in and do it. The kids on those CW shows. They make it look so easy.

Hermes leans over to Sophie and kisses her lips. His lips and shoulders relax.

Sophie's eyes open wide.

"What?" she says.

"I'm sorry," says Hermes. "I didn't mean anything." He slides off the bed.

"It's," she says, but Hermes tumbles onto the ground and looks away. "It's fine," she says again.

"No, it's not. It's just that I was scared that." He pauses. "You know."

"Someone's coming," she says.

Of course. Change the conversation.

A burst of light glares through the rocks at long last and Hermes's fists deflate. He holds his hands up instead, to block out the light.

Maybe protect from a blow or a weapon.

He doesn't know.

Because he can't see a fucking thing.

"There you are," says a female voice.

Hermes doesn't know if he recognizes it, this voice. It sounds too beautiful to be Lilith.

When it sounds like the voice it closer to his face, Hermes takes a quick swing at the voice.

"Whoa there," says the female voice. "I'm here to help."

Hermes pries one eye open. A darkened face against the brightness behind her.

"Who?" he says.

"Your friend Herc sent me, runt."

Hermes launches a punch into the hole and connects with a warm face.

At least he thinks it's a face. The texture is soft and warm as sunlight. But underneath the thin layer of softness is something hard as stone.

Bones?

"Herc?" says Hermes. He shouts out his friend's name. "Where is Herc?"

Sophie covers her ears and rolls away. "Ow."

"I'm sorry," says Hermes.

"I found them!" the female voice shouts.

Feet come thundering down around them. More rocks start to move and a high-pitched squeal of excitement comes through the small holes in the walls.

Sophie sits up. "Brad?"

"You better say thank you, Herm, or I swear in Zeus's name, I'll leave your pathetic ass down there."

49

Hermes grabs a hand and lets the owner's strength pull them out of the room. He emerges from the darkness, the light wrapping around him and for a moment, everything is too bright for him to see.

"Is the human still down there?" the female voice says.

Hermes turns around. "What the fuck is she doing here?"

Herc rests his arm around her shoulder. "This is Jamaerah, remember her? She's helping us now."

Jamaerah shrugs him off. "You are welcomed."

The other angel, the one he remembered being called Michael, stands at the entrance to the hallway. He nods, saying nothing.

Hermes turns around. "I need to go back in and get her."

Herc grabs Hermes by the back of his shirt. "You can stay out here. Let us help."

"But—"

Jamaerah rips open the entrance to the hole a bit wider and climbs in through.

"Do not worry," she says. Her soft voice echoes from around the room and comes out sounding hollow but warm. "I am here to help you."

Jamaerah appears at the hole with her wings wrapped around her. She has to crawl to move, the angels being so much larger than the other humans. And as she scrapes along on her kneepads, the room begins to shift.

"The hole," says Hermes. "We weakened the walls." He holds his hands out. "Give her to me."

Jamaerah shakes her head. "She is too fragile right now. She has lost a lot of blood."

Brad once again and drops to his knees. His face grows red, the lower lip of his mouth juts out. But he doesn't cry.

Hermes thinks that maybe he's been all cried out. His cheeks and nose are stained with the streaks of tears and dirt and dust from the previous fight.

He has nothing left to offer. Just hope and watch.

Hermes knows the feeling well.

"But I can help," Hermes says. He lowers one leg into the hole. Herc jerks him out.

"I said just stay here."

"I need to help," he says. "I didn't help out here, I wasn't here for the fighting. All I could do was sit in there and watch her die. Watch her." His voice trails off.

"I know, buddy." Herc grabs Hermes in a giant bear hug.

Hermes squeezes his hands between his and Herc's chest. "Get off me."

The walls creak.

"The walls," says Brad.

Hermes falls to the hole and stretches himself across the entrance. His hands and feet stretch out to keep the entirety of the hole from crumbling.

"Hurry up, beautiful," says Herc. He pokes his head around the wall and winks.

Jamaerah groans, disapproving.

She pushes past Hermes's eager head and finds a bed lying on its side.

"Please?" she says.

Herc wastes no time rushing to her side and bending over,

making sure that she sees his tight ass. Then, with only an index finger, he lifts the bed upwards while flexing his biceps for her.

Jamaerah rolls her eyes and rests Sophie on the bed.

"You are in need of a human doctor," she says.

"Can't you do anything? Help to heal her?" says Brad. He pushes the others to the side and grabs his mother's hand between his strong hands.

The female angel shakes her head. "It would be pointless to try," she says. "This human has little time left, it seems."

"This human has a name," says Hermes. He shoves the angel away and rests his hand on Sophie's twitching leg. "Her name is Sophie."

Jamaerah thrusts her right fist against her chest and bows halfway. "I am Jamaerah. I am pleased to make your acquaintance."

Herc nudges Hermes in the ribs. "See? Ain't she awesome?"

Hermes nods for lack of something better to do. "Yeah. Sure."

"If there is anything we can do, however, please allow us to do so," says Michael. He appears over around the corner of the hallway and into the room—or what used to be Sophie's hospital room. The mint green of the walls are now dusted with gray and brown. Machines turned upwards and fizzing out. The lights beeping faintly and getting fainter.

"You," says Hermes. He takes a step forward and holds his hands to his side in tight, closed fists. "You did this."

"I must apologize."

"You fucking bastard!" The wings on Hermes's feet launch him into the air at full speed.

But the angel reacts anyway, grabbing Hermes by his sides and holding him still. Hermes's hands fall flat to the ground, his feet kicking like a small child.

"I am sure I may have deserved that," says Michael, "but if you are quite done now, I would love to get to helping your human woman."

"Why is everyone calling her a human woman?" says Brad.

Jamaerah smiles and rests her armored hand onto Brad's left

shoulder. "He's right," she says. "The human woman's name is Sophie, and she needs our help."

Michael nods, but rests his eyes to the ground. "I am so sorry."

The room falls silent. The Greek gods look amongst themselves out of confusion. Hermes falls to the ground and stands back up, his arms folded across his chest.

"Sorry for what?"

"Because of the war waged by Heaven, humanity seems to have lost its right to die."

"Right to die?" Herc says.

"Indeed. When Gabriel came down to Earth Realm, he brought with him the rules of Heaven. The spirits are here, with the gates of Hell, Heaven, and Purgatory closed, no souls are welcome to leave into the afterlife. Any of them, for that matter."

Hermes shifts his weight. "That doesn't make sense. You embargoed human souls?"

"It was a logical consequence of bringing the war here, it seems."

Brad rests his mom's hand on her chest. "So my mom is never going to die?"

"This is true, young one, but she will not get better, either. It seems your bodies are in a state of stasis until the gates of Heaven and Hell are opened again."

"I get Heaven's gates being closed," says Hermes. "That makes sense if this is a war. But who closed Hell's gates?"

"That bitch," says Herc. "Where is she anyway?"

Brad shrugs. "I haven't seen her."

"Nor me," says Hermes.

Herc nods. "I've been too busy keeping an eye on this one over here." He points to Brad.

Brad smirks. "Thanks?"

Sophie tries to sit up in the bed, but she only makes something like a half-assed sit up.

"What are you doing?" says Hermes. "Stay down."

"I wanted," she says. Takes a deep breath. "To say thank you."

Sophie smiles and then raises a hand. She wiggles her fingers to wave Jamaerah in to her. "Come here."

Jamaerah pauses and looks to Brad and Hermes and Herc for an answer.

"Who cares?" says Sophie. "Come here."

Jamaerah bends over and wraps an arm around Sophie. She looks like she barely hugs her, keeping a safe distance while eyeing Herc's expression.

"You're not hurting, are you?" says Herc.

Sophie lets go of the angel. "No, no."

"We're going to have to move her," says Hermes.

"We need to find out just what the Hell's going on up there." Herc looks around the room and squirms. Judgment is everywhere. "I mean, no offense?"

"When she's safe and sound, then we can figure out what the Hell's going on," says Hermes. He takes his hands underneath Sophie's shoulders and knees, but doesn't lift her yet.

"Why don't we just go ask God why he's being quiet?" says Brad.

The room freezes still. All shift their heads to Brad's tiny stature, standing by his mother and staring at everyone in the eye.

"What?" he says.

50

The two angels, three gods and humans sit around in a circle in what used to be the lobby of the hospital's emergency room. This one story building that served as the source of medical care for the humans of Saraday was destroyed thanks to overly eager angels, ready to seize the humans and godlings responsible for the destruction of their kind.

A fact that makes sitting in this circle awkward for Hermes. He holds a cup of coffee—his latest addiction since watching so many of his favorite Friends on television drinking and enjoying themselves—in his hands. He regrets that there's no sweetener.

But he considers himself thankful. After all, he had to wait for the coffee machine, now tilted in a forty-five degree angle along the wall, to drip enough of the black liquid to fill the soft Styrofoam cup.

He slurps it into his mouth and realizes that he's only doing it for effect. Having lost the electricity to the place, the coffee couldn't be warm if he wanted it to be. No heat, no cooling. No fucking sweetener.

Still, he lets the mild, watered down liquid trickle in thin streams down his throat. Now if only there were some chocolate.

The angel Jamaerah stands from her seated position and stretches out her wings. Then, looking down at the seated Greek gods, she shakes her head.

"It's never that simple," she says. "We cannot just march into Heaven. After all, you three are demons by His command. You are barred from entering Heaven."

"But if God has gone missing, can we not just bypass his ruling about demons and such?" says Hermes. He considers it a fair question, but the looks of the two angels—Jamaerah and her commander and, he suspects, something more—make him feel small.

And not just because they are nearly seven feet tall and have to hunch over to fit in the hospital at all.

And not because he's seated.

And not because he's just small statured.

Okay. Maybe all of the above.

"The laws of nature are not so manipulated," says the male angel, Michael. His long blond hair comes at tight curls around the edges. He looks classically handsome, the type of chiseled features he's seen in Roman statues. Those copies of Hellenic statues that were really just mock ups of himself and his brethren.

Still, he wonders if the Muses weren't really on to something when they told the human artists how to mold the marble into something more.

"I do not see why you cannot just bypass them. You have already made it impossible for humans to—" Hermes's voice trails off. The word "die" lodges in his throat, so he swallows it down and chases it with a sip of cold coffee.

"That is not our doing," says Michael.

He feels irritated but tries to hide it for sake of being genial and productive. But Hermes likes the fact that he's pushed a button.

Maybe it's what he's needed to.

Herc stands up next to Jamaerah and attempts to put his arm around her shoulder again, but Jamaerah says, "I dare you to."

Herc rests his arm slowly back down to his side and smiles it off.

"But he's not a demon. At least not whole demon." Herc points a thick, meaty finger at Brad.

All eyes follow Herc's finger to Brad's face.

"Wait. What?" Brad tucks his knees in to his chest.

"He is only half god. A demigod. He is still half human, at least by decree of Zeus," says Hermes. "Technically, he has not been recognized as a demon and has not been cast into Hell."

Michael nods and rests his chin in his hands. His golden eyes stare into Brad's face.

Brad's eyes widen and he looks away at the wall. The ceiling. Anything but the giant seraph staring him down.

"You're not suggesting that we send him, do you?" Herc says.

Jamaerah stands by Brad. "We cannot be certain that he can do what we need him to do. Michael and Gabriel have both failed in their attempts separately."

"Failed?" Hermes's eyes wander from person to person in the room. All of them, celestial beings of some sort or another. Michael diverts his attention to the ceiling, staring up through a fist-sized hole in the wall.

"What do you mean by that?" says Herc.

"Michael and Gabriel are the only ones who now hear the voice of God. They attempted to communicate with him, to foresee what they should do about the War of the Souls. The Battle of Good and Evil was coming to an end. We needed some kind of command. Then Jehova went silent."

"How do you just go silent?"

Michael shrugs. "It's not easily understood by human minds. Gabriel believed that he did so to teach us angels a lesson. That He was unhappy with us. To gain his favor, we sought to gain his favor. That was when Gabriel decided that it was best that we attempt to finish the War of the Souls."

Hermes studies the face of Michael as he speaks. His mouth moves in thin, quick motions. His eyes do not blink and seem to avoid all direct connection with the others. Hermes sips the rest of his coffee and rests the cup next to him.

"You haven't heard the voice of God in a while now, have you?" says Hermes.

Michael shifts his weight and stands up.

"Michael, is this true?" Jamaerah moves to stand in front of Michael's line of sight. "Do not look away from me. Answer truthfully. Have you both stopped hearing the voice of Jehova?"

Michael nods.

"But that means that everything Gabriel has been doing has been meaningless."

Michael stands. "Not meaningless. He has been forwarding his own agenda. He fears that we will lose our grip here on Earth Realm. He seeks to keep its control by taking it over for himself."

"But that is not the way of Heaven."

"Nor is it the way of angels. But he wishes to wage war with Hell while they, too, are silent."

"But your little war up there is causing the rest of humanity to suffer. You invade, you kill, you cause massive paranoia and destruction," says Hermes. He tosses the cup away to a trash can, tilted over and half-empty. "I mean, Yeah we Olympians caused some massive destruction in our time, but we left the whole of humanity alone. You guys are just dicks."

"Do not blame all of us for the shortcomings of the worst among us."

"The problem is, buddy, that the worst among you has a high position in Heaven's army." Hermes feels the heat rush to his face. He has been craving this. Not being a physical person, a war of words needed to be his release. "You are looking at having a whole other Lucifer on your hands."

Herc stomps his foot on the floor and causes it rumble slightly under Hermes's ass. "Stop it, Herm."

Hermes points to Sophie. "Look at her! Look at how she barely hangs on to life and we're arguing over whether or not we can speak to God?" says Hermes. "You want to argue who is good and who is bad? Well look at this! Tell me that they have not fucked up in the worst ways."

Hermes stands up and leaves the room, floating on his wings just inches over the ground.

As he leaves, he hears the group begin to chatter amongst themselves but one voice—a young high-pitched one—rings out over all of them.

"Then let me do it."

51

"You said yourself that I'm not a demon," says Brad. His thunder blue eyes light up, flaring almost, into a heavenly light blue as he looks at the gods and angels before him.

"This is madness," says Hermes. He pushes himself through the crowd and kneels down before Brad. "You are only nine years old, and I promised your mother that I would keep you safe. I cannot keep you safe if you are in Heaven. However the Hell you get up there."

"There are ways," says Jamaerah.

Hermes looks backwards at the female angel and scowls. "You can keep your mouth shut at any time now," he says.

She bites her lip and looks away.

"But I can do it," Brad says. "I'm strong. I trained with Uncle Herc."

"Uncle Herc?" says Herakles. "I like it."

"And I can keep up with you guys in battle. Look what I did to the angels in there."

"You did that?" says Hermes, pointing over his shoulder.

Brad nods.

Herc nods and smiles.

DAVID GEARING

Hermes reaches out to grab Brad and hug him, but Brad slaps away his hands.

"I was there when my mom got hurt and I couldn't do anything. I can do something now and I want to. I'm strong, I promise." Brad's words collapse into tears. His face and cheeks glow bright red. "Why can't I just help."

With Brad under the control if his tears, Hermes reaches forward and hugs Brad.

He offers a bit of resistance at first, but gives in to Hermes's tiny arms.

"Please don't hate me," says Herc. This means that Hermes most certainly will. "But what if we were to actually let him go?" Herc pulls up a sleeve just past his shoulder and points at a little red dot on his skin. It looks like a human pimple, a reddish dot with a darker red pinpoint in the middle. "You see that? That was this little guy."

Jamaerah shrugs. "Impressive?"

Hermes waves him away. "He is not going. That is final."

"But you're not listening to me," says Herc.

"I am listening and I am saying no. Disagreeing with you is not the same thing as not listening to you."

"To me it is," says Herc under his breath.

Hermes tries to pick up Brad to take him out of the room, but he stops just short of lifting Brad off the ground.

"You have gained a little bit of weight. What has your mother been feeding you?"

"I'm not going," Brad says.

"Exactly, you are not going to Heaven. Forget it."

"I mean with you," says Brad. "I am not going with you. Leave me here."

"What has gotten into you?" says Hermes. "Do you see your mother? Do you see how ill she is? We do not even know if we can save her," he says. "I will not risk losing you, too."

"Who says you will lose me? I can kick ass. I can do what you guys tell me to do. I can go find God. I promise."

"I don't want to lose Mom either," says Brad. He rubs the tears

234

from his eyes. "But it's my fault she's hurt and it's gotta be me that fixes her. Okay? It has to be me!" Brad stomps his foot onto the ground and Hermes falls backwards.

Brad does not offer a hand to help Hermes up. He crosses his arms—his trademark mimicry of Herc—and frowns. "I'm not going with you. I'm going to Heaven whether you like it or not."

Hermes shakes his head. "But," he says, then gives in.

Sophie's head rolls over to watch the struggle, her eyes glisten with tears. She blinks and pushes a single tear down her cheek that falls off the side of her face and darkens the red-orange carpet beneath her.

"Let him go," she says.

Hermes looks to Sophie, his mouth opens. "Fine." Hermes stands up and shrugs. "If she says he goes, then he goes."

Brad rushes to his mother and hugs her. "Thank you, Mommy."

Sophie wraps her weakened arms around Brad and smiles a weak, trembling smile. "I love you, Brad, you know that."

"Yes, Mom," says Brad. "I love you, too."

The two hold each other in silence amongst the gods and angels until Herc finally breaks the silence.

"Um, I don't mean to be the cynic here. Is that the right word? Cynic?"

Hermes sighs. "Yeah, sure. Cynic. Right."

"Well, I don't mean to be a cynic, but just how do we get a half-god, half-human boy up into Heaven?"

Michael and Jamaerah look at each other in silence. Hermes sees from their faces that they have an idea. Either a great idea. Or a very, very, very bad one.

"Well, there is one way, but it's never been explored before," says Jamaerah. "And it might hurt a little."

52

Hermes grabs Jamaerah by the shoulder and moves the conversation into an adjoining room. The holes in the room allow for a slight breeze to come in. Enough of a breeze, Hermes hopes, for the hushed conversation to be completely invisible to Sophie.

"No, death is out of the option," Hermes says.

"You asked a simple question and I offered you a simple answer," the angel says. Her silver eyes reflect the springtime light back into Hermes's own green ones. "He is mortal and not bound by the same rules as you are. Death is an option."

"He is half mortal," says Hermes. "Death is not an option. Do you know how easy it is to kill a demigod? Not very easy. Believe me. Many have tried."

Jamaerah sighs.

"And besides, he just turned nine-years old. I cannot kill a nine year old. I do not know about you, but it is considered a bit of a faux pas around these parts."

"Faux pas?" says the angel. "I thought you were Greek. You speak French as well?"

"I am Greek. I just watch a lot of television."

"If you are not okay with killing a child, then we can try something else, but it could be messy. And we would need to require that he is clean enough to go in."

"Clean?" says Hermes. "I mean, he washes his hands after going to the bathroom."

Jamaerah's face twists into a sort of disgust. "What? No, I do not mean that." She pauses. "Do not speak to me of such things. That is disgusting."

"You angels do not pee?"

Jamaerah raises an eyebrow. "Pee?"

"You know. Urinate?"

"Yes, yes. I know what you humans do. Get rid of physical matter. Yes, I get it." She shivers in disgust. "We angels do not have to pee, as you call it. We simply do not eat. We have no reason to get rid of any physical, bodily waste. That was simply a God kind of thing."

Hermes scoffs. "God kind of thing? You still confinced that God made us, even though you came way after and had a bunch of human tribes to control from the get-go?"

"I am confused by your question."

"Of course you are." Hermes takes a step back and points a finger at her. "You guys came after me and my family."

Jamaerah nods.

"And then you angels were put in power after God—or Jehova or Yaweh or whatever you guys call him these days—until he decides that he needs an army. You know, a little harem if you will."

"I object to the term harem."

"So you are telling me that you believe that humans were created by your boss, even though you recognize that we predate you?"

Jamaerah shakes her head. "I do not understand what you are getting at."

Hermes nods. "Never mind. How else can we get Brad up into Heaven?"

"First, we make sure that he is clean."

"Clean?"

"Without sin."

"But what if he is not Catholic? Does it matter?"

"It does if he is to enter the Gates of Heaven."

"So you have gates, too?"

"I do not understand your question."

Hermes raises his hands up into the air and walks away. "Forget it. We need to find Brad and Herc."

Hermes finds Brad and Hermes fixing up the room with Sophie's half-assed bed. The white sheets drip red, soaked with blood and looking as if they need to be changed.

The problem being, any sheets in this place are not covered in a thin film of dirt and debris that will only get her wound infected. Hermes considers for a moment looking elsewhere, but he couldn't risk leaving.

Not for stupid sheets. Even if it did make Sophie more comfortable.

Was he really wanting to change the sheets for her? Did it really matter to her if she was spending her last moments on red sheets rather than white, fresh ones?

For her or for him?

Hermes takes the end of another chair, made of light wood and completely covered in a dark blue fabric with pink and purple zigzagged lines. He flips it over and rests on the armrest.

"Hey, guys. We might have a solution, but it is a little strange."

"Strange how?" says Herc.

"Hermes, Herc. I am a nine-year-old boy who fought angels. Strange is a little ordinary, don't you think?"

"Well, it may involve a church, if I remember how the Christian religion works."

Herc drops the chair and sits on the edge of it. "What do you mean it may involved a church?"

"And a pastor. Or Father. Or really, I am unsure."

Jamaerah's shadow comes into the room before she does. "We must have a religious figure, a Christian religious figure, bless him before he can go into Heaven. He must be purged of all sins that are inherent in all humans when they are born."

"Man, you guys are really hung up on your rules and regulations, aren't you?" Herc chuckles and looks at Brad, who sits on the ground like it's story time.

Jamaerah nods. "If you want into the Nine Spheres of Heaven, then you must play by our rules, as it were."

"Fine," says Hermes. "Just how do we play by your rules."

"The child has been past the age of infancy, and therefore has committed sin. If we can get him forgiven for those sins, then we can travel with him to Heaven."

"Travel?"

"It is not a physical traveling, but a spiritual one."

"But we can just march into Hell no problem," says Hermes. "Why is Heaven so different?"

"Hell is a realm of carnal sins and physical transgressions. It is a physical realm as you know it. Yes, spirits do reside there, but the underworld has always been about physical, not spiritual power." She takes a step into the room. "Heaven is about spiritual well-being and balance. We are about the internal mechanisms that make a human good and proper in the eyes of the Lord. Therefore, we are a spiritual realm and we must travel accordingly."

"This is complicated," says Brad.

"It is nothing," says Jamaerah. "But we have never had a half mortal amongst us before. We have had one mortal and one mortal only up there. But that was nearly six hundred years ago. You will be quite the odd duck out up there."

Brad smiles as if it's a compliment.

"I'm sure you will like it," says Jamaerah. "I'm excited to show it to you."

"I want to go," says Sophie. She manages to pull herself up into a seated position by gripping along the wall. The sweat from her hands makes a squeaking sound as she slides it down the painted walls.

"But you are hardly in a position to leave this hospital. What if you get worse?"

Sophie pushes the blonde hair back over her ears. "Look at me, Hermes. Do I really look like I can get worse?"

She lowers one foot to the ground and tests the strength of her leg.

"Besides, I wouldn't want to miss my baby's first blessing."

Brad rushes to her side and steadies her stomach with his hand. "Are you sure you can stand?"

"Of course I can." Sophie's second foot lands onto the ground. Her legs wobble. But she stands. "See? Just need to get my strength back."

Hermes rushes to her side, but Sophie's outstretched and trembling hand stops him from coming closer. "I do not know about this," he says.

"Too bad it's not your decision." Her voice grows stronger as she speaks, but Hermes sees her legs twitching.

To Brad and Jamaerah, it looks as if she's standing. But Hermes sees that she rests her weight against the sides of the bed. Hoping that friction will keep her from falling to the ground.

"I die out here or I die in there," she says. "Either way, I'm dead. At least let me die with my family."

Hermes wipes away a tear from his eye with the back of his hand. "Fine," he says. "If that is what you wish."

"Of course. That is what I wish," she says.

Jamaerah nudges Brad aside and picks up Sophie so she lays in her arms. "Then let us make this quick," she says. "We do not want to waste much more time."

53

The only Catholic church in town lies at the center of the town. At the top of the giant hill that separates the houses from the rest of the stores. Brad remembers passing by the church over and over again, but never dared go in.

Of course he was curious, but you don't just walk into a church to take a look around.

At least that's what he told himself.

The church itself is not that big, but it as a steeple on it because he swore that all churches—at least the big religious ones—always have steeples. The large pointed towers that make them look older than they really are.

Almost two hundred years ago Saraday had a fire. A big one that only left one house intact. The house, Sophie warned Brad, was off limits. She told him so when he was only five.

And that must have traveled with him, because up until now, he thought all old buildings were supposed to be off limits. And this building only looks old, Brad sees. After all, the building is made of red bricks and not the large stones he sees on European gothic churches. His fascination with history books has led him to want to travel to Europe and see the great big buildings dedicated to the gods in the sky.

Little did people know that gods, like his step-brothers Herakles and Hermes, walk the earth all the time. Just don't announce it.

Now, Brad finds himself a little weirded out by the irony of approaching a church with narrow, stained glass windows at the front of the church like painted, watercolor eyes. Himself a demigod, going to gain the blessings to see a god. In the house of God.

The parking lot is bare except for only a few cars. Of course there's a Cadillac because old people are here. His mother likes to say that all Cadillacs are built to take an beating because the people inside—old people, she meant—didn't know how to drive them.

Brad rests his large nine-year-old hands on the rustic metal door handle and pulls. The door did not creak.

Funny, judging by the size of the door, it should have creaked. They always creak in the movies.

He takes small, cautious steps toward the two large wooden boxes that look like those things Superman flies out of in those old cartoons his mom shows him. The boxes, however, are near the front of the church. A million miles away. But that's where they told him to go—Hermes and his mother.

And no matter how many steps he takes, it's not fast enough to get this over and done with.

The church has wooden floors, not like the video games he plays on Xbox. The colorful stained glass pictures take up the top half of the wall. And whoever did it is a fan of guys in cloaks and hoods.

Except the women. They're always fancy, in white togas or something. One of them holds a little baby. Probably Jesus. At least that's what his teacher tells him at Christmastime.

Also unlike the video games, Brad notices, the church itself is really bright. Not dark, gloomy, and made of stone.

He slumps in his seat. In his head, he imagines a wooden altar, thick white candles, and red tapestries hanging from the sides.

And choral music. Creepy, choral music.

There is a line of three people sitting on the light wood pews. Each with his or her hands folded in their laps.

So, Brad sits down and folds his hands on his lap. The large—larger than Herakles—figure of a wooden Jesus stares at them in agony or joy. He can't tell which. Not even sure he wants to.

He looks at the others sitting on the bench. All women. At least his mothers age. Maybe a bit older.

Brad sighs. This makes him the smallest, youngest person in the room.

One of the boxes opens and an old man steps out. "Thank you, Father," he says. He tips his hat and smiles at Brad. He's not sure, but there might have been a wink. Old guys always like to wink.

"You can go along first, dear," says the woman in front of him. The woman smiles. She's so old, her lips keep her wrinkles when stretched out in a friendly smile.

Brad shakes his head and smiles. "No, thank you, ma'am." He knows he should go first, so he can get the Hell out of there, but the mental voice that tells him to be polite is his mother's.

"You're such a sweet boy," the woman says. "Are you here alone?"

Brad nods. "No, ma'am."

There's a pause. The woman looks a bit confused. She searches behind them with a quick glance. "And where are your parents?"

"My mom is waiting outside. She doesn't like churches. She says they give her the willies."

The woman frowns. She disapproves of Sophie's words. She pats Brad on the knee. "Well it's good that you have accepted the Lord as your savior in spite of your mother."

"She's not that bad," says Brad.

The woman buttons her lip. She pretends to smile by pushing her mouth upwards with her lower lip. The same way his mom does when she's pissed and doesn't want to talk about it. Usually once a month.

When the door opens again, the woman swings an open palm gently to the door. "Your turn, son."

Brad scoots off the wooden pew and nods at the woman. "Thank you, ma'am."

Do you start with the big stuff first? Or last? Is there an order?

Brad fumbles through his pocket, searching for the piece of paper. The notebook paper with instructions. In case he forgot.

He knew he would forget. He always forgets when things get awkward.

He takes a seat in the box and closes the door behind him. It's dark, but not creepy dark. Almost a relaxing dark. A small beam of light comes in through a slim window along his left side.

Brad's heart jumps in his chest at the sound of something sliding open.

"Did I startle you?" says the man on the other side.

"Yes, sir."

Brad is sure he can hear the other guy smiling at his politeness. He waits, patiently at first, twitching his thumbs and swinging his feet back and forth on the seat.

The man on the other side clears his throat.

"Oh, right." Brad takes a piece of paper out of his shorts pocket and unfolds it. It rustles loud enough for the rest of the church to hear it.

"What are you doing?" says the man.

"Bless me, Father, for I have sinned. It has been state how long since my last confession. These are my sins."

A snort and then stifled laughter erupts from the other side of the wall. "My apologies," he says. His voice is calm, soothing.

Brad's is, however, shaky and cracks his voice about five years before its time. "Um, do we start with the big stuff first or the little stuff first?"

"That is completely up to you," the man says. He sounds young-ish. Deep voice. Kinda like Herakles. But not as drunk.

More silence.

Brad twiddles his thumbs.

The man on the other side clears his throat again. And again.

"Oh, sorry," says Brad. "This is my first time here."

"So I've gathered," he says. "What can I help you with?"

Brad bites his lower lip. Hermes said to do this honestly. Openly.

Before he walked in, his mother kissed him on the forehead and told him there is nothing to fear. Just confess everything. It was vital to his mission.

"So no one will judge?" says Brad.

"Well," says the man, "I suppose you could say that God is always watching, judging. But his goal is forgiveness. He loves us and wants us to become better people."

Hermes rolled his eyes; they simply weren't church-going people. But this was important, his mother said. So very important.

Brad nods. "Right. So here we go."

The man's clothes seem to rustle, getting comfortable in his side of the wall. "Any time you are ready, son."

"Okay. Well, one time when I was five, I stole a piece of candy from a store. My mom never found out about it. And another time I hit this little girl because she was being mean to me. And every day before dinner, I sneak cookies as a snack even though I'm not supposed to. And there was that one day when I left the house without telling my mom first."

"Whoa, there. You might want to slow down," he says. "First, answer me this. Do these things you've done, do they make you feel guilty or bad for doing them?"

Brad taps his chin. "Not really. I feel bad when the teacher calls and tells my mom."

"So you understand that you are not supposed to hurt other people's feelings?"

"I think so. It's not nice."

The man makes some kind of noise on the other side. Like "Mmhm," but quieter. Does that mean he agrees?

"Okay, so time to get to the big stuff?" Brad asks.

"If you wish."

Brad takes a deep breath. "So yesterday I killed some man."

54

The priest seems to cough, then says, "I'm sorry, you what?"

Brad hears the man struggling to sit up, grasping the walls and he coughs.

"Too big?" says Brad.

There's a pause. An uncomfortable one.

Brad can see it now, the police opening the door and handcuffing him in the church. That nice old lady who let him go first, she will yell at him, telling him he's a bad boy and should have known better. Maybe that he's going to Hell and will never see his mom or his step-brothers again.

"You can't tell anyone, can you?"

There's a pause.

"Are you in danger?" says the man slowly.

Brad tries to hide his smile, even if the priest can't see him. "Well, not anymore."

"How old are you?" says the man.

"I just turned nine. But I'm not a little boy."

"And why would you feel compelled to kill another human being?"

"I don't want to talk about it." Brad twitches in the chair, pulling himself off of it, then sitting back down. To leave or not to leave?

"And yet you want me to tell you that it's okay?"

Brad climbs up onto the chair and peers through the hole between him and the priest. "Isn't that what you're supposed to do?"

The man looks upwards. His eyes are wide, round like cereal bowls. His mouth open wide. Like he got caught in a lie. "How can I help you if you won't tell me about the sin?"

Brad rests his hand on the door. He takes a breath to wrangle the stampeding thoughts tearing his emotions away from him. "I don't want to talk about it. I just need forgiveness so I can go to Heaven and save my friends."

"I'm sorry," says the priest. "If you are in danger, you can tell me."

Brad puts one foot outside the confessional.

The priest's voice gets louder. "If you walk away, I may have to tell the police."

Brad closes the door politely and waves to the old lady.

She waves back.

The priest opens the door. "Please do not walk away. Come back and talk."

Brad stops and turns around. "Does this mean I get my forgiveness?"

The priest looks downward. He shakes his head.

Brad turns around and continues to the door. "Fine," he says. "But I'm not spending the night."

The old women at the pews gasp in unison.

The confessional door slams behind him and Brad leaves the church in a huff.

"It didn't work," he says when he gets outside. He looks around and rests his hands in his pocket.

He's greeted by his friends and family. A short, curly haired man with a boyish face—Hermes, his step-brother by Zeus.

Then there's Hermes's best friend, Herc, who towers over all of them like a body-building mountain. His hair is brown, pulled back and tied up underneath a baseball cap that looks like it has a lion's head sketched onto it. He's dressed fashionably, with bright blue shirt and gray slacks.

And of course his mother, who kneels down and gives him the biggest hug ever. Like always. She is where Brad gets his curly blond hair from. And her blue eyes. His grandma once told him that his mother couldn't deny Brad if she tried.

Whatever that meant.

"What do you mean, it didn't work?" says Hermes. He grabs hold of the door and opens it up, moving his eyes so he can see inside the church.

"I mean the man inside—"

"The Father," says Sophie.

Brad pauses and huff. "The father didn't want to forgive me."

"Why wouldn't he do that?" Sophie says. "Did you do as we practiced?"

Brad nods.

"Then none of this makes sense. What did you tell him?"

Brad eyes Herc.

He jumps to Brad's side. "You know what, maybe it just isn't going to be the best way to get forgiveness. Maybe there's something else we can try."

Brad smiles. "Yeah, we can try something else."

The great big wooden door opens up with Hermes's hands still resting on it. Hermes jumps backwards, causing a chain reaction of all four of them leaping back.

"Excuse me, young man," says the priest. He looks up and catches a glimpse of one of Herc's massive, body-builder legs. He follows the trail up to see Herc's smiling, bearded face.

"Hi," Herc waves.

The man lets go of the door and steps outside. He waves just a little.

"Hi," he says. He clears his throat. "This man was just in confessional," he says, "and he rushed out so quickly, I didn't get a chance to talk to him further."

Sophie smiles. A drop of sweat falls off her cheek.

"Dear Lord, ma'am," says the priest. "Are you okay?" The priest looks to all of the other men to check for reactions.

"Yes, yes," she says. "Thank you, Father."

"Please," says the man. "Just call me Pete." He extends his hand out to Hermes and Brad, and then Herc. Herc's hand completely envelopes the poor priest's shaking hand.

"Maybe Brad here can go back in and finish talking to you?"

Brad shakes his head. "I told him that I killed someone."

The priest checks for the reaction from the others. Seeing none, he kneels back down to Brad.

"You're quite the unusual little kid," he says.

Brad nods. "I know."

Pete smiles. "I knew a young man who was different as well," he says. "It did not work out so well. But you," he says, "you will have an interesting future before you. I can just tell."

"So uh, what about his forgiveness?" says Herc. He steps backwards, blocking out the sun from Pete's eyes.

"The forgiveness?" says Pete. "What you did," he says. "You meant it?"

Brad nods. "I had to protect my mom."

Pete nods, mimicking Brad. "Protect your mother," he mutters.

"Yes, sir."

Pete smiles and waves for Brad to come back into the church.

The door closes behind Pete. Brad stands outside with his mother, Herc, and Hermes waiting for instructions.

"Well, go inside. If he is willing to help, then we take it," says Hermes.

Herc taps Brad on the head with his knuckle. "Go get all that forgiveness so we can help out some good people," he says.

Brad smiles a great big smile.

Sophie, with Hermes holding her still, leans over and kisses Brad on the forehead. "You are very special," she says. "And I love you."

Brad kisses his mother on the cheek. "I love you, too."

He opens the door and follows Pete back into the confessionals.

55

M ichael decides that maybe it's best to just wait outside of the hospital.

Inside the disaster that his troops caused without his consent, his first and best soldier, Jamaerah, attempts to fuse pieces of the shattered walls together. The white and pinkish plaster lays in tiny pieces that normal humans will end up finding for weeks, if not months, from now.

Only angel eyes, and some animals, could be able to see the remnants of this kind of destruction.

This fact keeps Michael out of the hospital and out into the lawn. His eyes scan down the street, but he sees no movement. The people of this town have decided to barricade themselves inside. A well-intentioned, if not stupid, mistake on the part of the humans.

If the angels wanted to get inside the house, there is little that can stop the seven to eight-foot giants from doing so. When one swings the flame of faith, few can stand in its way or withstand its heat.

But the humans know no better.

It's this fact that he keeps telling himself as he replays the events in the Vatican over and over again. He remembers the mother offering her child to Gabriel. She wished her child to be well.

From her thoughts and feelings, Michael sensed cancer in the child.

Gabriel only sensed insults and sarcasm from the people. This angry, angry angel.

Michael had wondered to himself—was the one they called Hermes correct? Is he to face another Lightbringer, ready to claim the throne of Heaven for himself?

Michael checks the skies for signs of life from the Heavens above. The moon's face just begins to appear though clouds. The sky is still too light to see the edges of the moon, so it just hangs there, fading in and out of view.

The afternoon wind begins to blow and carries with it the smell of dust and flowers, intermixed into a peppery and herbal scent that Michael finds distasteful. He much prefers the sweet smell of the middle east. The tart spices and the smell of salty waters nearby.

Here there is nothing more than the smell of artificial everything. Smoke in the air, paint on houses and cars. Even these scents on humans. Fake flowers and fake natural scents.

As much as he adores the potential of humans, he has a hard time defending their choices in how they use up the Earth Realm's resources.

And yet, here he is, helping them to keep this planet and their realm free from celestial hands.

He does not pity the humans. He learned early that pitying the humans serves no one. No. Instead, he prefers to respect them and show them the way.

And this he struggles to do so, feeling irrelevant amidst a war that he has been charged to win.

A war, now, that includes a battle with his brethren.

Michael stares across the sea and sniffs the air, but his attention turns to his ears and chest. He shifts his head to the side and sniffs.

More angels on the horizon. Hiding somewhere out there.

Michael guards against making any quick moves. He sees any twitchy behavior as a sign that he knows he is being watched.

Watched because Gabriel commands it.

But few are familiar with Michael's gifts. His ability to reason with people by sensing their thoughts, their feelings. Their desires. By knowing one's enemy, the human writer Sun Tzu once wrote, one may know how to win.

It was a crass description, but one in which Michael felt best described his gifts.

At least as far as the military was concerned.

Michael turns his head to listen to the movement of furniture and drywall and people inside the building. He stands watch outside, however, really listening to the movement outside.

Listening to the hearts of the angels and others who watch with commands. Spying.

But for what? Do they suspect that they have turned on them?

When Michael stands up from his seated position, he lets his wings stretch out. A sign that he knows the other angels will see. A sign that he wants to be seen. He knows they are out there.

Michael's heart and head feel as if they are spinning.

It has worked. He's gotten his watchers' attention.

"He seeks to destroy the Throne of Heaven, you know," says Michael. The trees rustle. Shadows move about downtown. His own chest beats a beat per second faster. "And tell him that Pride cometh before the Fall. Warn him well," he tells the afternoon air. "Tell him that I will be there when he falls."

Michael turns his back on the outside and faces the hospital. He rubs his hands together and grabs rocks from the outside wall in his pale, white fists.

From behind him, rustling catches his attention. Then bursts of thunderous flapping.

The spies have gone to their master.

Jamaerah comes from the back rooms. Dust covers her silver and golden armor. Her hair is pulled back into a pony-tail, a suggestion from Herc. She smiles and says, "And what do we do about Gabriel now that we have committed to this plan? We were supposed to have gone back by now."

Michael says, "I have a feeling he already knows."

56

B rad points at the wooden boxes that look like the booths Superman changes in and says, "Do we need to go back in there?"

Father Pete shakes his head. "I suppose it's not really that necessary. Those are built for privacy. And well, I suppose we've already broken that sanctity."

Brad nods. "Right," he says. Whatever "sanctity" meant.

"But could we?" says Brad.

Pete looks out into the pews.

The old lady waiting patiently for her own turn smiles and waves them in. "I can wait a little while longer, I suppose," she says.

Pete smiles and takes her hand in his. "Thank you, so much, sister. We'll be right back. I promise."

Walking back to the booths, Brad blocks one side of his face from the woman's view and says, "Your sister is really, really old."

"She's not my real sister."

Brad opens the door and goes inside.

"It's a think we do within the congregation," says Pete. "We call everyone brother or sister out of love and respect. A way of acknowledging that we are all God's children."

Brad nods. "God's children?" he says. "So you have powers, too."

There is silence. Brad feels the confusion from the other side.

"Well, no, not powers." He pauses. "Just what kind of powers are you talking about?"

"Nothing," says Brad. "So can I be forgiven or not?"

"Son," says Pete. "It is never just that simple. It requires that you go about seeking forgiveness. There has to be some sense of regret. A sense that you want to become a better person."

Brad wipes his eyes with the back of his hand. "But I have to be a better person, Father. If I don't become a better person, then I can't go save my mom. She's hurt. Really bad, and I need to get stronger and better so I can go save her."

"You are only a child," says Pete. "You cannot be expected to save the world, my son."

"No one expects me to except me," says Brad. He stands up and rests his hand on the door.

He likes the darkness of the room, the bits of light that come in thin rays over his head. It is the most sense of privacy he's had in almost two days. A large part of his heart tells him to stay in the box, to keep talking. Take advantage of the time away from his family to feel better.

"I'm just afraid of myself," he says.

Silence. The long, dark kind that only helps Brad pay attention to everything outside of his door. Including a bright, shining light followed by a sucking sound.

"Father Pete?" says Brad.

More silence.

Brad opens the door and steps outside. The door to the booth next to his swings open. A bloody hand lays flopped out of the doorway, leering across the doorway.

Brad takes a step forward and peeks in.

Pete's face is still, his eyes pointed upwards. A thin trail of blood falls down his chin.

Brad's hands react immediately, slapping his face.

"Oh my god," he says.

A cold hand grabs the back of Brad's neck and squeezes. "God is not here at the moment."

Brad's jaw starts to open, but he feels the squeezing from the giant thumb against his neck. It pressure is too much for him to scream or open his jaw.

"Scream and I kill you right here, right now."

Brad stares at the front door.

Everyone, Hermes, Herc, his mom. Everyone is just right out there.

The could save him. He knows he can.

The old woman from before sits on the bench and cowering behind the pew in front of her. Her eyes gape open wide, her mouth caught in a permanent "o" shape. She trembles.

Brad looks downward. He is at least his own height away from the ground. His feet dangle from his legs, swinging back and forth.

He wants to kick the guy in the stomach. Maybe his arms, if he can reach that high.

But all attempts leave him grunting in pain. His windpipe is pulled tight against itself. His head feels light as a balloon and his vision blurs.

"Mom," he mutters through his tightened jaw.

"Just what is it that everyone sees in you, anyway?" says the man behind him. The man's voice shakes Brad's body with the deep bass. A sense of commanding others, not simply stating a fact.

Whoever he is, he sounds strong than his friend and step-brother Herc.

The room spins as the man turns Brad around to face him. The first thing Brad sees as he pries his eyes open are wings. White snow-like wings that twitch and flutter behind this giant man.

His hair is black, straight and cut short around the sides of his head. His strength must come from his size, Brad realizes. The man's narrow and thin arms could be broken by Herc in a simple gesture.

Brad smiles. "You're one of them?"

"One of them?" the male angel's eyes flare into a golden flame and fizzle out. "What do they teach you in Catholic school these days?"

"I'm not Catholic," Brad squeezes out of his throat.

"Then I suppose that makes it okay?" says the angel.

"I am the one they call Gabriel." He bows his head while keeping Brad still. "I am the Deus Vox, the—"

"Voice of God," says Brad. "I know a little bit of Latin."

"That is most impressive, young one. Maybe you humans are not as stupid as you may seem at first. Perhaps there is hope for you yet." Gabriel's eyes nod toward the front door. "That door there is the only thing separating your friends from me and you. It's rather poetic, don't you think?"

Brad's hands clutch at the angel's wrist and he squeezes.

Gabriel shakes his hand until Brad's hands slap around him. "Get off of me, you little twit." The angel's fingers squeeze tighter around Brad's throat. "It is a good thing that I need you," he says, "or you would end up like the good father over there."

For now the blood stays inside the booth. But the hand, the hand has gotten paler in this light. The woman on the pews, she tries to run out of the door but is stopped frozen by Gabriel's words.

"You will go nowhere," he says.

There is something different about his voice. A sense of intensity yet natural. Like a tropical storm or a hurricane.

"We have a trip to make," he says. "A little birdy says that we can use you a little bit later."

Brad's eyes open. He watches as a blue circle pokes through the air and widens. It grows and grows, taking up the majority of the wall and stops when it is big enough for the angel to step through.

Brad reaches out toward the front door. He kicks his feet about, but the angel's grip on the boy stays tight.

"Stop it," he says. "Stop this and I just might let you see your mother again."

The angel tosses Brad's body through the portal with a flick of his wrist.

Brad screams out for his mother. He flaps his arms to keep himself afloat. It seemed natural, if not stupid. His feet kicked.

"Mom!" he screams.

The blue light envelopes him completely.

57

"Should we be worried?" Sophie rests against he side of the church's plaster wall. The rough outside surface scratches against her back. The blood that leaks from her shoulder crusts up in a small black blanket that Jamaerah gave to her before they left.

The afternoon begins to cool down outside. The humidity, however, remains high and just as Sophie hates, she feels the sweat collect in itchy patches along her lower back.

Hermes's body stands up straight. "Did you guys hear are bang? I think I heard a bang."

"I did not hear a bang," says Herc. He stares at the empty streets. At mid afternoon, it was typical for the old folks to start wandering to the Lil Teapot Café. But today, even that restaurant remains closed.

Hermes perks up from his seat. "You see? There it is again."

Hermes rests his ear against he solid wood door and closes his eyes.

"You are not seriously trying to spy on a church?" says Herc.

Sophie looks down the street.

"Shh," says Hermes. He rests his ears against he door again. "I hear something," he says. He rests his hand on the solid brass doorknob. "And we are going in."

"We are not going in. Let Brad do his confessional thing all alone."

"But they have booths for that," says Hermes. "We could be waiting in there while they talk."

"With your hearing," says Herc, "you'll be judging and listening in on them anyway."

"Why did you say judging first?"

Herc rests his giant bear paw of a hand on the door. "We're not going in."

"We are going in," says Hermes.

The door rattles underneath both Hermes's and Herc's hand.

"There," Hermes says. "Do you believe me now?"

Herc nods. He digs his fingers into the solid wood and hurls the door open. "Brad?" he shouts. His voice echoes into the white room. Off to the side are two passageways. Probably bathrooms, Hermes things.

After all, religious people poop, too.

Sophie follows them in but rests herself against he back wall. "I'll stay here, if it's okay with you guys."

Hermes feels the pull of disapproval in his stomach. She shouldn't have come. It was stupid, reckless.

"Okay," he says anyway.

Hermes follows Herc's giant steps into the center room. White and full of pictures of God and other people in robes and hoods.

Like one of Brad's video games. Except not as dark. Or bloody.

"What the hell happened here?" says Herc. He approaches the confessional boxes but stops cold and then looks away. "Someone killed him."

Sophie's voice rings from the hallway. "The fuck?"

"Not Brad," says Hermes. He floats to Sophie's position and holds her in his arms. "Not Brad." To Herc, "Right, Herc? Not Brad."

Herc turns his head and nods. "Not Brad. But Father Pete is dead."

"Brad?" says Sophie.

"Brad would not kill him and then just disappear," says Hermes. "This does not make sense."

"Did someone. Get him?" says Sophie.

Hermes ponders for a moment. "Lilith?" he says under his breath.

Sophie shoots him a look, a raised eyebrow. "That bitch."

"We have no proof it is her," says Hermes. "Besides, she would only do it to get my attention. This is missing her touch. It is too messy for her. She is a selfish bitch, not a homicidal one."

Sophie's heart rate slows down. Hermes shifts his weight away from her chest and lets her breathe for a moment.

"We need to figure out who took him," says Herc.

"That is genius!" says Hermes. "Why did I not think of that?"

"There is no reason to get snippy, buddy." Herc rests his hands on his hips. "Too much TV for you."

"Why does everyone say I watch too much TV?"

"Because. You do." Sophie smiles.

Hermes smiles back, but he doesn't mean a damn part of it. "We will talk about this later," he says monotone.

"If it's not Lilith, then who would grab Brad?" says Herc.

Hermes holds up his hand. "Do you hear that?"

"Hear what?"

Hermes listens closer, bending over closer to the sound. "Sliding? On the ground."

Herc looks down around his feet. "I don't see anything."

Hermes follows a sound to the edge of the hallway and then turns around the corner. He tiptoes to the end of the pews and turns left.

"Whoa, shit!" he says. Hermes takes an overly excited step backward.

"Brad?" says Sophie.

Herc rests her against the wall. "Stay here."

"Where else am I going to go?" she says.

Herc tiptoes toward Hermes. "What did you see?"

"Not did. Do." Hermes waves Herc to his side, but holds his

hands up to tell him to stop when he's only three feet away. "Do you need help?"

"You could tell me what's going on," says Herc.

"Not you." Hermes runs to the end of the pews and scoops up an old woman.

Her white shirt with tiny pink flowers—the type with four petals and a bright yellow center that exists nowhere in nature—is dark with sweat. She stammers something in her shocked state. Her eyes don't blink.

Hermes holds her head full of curly gray and white hair in his hand. "What happened here?"

Her lips move, but no sound comes out.

Hermes rests his ear against the woman's mouth. "Say that again."

The woman's mouth moves. Hermes's head nods up and down. "I see."

"What did she say?" says Herc.

"A giant," Hermes says.

"A giant?" says Herc. He snaps his fingers. "An angel."

"Got that all by yourself did you?" Hermes rests the woman on one of the pews, propping her up against the side of the armrest. "We shall call an ambulance for you, okay?"

Herc pulls Hermes over to the side. "The hospital is a little busy at the moment," he says in a whisper.

"She does not have to know that just yet," says Hermes. "Besides, we will deal with our problem and come back for her later."

"You really gonna remember that, dude?"

"What did I say about dude? And no, probably not. Can you try to remind me?"

"Well, no."

Hermes floats to Sophie's side and pulls her from the wall. "We think we know what's going on. We have to go back to the hospital and fast. We are going to need a lot of help."

"What happened? Where is my son?"

"Don't be alarmed," says Herc, "but we know who has him."

"Don't be. Alarmed?" she says between breaths. "How am I. Supposed to be. Not alarmed? When you say. It that. Way?"

Hermes bunches up his fingers into a tight fist and punches Herc in the shoulder.

Pain and pressure of strained muscles in his fingers reminds him why he never does that in the first place.

"Yeah, you moron."

Herc shrugs. "Come here." He picks up Sophie from Hermes's arms. "I'll carry her, you hurry up to the emergency room."

"Since when are you the one to come up with plans?" says Hermes.

"Since you've been a bit preoccupied lately."

"I am not preoccupied."

He stares at Sophie, who looks as if she's already half asleep. Her eyes fall halfway over her eyeballs. The whites of her eyes turn pink and red.

"She needs rest," says Hermes. "Come on."

Herc nods and beats Hermes to the front door. He steps over the busted frame and into the pink and blue mix of the afternoon sky. The streets are still silent except for the faint sound of thunder above.

"Are we due for a storm?" says Herc. He looks upward.

Jamaerah falls from the sky and lands on her hands and knees. Her eyes flash with a blue light that colors her face, making her look pale. "We have grave news," she says.

"So do we," says Hermes.

Jamaerah stands up. So close together, Hermes begins to see that she and Herc are almost the same height. Jamaerah may be only a few inches taller.

Hermes's wings take flight and pull him up to eye level with his two taller friends.

Jamaerah nods and salutes, throwing her fist to her chest and bowing her head. "We have reason to believe that Gabriel will make a move sometime soon. He has been spying on us."

"Then I guess that means we know what his move was."

"Was?" Jamaerah searches both Sophie and Herc for a further explanation.

Herc clears his throat. "He took Brad, we think."

"Did he at least get his blessing?" she says.

Hermes shakes his head. "We don't know. Maybe. Yes? The priest was nice enough to talk to him."

"The safest place to take Brad is in Heaven. No doubt he knows that he has more power up there than he does in this realm. But if Brad has not been blessed yet and forgiven of his sins, then I cannot be sure that he will have survived the trip."

"Gabriel wouldn't try that." Herc looks to Hermes. "Would he?"

Jamaerah looks away. "I do not know that angel anymore. He has chosen to follow the Pride and not the word of Jehova."

"But isn't he the Voice of God?" says Herc.

"In title, yes. But it is a long explanation that we simply don't have time for." She takes to the air. "We must consult with Michael at once."

58

Hermes steps outside from the hospital. Having laid Sophie for a nap in the waiting room, he comes to join the rest of the conversation. The further he gets from Sophie, however, the more she remains on his mind.

Her son Brad may be dead. Immaterialized by the travel to Heaven.

She may be dead in a matter of days or hours if Heaven ever decides to change its mind on the whole mortality thing.

And Hermes, the smallest of the Olympians, wallows in his inability to do precisely jack and shit about it all.

The sun sets over the horizon. Hermes welcomes the scent of the fresh flowers blooming in the garden along the walls of the hospital. The walls have crumbled but flowers bloom—blue and red ones—just underneath each of the windows.

The scent is a sweet refreshment after the ointment and allergenic smell of the hospital. Jamaerah and Michael had done a great job putting the walls back up and giving the room some order.

But even their strength could not repair the full extent of the hospital in just a few days.

While fixing the walls, Jamaerah had noticed that her own

strength had begun to wane. She was hesitant to say anything to Michael, for no doubt he felt it, too.

But she let it slip on the way to the hospital, telling Herc in a subtle gesture and joke about feeling exhausted.

His own powers disappearing and Herc's strength remaining stagnant. Why is Brad the only one on the Earht Realm getting stronger?

The question digs at Hermes's mind and he can't help but feel the answer is right in front of him. If only he knew exactly just where to look.

Michael turns at the sound of the once electric door to the hospital sliding open under Hermes's limited arm strength.

"Good," says Michael.

"That does not sound like a good good," says Hermes. He takes small steps outside. As if not arriving in their circle would really make the bad news never come at all.

"It is probably not," says Michael. "But it could be a blessing in disguise. Indeed, He does work in mysterious ways."

Hermes resists the urge to roll his eyes yet again at all of this God talk. "Okay," he says. "So?"

"So it appears that Brad is most likely in Heaven," says Michael with a smile.

"We knew that already," says Hermes.

"This is true," says Michael. "But that also means that Brad must be alive. He would not take Brad to Heaven if he wanted to kill him. He has other plans for him to be sure."

"And how would you know that?"

"Your friend alluded to other killings in the church," says Michael.

Hermes nods.

Herc raises his hand and grins. "Hi."

Hermes sighs. "And?"

"And so this means that if he wanted Brad dead, you would have already found his body."

Hermes feels the pull of the words hitting his throat. "That seems rather harsh, do you not think?" he whispers. He peers back over his shoulder into the hospital.

"Quite the contrary." Michael rests his hands on Hermes' shoulder. "He works in mysterious ways, like I told you. Perhaps this is a good thing, for a boy so strong to be in Heaven already. He can do what we planned."

"And what do we do?" says Hermes.

"We just wait," says Michael.

"Wait for what?" says Hermes. "For those sick assholes to just return Brad's body back to us?"

"If he is indeed dead, then there will be no reason to return his body. He'll already be in Heaven," says Michael.

Hermes points a short, shaky finger at Michael. Words lock up in his mouth and he turns around, running his hands through his short brown hair and then kneeling down.

"This is impossible," he says. "Seriously, what are we going to do?"

Michael shrugs. "We can attempt to strike back, but that does not seem like a logical thing to do. They have the entire chorus of angels on their side. We're but a few."

"But I hit like a few more," says Herc. He slams one fist into his open palm. "We can take them."

"It is not a question of whether or not we can take them, as you so put it. But a question of whether or not we can survive the coming onslaught."

"Coming onslaught?" Hermes raises his head from his huddled position.

Michael nods. "Indeed."

59

B rad feels like he should be cold, but isn't. The lack of colors anywhere in this square box he's placed in suggests to his body that he should be freezing right now.

But the light that seems to pulse from the inside of the room, from the walls, has a light warmth to it, like sitting next to his mother on his bed before nighttime stories when he was little

Nine years old is way too old for nighttime stories. All the kids at the school will make fun of him.

If they find out.

Brad stands up and checks his clothing for dirt and holes.

Nothing. Though the passage through the blue oval—this fiery thingy that looks like something out of a video game—it looked like it should have been on fire.

He pounds his hands on the white walls. Everything is featureless, flawless. The kind of clean that his grandmother would be proud to call "accomplished."

The walls have some kind of give, like rubber against his fists. He scratches against it with his fingernail. Nothing comes out, the surface feeling tight together like cloth.

"Why is everything so backward?" he says. Brad falls to his

behind and bounces on the ground.

He smiles.

"No way," he says.

Brad stands up and falls down again.

Once more, he bounces a little bit.

"This is cool," he says. He gives it one more bounce before standing up and pounding his fists on the side that he figures is most like a door.

The cube feels like a room. A prison of no windows. No obvious doors. No anything.

Not even any furniture.

Brad remembers his step-brother Hermes mumbling something about cruel and unusual punishment. He looks around the room.

Does this apply?

"Where am I?" he shouts into the room.

His fists pound against he door again.

"Hello?"

He waits for an answer, but he hears nothing. Even his echo appears to disappear into the walls. Absorbed into them, his words never to be heard from again.

This is beginning to get weird.

He knocks on the soft walls again. "Hello?"

He rests his head against the soft walls. Closing his eyes, he concentrates his energy into his ears, but hears nothing.

"This has got to be a joke." He can already feel the tears welling up in his eyes. Every breath comes in shorter and shorter until he feels like he's barely breathing.

He collapses onto the ground and pulls his knees toward his chest.

"Just. Breathe," he says.

His words disappear into the surface of the floor.

His mother's face appears in his mind's eye. The battered and bruised face, with a purple patch extending up her shoulder to her neck and left ear. He opens his eyes and focuses on what he thinks is a corner.

With no light and no shadows, the room could be a cube. Could be a sphere. Could be anything, really.

He forces himself to take a deep breath.

He closes his eyes again. His mother's face appears in his mind again.

This time, her eyes are not bruised. She smiles, but the purple blotch—the bruise from her wounds—bursts and leaks blood all over her side.

Still, she keeps on smiling. Her eyes look warm. Her smile soft.

"I'm so sorry, mom."

"She cannot hear you, you know." A voice comes through the walls, but doesn't echo.

Brad opens his eyes. His eyes cross from trying to gain a sense of direction in the featureless room.

The room's warm heat and scentless air causes him to feel dizzy.

He just wishes he knew which way was the corner so he could throw up.

A foot, a nose, and then a whole face appears from the wall opposite Brad. Gabriel walks from the walls. "We are not going to kill you, if that is of your concerns at the moment."

"Where is my mom?" Brad shouts. "And where am I?"

"Your mother is still in the Earth Realm," says Gabriel. His silver and golden armor looks cleaner than it did on earth. Like pearls. The golden eagle across his chest appears to glow like he would expect a halo to glow.

"Earth realm?" says Brad. "So I'm not on earth?"

Gabriel shakes his head. "We had to take you away somewhere safe. So we can keep an eye on you."

Brad smirks. "So this is Heaven," he mutters. He stands up and wipes the sweat from his palms on his blue shirt. "I expected more clouds."

Gabriel's eyes narrow. "One second you are whimpering for your mother. The next you cast this false bravado in the face of danger," he says. "You are an Olympian after all, aren't you?"

"I am Brad, Son of Zeus."

"Yes, yes, I quite know who you are." Gabriel walks around Brad's unsteady posture.

Brad tries to follow him around the room, a center of focus amidst this confusing and upturning room, but he cannot focus. His stomach, his head begins to twist and turn. His eyes feel like they are upside down and inside out. So he picks a spot on his shoe—probably golden angel blood—and focuses on it instead.

"Son of Zeus." Gabriel folds his arms behind his back. "You did quite a number on my soldiers."

"You have soldiers in Heaven?" says Brad.

"Of course we have soldiers in Heaven. We have soldiers everywhere. Keeping an eye on you and your kin. The last thing we need is a series of old gods coming and usurping our place. You were placed in Hell for a reason," he says. "You should have learned your place and stayed there."

"I'm not from Hell," says Brad. "I'm from South Carolina."

"Yes, your father is known for his extra escapades away from home." Gabriel looks at Brad's strong shoulders, the muscles tensing up on his arms. "You look strong. Strong enough to take out a number of my own men and women."

Gabriel kneels down in front of Brad. He takes a finger and lifts up Brad's head to meet him eye-to-eye.

"I have a proposition for you," he says.

"No," says Brad.

"But I barely said anything."

"I know what a proposition is," says Brad. "And whatever you are going to tell me, no."

Gabriel stands up and holds his hand up, ready to backhand him. Gabriel lowers his hand and roars at him, screaming enough for spittle to hit Brad on the nose. "You will speak to me with more respect, boy! I could have killed you when I had the chance."

"Then do it already," says Brad. He rests his hands on his hips. "Just shut up and do it."

Brad watches both of the angel's hands make tight fists and he braces for impact just in case.

He's never pushed his limit before. It's always frightened him, the idea of losing control.

Whenever he does so, he manages to kill and destroy. Never to help and save.

Gabriel's grimaces softens in his face, turning into a smile. "I can see it in your eyes, pup. You want to hurt me. You want to destroy me."

He kneels down and points at his own chin.

"Take your own advice, pup. Hit me. Destroy me. If you can."

Brad pulls his fist back and stops. He studies the angel's jaw. He knows right where to hit it.

Or if he aims up and into the angel's nose, he can force the little bone in his into the angel's brain.

Wait. Do angels even have brains?

"Well?" says the angel. He stands up and takes a step back. "I thought so. You see, you humans are not worth the effort. None of you are. You are half evil, half ambivalent. Jehova himself made a gross mistake keeping you all alive. He should have flooded the planet for real. Start over."

Brad lets his fist go and drops his hands to his side.

"And you lack the strength of will to do even do what you were born to do. What good is free will if you aren't even strong enough, smart enough, to use the damnable thing?"

"My family will come for me," says Brad.

"No doubt they would try, if they knew how to break the realm's barrier. But gods such as you? You only know the physical planes. You know nothing of the spiritual planes." Gabriel looks toward the wall and steps toward it. "Like it or not, you are stuck here until I say you are free to go."

Gabriel disappears into the room.

Brad rushes to the wall and bounces off the soft white cloth but not cloth that covers it.

His brain rushes with feelings and images, not knowing which one to do first. Shout or cry? Scream or punch?

They all seem like great options at the moment.

So his body turns inward and he drops to his knees and waits.

A tear tickles the skin of his nose as it drips off the tip and lands onto the white ground. It softens up and then disappears, leaving the floor pure and white once again.

60

Michael literally puts his foot down onto the ground. It was the first time Hermes had ever seen anyone actually do it before.

"No," says the giant angel. "They will never survive the traveling process."

"We've never tried," says Jamaerah.

She stands opposite Michael outside of the hospital. The sun turns pink and blue behind them. The light breeze carries with it the pine scent of the patch of evergreens across the street. Even if there wasn't a show, Hermes would consider this another beautiful day. The streets remain silent and human-free. All of them locked up in their own homes out of fear and threats.

Gabriel had threatened war. A war that never officially came, but the lurking soldier angels in their white and silver armor—and their eight foot presence—gave the humans enough to worry about.

Nearly ten miles away from the city's limits, soldiers gather in tanks and trucks with weapons that they hope will shoot and kill these winged aliens.

Herc and Hermes sit, cross-legged in the grass, watching the intense debate.

"We would be going against the word of Jehova," says Michael. "We cannot risk it."

"But with Jehova out of the picture."

"Out of the picture?" he says. "Have you lost your mind, Jamaerah? Just because he is silent does not mean that he is dead."

"Doesn't it?" says Jamaerah. "For nearly a century, the humans have been claiming that God is dead. What if they wished it into existence?"

"They can do that?" Herc whispers.

"Our powers come from those who believe in us," says Hermes. "Technically, they can do whatever they want to. They just don't know it yet."

"But I thought—"

Hermes taps Herc's head and points at the ensuing argument.

"Then I will not allow it," says Michael. He rests his foot down again onto the ground. "End of discussion."

"Then I go myself."

"You will do no such thing. You'll be walking into a trap."

"I can fend for myself," she says. "I am the best soldier you have."

"Technically, isn't she the only soldier he has?" Herc whispers.

Hermes stifles back his smirk and taps Herc on the knee. "Watch and shut up."

Jamaerah holds her hand up to Michael's face. "Hold on a minute," she says. She turns to Herc and Hermes. "I can hear you, you know."

Herc turns away and looks at the swaying branches of the trees next to the hospital.

Hermes whistles and nudges Herc. "Stop pretending you were not talking."

Jamaerah turns to face her argument once again.

But Hermes interjects. "But you know, he has a point. Why are you willing to sacrifice yourself if you go up there? You are only good to us if you can bring Brad back with you. Two dead people— uh, angels—will not do us much good."

Herc shrugs. "What he said."

"I cannot believe this," says Jamaerah. "I am trying to help you get your brother back, and even you stand in my way?"

Herc stands up. "We just want you alive, Jamaerah."

"This is not about emotions, Herakles of Greece. This is about getting your brother back and stopping the next prideful angel from taking over the throne of Heaven."

"Why can it not be about both?"

Hermes swallows and looks away. This won't be good.

"Because you are the only one with emotions," she says. "I like you, Herc. You are a brave warrior and you do, indeed, dole out a fine beating. But you are trying to force something that I am not allowed to feel."

"You are not allowed to feel love?"

Jamaerah looks to Michael. He turns his back on the conversation.

"It is complicated," she says.

Herc throws his hands up into the air and walks back into the hospital. "It's complicated, she say. It's always complicated."

His rantings disappear into the hospital hallways.

"I am so, so sorry," she says.

Hermes nods and taps Jamaerah on the foot. "It is quite okay. He needs to get used to hearing no."

"I did not mean to simply say no."

"But you did. It is how things go."

"I will save Brad."

Michael raises his hand. "You will die in the process. You really think Gabriel will not have some kind of contingency plan? He took Brad to Heaven for a reason."

"And we don't know what that reason is just yet. We cannot find out until we bring the battle to him."

"You are as infuriating as ever," says Michael with a smile. "Go with God."

"You as well, Michael," says Jamaerah.

He hugs her and pulls away, staring into her eyes.

Hermes says, "Oh, now I see."

Michael leans in and kisses her on the lips. The kiss lasts only a few seconds but Hermes looks over his shoulder to look for Herc's lurking eyes.

He thinks he sees him in the shadows, hiding out amongst the furniture and rubble.

Hermes waves, then frowns.

Michael and Jamaerah break from their embrace and she takes a step back.

She looks downward, then upwards and salutes, holding her closed fist to her chest.

A blue flaming portal opens behind her and she waves. Drawing her sword, she enters into the portal and it closes behind her with a loud sucking sound.

61

B rad has mixed feelings about being able to tell time right about
now. His eyes stay fixed onto his white shoes. They are
streaked with golden blood, splattered from the blood of angels that
he destroyed only hours ago. Or was that half a day?

The streaks start out thick at first near the front of his shoe, but
turn thin and jagged like lightning bolts as they travel up and along
the sides of his shoe.

They dried almost instantly, it seems. Brad toyed with the idea
of pressing on them and touching them, but the idea of getting
angel blood anywhere on his skin seemed a bit wrong.

Not to mention disgusting.

He begins to hear a tapping so he looks up, wishing immediately
that he didn't.

The walls and the light don't ever appear to change. He cannot
tell which way he is really facing, and with the corners not really
being corners, Brad finds it best to just face one way and look down
at his shoes.

And count the fibers in his shoelaces as best he can. Anything to
keep himself preoccupied.

But deep down, he's clenching his teeth and waiting for the next time the angel comes into his room.

Next time, he'll kick its ass and then break free.

Somehow. Some way. It always seems easier on the TV shows his brother Hermes likes to watch.

Brad stands up and approaches what he thinks is a wall. He walks almost as if blinded, his hands extended out in front of him. Reaching, waving back and forth. Looking for something that resembles a wall.

When he finds the solid fabric-like wall, he begins pounding his fists into it.

Each fist going deeper and deeper into the wall.

But not making a single dent.

Brad closes his eyes.

No crying. Not now. No crying. Herc wouldn't cry. Herc doesn't cry.

Brad clenches a tight fist and slams it into the wall again.

He thinks about Herc fighting alongside him in the hospital.

Slam.

He imagines Hermes holding his mother tight in his arms, keeping her from bleeding too much.

Slam.

Brad closes his eyes and tries to imagine his mother without the wounds, without the blood, without the thoughts of death teasing and tempting his imagination in the back of his mind.

Slam.

Slam.

Slam.

The wall begins to rumble, but Brad falls forward and leans against it. He begins to slide down the wall until he rests on his knees.

"I'm sorry, mom. I'm so sorry."

He feels the gentle tug of tears pulling at his eyes.

Brad tries to stand up, but cannot get a solid grip on the wall. He tries to pull himself up but slides down the wall again.

When he slaps the ground with his hands, the tip of his fingers trace the sides of a shoe.

Someone's in the wall.

Brad makes a strong fist and raises his hand up. "You won't get me this time, Gabriel."

Brad lowers his fist but something stops it. A warm hand, soft skin like his mother's.

"Who?" says Brad.

The face and body of Jamaerah emerge from the wall.

"You found me," says Brad. He pulls forward and yanks Jamaerah into his arms. "I cannot believe you found me."

His eyes and his chest give in, and he sobs at the feet of Jamaerah.

She picks him up by the armpits, lifting him up and holding him out in front of her.

"You must stop crying," she says. "You have a job to do."

Brad shakes his head. "I can't do it."

"Cannot or will not?" says Jamaerah. Her grip on the Brad tightens around his shoulder and she brings him in for a hug. "You poor, sweet boy. You are unharmed, are you not?"

She holds him out and examines his forearms and feet. "No torn clothing."

"I'm fine, I'm fine." Brad wipes away a few tears. "How did you get here?"

"I am an angel. And this is my home," she says. "But since you are already here, then we can proceed with our plan."

"But I don't know where to go. Or what to do."

Jamaerah lowers Brad onto his feet. He wobbles at first but stands tall.

For Herc and Hermes and his mother.

"But you can do this. You are mighty, small one."

"I was captured," says Brad. "You guys are the fighters not me. I couldn't even save my mom."

Jamaerah pushes against the wall. Brad feels something radiate from the white wall, something warm.

Soon, Jamaerah's fist disappears into the wall and she continues to walk past it.

"You can pass through?" Brad says.

"It is a celestial magic. None pass through without the will to do so."

"You mean I could have escaped any time I wanted to?"

Jamaerah nodded. "This is Gabriel trying to prove his point. That Jehova was misguided in giving humans free will. What good is will if they are not strong enough to use it."

Brad sighs. "So he made an idiot again."

"Not an idiot." Despite her saying the opposite of what Brad is thinking, she seems genuine in her compliments.

Brad wants to believe what she's saying.

"Can angels lie?" says Brad.

Jamaerah's footsteps seem to skip for a moment, caught off guard. "Why do you ask?"

"Nothing," he mutters.

Jamaerah nods. "I believe we could lie if we need to, but rarely is there an instance served in which lying is the best approach."

Brad nods, trying to follow the line or reasoning. "So you guys don't really lie often?"

Jamaerah looks at him through the corner of her eye as they walk down a long white corridor. She smiles. "No, I suppose we do not."

The corridor is crystalline and smells like cloud vapor. Thick and humid, but pure. Not like South Carolina's humid summers in the midday sun. This was a place that feels warm all over. An entire realm made to make you feel more comfortable.

"Why is it so empty here?" Brad asks.

"It is not that empty. But the armies are preparing to march."

"The armies of Heaven."

Jamaerah points to a corner and nods. She turns down the corner. "The choruses of Heaven are what Jehova used to gain prominence and speak with the humans. Those that hear his voice are supposed to be deafened. Possibly even death. This is why he takes various forms and sends Gabriel in his place."

Brad nods. "I don't know if I believe in God."

He looks around at the white walls with a crystalline sheen, as if carved out a white diamond. He realizes as he turns down the corner with Jamaerah just how stupid the words sounded coming out of his mouth.

"I mean, I guess before now," he says.

Jamaerah smirks. "I suppose I would not have believed in him either if I had a life such as yours."

"What's that supposed to mean?"

"You have lived an incredibly unique and challenge life, Brad. And yet, here you are. Strong, healthy, and about to save the world. You have been tested and found worthy of an incredible future."

"I have?"

"You have." She taps Brad on the head, just as she had seen Herc and Hermes do back on Earth Realm.

Brad looks up at her hand.

"Did I do something wrong?" she says.

Brad shakes his head. "No, but I miss Hermes and Herc."

"They miss you, too," she says.

"What are we looking for?" Brad's eyes search the walls. Mostly they are white with bits of a white pearly substance that splits the wall in a thin line down the center. Brad felt it was something to follow, so he followed it.

It's not that Jamaerah ever told him not to.

But now, he looks down the hallway and sees a series of doorway. No doors, or at least, no doors that look recognizeable to him. They have only a hole where the doorknob should be. No sign of hinges.

"I don't know where I'm going," he says.

Jamaerah puts her hands on Brad's shoulder. "When I tell you to run, I want you to run."

Brad stops. "What? Why?"

Jamaerah draws her blade. It ignites into flame in a burst that blinds Brad for a moment.

When he opens his eyes and turns around, a shadow looms around the corner.

"I need you to run," she says.

"But where? Where do I run?"

"Run all you want," says Gabriel, "but you will not hide from me in my realm."

62

The white crystalline walls soon blend together as Brad runs down the hallways. He struggles to catch his breath and tells himself to not look back.

So of course, when he least wants to, he looks back.

A flash of blue and white light flares into his hallway from around the corner.

Gabriel is coming for him. And Brad isn't sure if he can take him. At least not like this.

Brad considers for a moment to go back. To rescue the pretty girl angel before she gets herself killed.

The way she came in and protected him.

He starts to walk fast down the halls, his fingers tracing the path along the walls. As if somehow that will help him find where he's supposed to go.

Yet he feels pulled forward. An instinct, like when he fights and he knows to turn left or right and then counterpunch.

This same voice in the back of his head tells him to keep walking. Let her fight. It was her idea.

But he ignores that voice.

He knows he shouldn't because it was Herc who taught him all about that voice. Herc, who had taught him that to fight and survive, he had to learn to be not so human as a force of nature. Because all Olympians everywhere are force of nature.

Brad's feet turn him around and he stops. The white and blue flashing lights up the room faster and faster.

Flames? Portals?

Brad feels his heart swimming in the top of his stomach. He needs to get there and help her out.

He runs. His fists clench into tight balls and he feels every muscle in his arms and legs tense up. Going into battle. For real. Without anyone pulling punches.

Brad gets to the corner of the hallway and stops cold.

Jamaerah sits on her knees and holds her hands out toward Brad. Gabriel has her in a headlock, his hand twisting her head as if trying to rip it right off. Their swords lay crossed next to them, tossed apparently in the battle.

"What are you doing?" says Jamaerah. Her hands grip the sides of Gabriel's arm and she tries to pull his forearm away from her throat. "I said leave!"

Brad's hands tremble as he trips the corner of the hallway. He shakes his head. "No," he says. "I want to help you."

Jamaerah's eyes widen. "No," she mouths.

Gabriel grips tighter in Jamearah's head and turns, jerking quickly, but he stops midway.

"She is correct in telling you to leave, boy. You are next when I catch you."

Brad runs toward the swords. He grabs them both and they flare up. His hands burn with intense flame, the fire melting his skin against the handles of the sword.

Gabriel gnashes his teeth and tosses Jamaerah off to the side. "Do you feel that burn, pup?" he says. Gabriel stetches his hand out to Brad. "Do you feel that intense heat? That sacred flame?" He steps closer to Brad. "That fire means you were not suppose to have that sword. These are not for mortal hands."

"I'm only half mortal," he says. He represses his screaming by biting into his lip. He swears he tastes the metal flavor of pennies touch the tip of his tongue.

"Half or whole, that burning has to hurt like Hell." Gabriel waves his hand toward him and one of the swords pulls away from Brad's hands.

It flies into Gabriel's hand. "And you should know that it knows me as its master."

Brad clutches the remaining sword tight in his hands. He waves it back and forth in front of Gabriel. He knows nothing of sword-fighting. His biggest sparring partner is a fan of punching bad guys in the face. Hard. With his fists.

There is no way he can figure out how to use a sword. Not like this.

Gabriel holds out his hand again. He waves for the other sword, but Brad lunges forward. The blade slashes into the angel's hands.

He growls in pain and pulls away. His hand drips with golden blood. Each droplet splats onto the ground and then disappears into the crystalline floors.

"Brat!" he roars. His hand stops bleeding in a few seconds. Gabriel, too, grabs his sword with both hands. The sword's tip bursts into flames.

Brad breathes in and holds it deep in his chest. He looks at the angel's shoulders and elbows. He can't go anywhere his elbows can't go.

Brad steps forward and swings the sword over his head. He nearly slices into the angel's forearm.

He brings the sword back around for another swing.

Gabriel seizes Brad's shoulder and yanks him into his grasp.

Before Brad can react, he feels Gabriel's warm body against his back and a flaming blade against his collar bone.

"You will move no further, Jamaerah, or this boy will die."

Jamaerah stands up and raises her hands. "Leave him be and you can have me."

Gabriel smiles. "But I already have you both."

Jamaerah unfurls her wings out into full span. She stretches, then stands straight up, her arms at her side. She looks at Brad directly into his eyes. "We will get out of here, do not worry."

Brad nods, though he's not quite sure he believes her.

Whenever Herc had him in a headlock like this, Brad remembered getting out any number of ways. But this blade makes Brad nervous. The flames are not hot, but make his neck muscles tense up. His chest feels tight, barely able to breathe.

All the while, he wants to escape. Find God.

Save his mother.

Jamaerah takes a step closer to Brad and Gabriel.

"What are you doing?" he says.

The blade draws closer to his throat.

Jamaerah's hands lower to directly in front of her to show that she's empty handed. "You are outnumbered, Gabriel. Two versus one. Without your armies, you cannot be victorious."

"You raise a good point, but it's moot. You seem to forget just what kinds of tricks I have up my sleeve." While keeping strong grip around Brad's neck, he feels the angel's blade swipe away from him.

Something explodes behind him, giving way to a sucking noise that Brad remembers from before.

A portal.

"Where are we going?" Brad says.

The sword's blade gets pressed up against Brad's jugular.

"Your friend here gave me a great idea. I'm going to get my army."

Brad's feet drag on the floor as they are turned toward the portal.

"To me, my armies," says Gabriel.

Brad peers into the portals, watching as the green grass on the other side blows in the breeze. They wave like a green ocean.

Brad doesn't know if it's possible, but thinks he even smells the piney air of the trees, the pastries cooking in the kitchen of the Lil Teapot Café.

"Home," says Brad.

"Do not get too excited," says Gabriel. "We cannot just arrive unannounced. What's the point after all?"

"You are beginning to sound like the Lightbringer," says Jamaerah.

"You have way too much faith in Jehova," says Gabriel. "Look at what he's done. Look at what he's created and tell me that he really knows what's best. He's allowed for the earthlings to take make their wars. He's allowed them to destroy the world they live on. And for what?" Gabriel points at the portal as if to prove his point.

Brad struggles to break free but the blade finds his throat again.

"And you think yourself better?" says Jamaerah. Brad watches her feet sink down into the ground. Getting ready. "You know where Pride will get you."

"Lucifer was an idiot who never understood how to rule properly. He barely has a handle on Hell. But I've watched. I've learned. I know the true value of what we can accomplish. I know how we can be the superior race. And we'll start by destroying these half-wit hybrids such as this."

Gabriel twirls Brad around so that the yare staring at each other face-to-face. Gabriel's face appears darker, the crevices of his mouth and eyebrows lit up by the fire of his blade.

"I have no idea why you were His favorite," Gabriel says.

Brad swallows. "Wait. What?"

"Gabriel, you will leave the boy alone," says Jamaerah.

Both Gabriel and Brad look up.

Jamaerah charges at them, her fists forward and her head tucked into her chest.

Brad closes his eyes and braces for the impact.

He body gets thrown forward into Gabriel's. They fall off balance into the portal.

Brad struggles to grab hold of something, anything, but his hands flail around in the air. The wind picks up past his face.

He's falling back to Earth.

"Brad," says Jamaerah, "give me your hand." Her hair flutters past her face, but her hand is outstretched at Brad.

He swallows first and then reaches out and grabs it.

Jamaerah flaps her wings as they fall, giving them a little bit of lift.

But Gabriel latches onto her wing and pulls backwards.

Jamaerah's eyes widen. She doesn't look back, but keeps her eyes on Brad.

"Go with God," she says. "No jump." Brad feels the pull and then sudden push from Jamaerah.

Brad looks backward and watches as the two angels wrestle in the air, getting smaller and smaller. Falling in the opposite direction.

Brad turns his head and falls through the portal once again.

He reaches out and clasps the side of the floor with a tight grip. He doesn't dare to look down.

With a grunt and a good, strong pull, he pulls himself out of the portal and it fades into back into the air, sucking in some of the atmosphere with it.

Brad looks back into the hallways. Everything is empty. Abandoned.

"Now how do I get home?" he says.

63

After trying eight doors, Brad would have expected at least one of them to be open.

If he was even opening them correctly.

Brad walks down the hallway slowly, looking for something that will get him closer to anywhere but in the same white crystal hallway with a silver line down the center of it. It cuts across the middle, leaving a top half and a bottom half, but they both look the same.

So not knowing where else to go, Brad follows the silver line down the endless hallways.

Nothing changes as he progresses down the halls, however. He's not even sure what these halls are to, or where he is exactly. All he knows is, he must be in Heaven.

Alone.

With no way to get home.

Brad takes a deep breath and comes upon something else that looks like a door.

He tries to push against it, but nothing happens. He clenches his teeth and looks to the left, then to the right. No one around.

Like always.

So he pulls back his fist and lets it go into the door. Or what he thinks is a door.

His fist hits the hard crystal wall thing and shakes.

Just as before, his entire arm vibrates through his shoulder.

He smiles and then punches the door again.

His arm vibrates deep through his bone.

"This tickles," he says and punches it one more time.

He shakes off his hand and keeps walking down the hallway.

Everything so white and clean, so alone. Too pristine for his own tastes.

Brad wishes that his mother could see this, how beautiful it all is. Beautiful and yet somehow lonely and cold.

"God," Brad sings aloud. "Where are you?"

He walks slowly, tracing the walls with his fingertips again. Hoping to feel some kind of crack or crevice that will tell him that the door can be opened. That he can look at something other than shiny white whatever this is as far as the eye can see.

Just where do they make all of this stuff anyway?

"Hello? God? It's me. Brad."

Brad takes a smaller step forward and begins tapping on the walls as he walks.

The beat starts to resemble a Beatles' song, so he keeps tapping and humming to himself.

He keeps tapping. Tapping. Humming. Tapping.

Then something in his brain tells him to stop. The same voice— Herc calls it instinct—that tells him to punch or dodge or run.

He stops in front of the wall and taps on it.

It sounds no different, so he rests his ear against the wall and taps again.

"Hello?" he says. He taps again with his ear against the wall.

Wait. Brad closes his eyes.

He just has to want to get through. Just like what Jamaerah told him when he was imprisoned.

Brad closes his eyes and pushes into the wall.

"I want to get through," he says. "I want to get through."

His hands push into he wall but he tries to walk forward.

His shoe hits the wall.

"Dammit," he shouts. His voice echoes in the halls.

He covers his mouth and looks both ways down the hallway.

He just swore in Heaven. He smiles but holds his breath.

"Sorry, God," he says.

He closes his eyes again. "I want to get through the wall," he whispers.

He rests his hands against the wall. Resting and pushing forward lightly.

He has no idea what's on the other side of the wall, but he presses anyway. Walking forward, but not using his strength.

Brad lets out another stream of steady air.

"I want to go through," he says.

Brad opens his eyes. "Are you working yet?"

His hands rest on the surface of the wall. Not in it.

"This isn't going to work," he says.

Brad pulls away but something comes from the wall and grabs his wrists.

"What is this? Let go."

Brad jerks his hands backward but goes nowhere. He pulls back again, resting his feet against the wall and jerks so hard he feels his shoulders pop.

"Let go," he says again.

Once more, he pulls backward, but instead feels the pulling motion of moving forward through the wall.

Brad closes his eyes and huddles into a ball.

He feels funny, coming through the wall.

But he didn't do it. Someone else did.

The stranger lets go of his wrist and Brad feels the familiar cool of air brushing past his fast, twirling in the air.

He lands with a hard roll onto the ground. He gradually unravels himself to slow himself down.

Something familiar tickles his nose.

"Grass?" he says.

Brad opens his eyes. His line of sight is filled with a bright green. With yellow flowers and a smell of fresh air.

Something dribbles along, splashing.

"Where am I?"

Brad stands up and looks around.

In front of him, standing in front of a white wall, the other side, he guesses, is a little boy in a blue hooded robe. The boy's head is covered mostly, but a lock of white hair sticks out near the boy's forehead.

"Who are you?" says Brad. "Where am I?"

"I am called Jehova," he says. "I can help you escape this place, if you want."

"Jehova? You're God?" says Brad.

He sizes up the boy. His feet are bare in the grass, his body is tan, not Hispanic or Arabian, but his eyes seem to be as green as the grass. Greener even. The boy's small lips perk up into a smile as he waits for Brad to finish his questions.

"That is one of my names," says the boy. He pulls back his robe to reveal a simple shirt and pants, held together by a golden braided rope that makes him seem like he's from an age long ago. Like before they even had jeans. "But if you prefer God, then that will work for me, too."

God's voice seems to be as childlike as his own. Maybe younger. If he had seen him in school, he would have guessed he would be a third grader or maybe a bigger second grader.

"Why are you so young?" Brad says.

"I am young because I am one of you." Jehova smiles.

"You are Greek?" he says.

Jehova lets out a slight laugh. "No, Bradley. I am a god like you."

"Hermes says I'm only half god. My mom is a human."

Jehova smiles and nods. "Yes, I know who you are, Bradley. I have been waiting for you here for quite some time. It is nice to finally meet you face to face."

64

Hermes still remains sitting outside the hospital. He keeps his eyes out to the sky, keeping the image of Brad's smiling face alive in his mind's eye.

The Greek god of communication. Of travelers. Of ferrying the dead spirits to the insides of Hades, and yet he can't even set a damned foot in Heaven.

Because of some old rules.

Hermes picks at some of the grass and pulls it up, taking large chunks of roots with it. He lets the dark soil dangle from the roots as he shakes it off and then tosses the clumps off into the distance.

Herc's sandals squeak as he walks from out of the hospital.

From tucking in Sophie and making sure she's okay. It was his idea. Not Hermes's.

He can't seem to even want to look at her right now. Her son, lost. She is on the brink of death for days and Hermes has decided that he just cannot take it anymore.

"Hey, are there supposed to be shooting stars tonight?" says Herc. His giant feet appear next to Hermes's hands. The sweat and dirt from the giant lug's unwashed feet make Hermes roll over and finally stand up.

"I do not know. I do not keep up wit things like that."

Herc points off into the sky. A burning ball of flame falls downward.

"That is a lot closer than it should be for a shooting star," says Hermes. "Maybe it is Brad. We must go." Hermes waves at the hospital. "Michael," he says. "I believe we have some news."

Michael stands at the entrance of the hospital. He rests against the doorway. "Then go. I will keep track of the humans in here. I am tired of fighting."

Hermes nods. "You cannot tire just yet. The battle is not won."

"That is the problem, godling. The battle never ends. It will never be done." Michael ducks his head downward and enters into the shadows of the interior of the hospital.

"Leave the Gloomy Gus. We need to go get Brad," says Herc. He picks Hermes up by the shoulders and hauls him on his side while running as fast as his muscular feet can take him.

Hermes had never wondered who would win in a footrace. Hands down, it would be Hermes, but Herc would definitely give him quite the competition. A run for his money, as it were.

As Herc builds speed, Hermes can see Herc's confidence begin to rise. They begin to not just run, but to leap and jump over things as well. When they get close to the Owl Foods store, Herc seems to pick up speed and leap over the building completely, falling to his feet and continuing his run.

In a straight and narrow kind of race, Hermes knows he would win.

In an obstacle course, Hermes would be hard-pressed to show some confidence.

"Watch it, there, will yeah?" says Hermes.

Herc smiles. "Sorry."

"No you are not." Hermes's words come out in herky-jerky motions from the running and rocky roads of the beach that lie next to the river's edge.

The two follow the line of sight straight down into the park near the river. Well, more like a stream. It's called a river during the rainy winters, but becomes much, much smaller during the summer months.

"You think they'll land here?" Herc drops Hermes onto the ground and peers upward. He blocks the sun with his hand.

Hermes looks upwards as well. "I have no clue. But probably."

"Come on," says Herc. "You're good at flying and shit. Why can't you tell where they are going to land?"

"Because I can figure it out from up there. Not from down here."

Herc shrugs. "Makes sense."

The ball of flame grows larger. Something black seems to wiggle inside of it.

"There's definitely people in there," Herc says.

Hermes nods. "Yup." The wings on his feet begin to flap and carry him upwards.

"Where ya going?"

"I want to get a closer look," Hermes says. His wings take him higher up, over Herc's head.

"Don't get caught on fire or something."

Hermes shrugs. "What?"

"Man, it sucks being down here." His voice fades as Hermes climbs higher into the sky.

The black thing wiggling inside the ball of flame comes clearer, growing.

It's two things. Black. Wiggling.

No. Fighting.

"Herc!" shouts Hermes. "Herc! I think it's Jamaerah and some one else."

"Brad?" shouts Herc.

Hermes shakes his head. "I don't think so. I think they're fighting."

Hermes looks back up and notes a thick black cloud coming in from the east. But the winds are coming from the east. They are coming from the south.

The clouds cannot travel where the wind isn't blowing.

"Oh shit," says Hermes. He drops to the ground and lands on his knees. "We have got more trouble than we thought."

"Good," Herc says. He cracks his knuckles.

"No, no. Not good. Bad. Very, very bad." Hermes points at the quickly approaching fireball. "That is Jamaerah and Gabriel." He takes Herc's hand and twirls him to face east. "And that? That is Gabriel's backup army."

Herc's shoulders drop. "Damn."

"Damn indeed."

The flaming ball of fire seems to extinguish as it gets closer ot the ground. The angels begin flapping their wings, but too late, Hermes suspects, as they are too close ot the ground and coming into too fast to reasonably slow themselves down.

Hermes feels like he should do something. Anything.

"Throw me," says Hermes.

"What?"

"Throw me." Hermes points up at the fighting angels. "At that."

Herc smiles. "That's an awesome idea. Too bad you can't throw me."

"I will never be able to throw you." Hermes flies up to Herc's hand and stands in his giant bear paw. "Ready?"

Herc nods. "Ready."

"Aim," Hermes says.

Herc's hand moves around a bit, back and forth until resting still. "Ready."

"Fire," Hermes says under his breath.

His stomach seems to hit his feet as he's thrown with an explosive force. His is launched into the air. He looks downward and watches as Herc's smiling, bearded face disappears and he quickly approaches the heating ball of fighting angels.

Hermes extends his hands out and flexes his fingers.

"Ready," he tells himself. "Ready."

The angels come closer to him.

"You shot too high," says Hermes.

He flies over the two struggling angels, but manages to cling hold of Jamaerah's armor, pulling her out of the fight.

"What are you doing?" she screams at him.

"Saving you," Hermes says.

The two go twirling, spiraling in the air and arcing back down toward the hopefully soft ground.

"You smell nice," says Hermes. Wrapped up in her grip, he can smell traces of freshness around her. Like clean clothing, but cleaner. Fresher.

"Hmm," Jamaerah groans under her breath. "Not you, too."

"What? No, not me, too."

Jamaerah's wings go full out and slow their descent. "Are you ready?" she says.

Hermes feels his ass muscles clench. "For what?"

Jamaerah's wings pull close to her body and they pick up speed. "For this."

The air thunders past Hermes's ears, pulling the skin on his face to the back of his head. His hair feels it may be pulled out of his skull.

"Is this necessary?" says Hermes, though he doubts that she can hear him.

As they come close to the ground, Jamaerah's grip on him tightens. Protection?

The ground comes closer. What were once tiny specks are now rocks are now boulders, it seems. Everything come at Hermes faster than he can breathe.

"You are crazy," he says.

Jamaerah nods. "Mhm." Her grip tightens once more an Hermes is caught mid-breath and unable to move his chest. The sun disappears behind Jamaerah's wings as they turn into one big feathery cocoon.

They meet the ground with an intense thud and intense vertigo as they roll in some direction. Hermes closes his eyes and realizes it may be better to keep them open.

If not for the vertigo but to be ready in case they hit something.

When the wings unravel, Jamaerah smiles. "Was that not fun?" she says.

Somewhere in the distance, Gabriel lands with a ground-pulsing thud.

Hermes shakes his head. "Hell no." He tries to stand but his head spins. In his youth, he used to be able to go that fast. Some days he had to go that fast.

But those days are behind him. His powers lost, he just doesn't have the stomach for it like he used to. A fact that came very, very painfully obvious just now.

"That was awesome," says Herc. He sprints over toward them, on the other side of the park. "That was good aiming."

Jamaerah stands up tall. "I was too close to stop, so I decided to just go with it." She looks around. "We did not harm anything, I trust?"

Herc looks around. "Just Hermes."

65

Jehova sits on a rock in the beautiful grassy garden. Thorny bushes grow along in hedges along the sides of the walls, giving Brad the impression that the room could quite literally last forever in any direction.

When he looks to see just where he may have come in, he cannot find the same wall. Everything is changed, but gradually.

"Why is this room different?" says Brad. He eyes the walls and hedges over Jehova's hooded little head.

Jehova smiles and pulls his hood back. His hair is longer than a boy's normally is. It comes down to his shoulders in the back, and it's all white. Not white and black like old people hair. But real white hair that shines in the light.

"You have excellent eyes," says Jehova. "You are a smart, little boy."

"So if you're Jehova, then that means you're God?" says Brad. "The capital G god?"

Jehova nods. "Yes."

Brad steps back and raises his tight fists in front of him like a boxer. "Then I'm here to kick your ass."

Brad waits. Slows his breathing. He anticipates that any time that God will stand up, grow up or something and stomp him into oblivion with a giant, sandaled foot.

But he sits there.

Waiting.

Smiling.

Brad bites his lower lip. He wants to scrape away the God's stupid, fucking face and make him cry the way he's cried because of his mother.

Because of the pain.

Because of he doesn't want any of this and now it's up to him.

To save the world.

Because to save the world, he has to be better.

And how else to be better than to beat up God?

"Well?" says Brad. "Stand up and fight me."

"Even if you could," says Jehova. "You do not want to do that." Jehova looks around and raises his arms.

The sun feels warmer. The flowers brighter.

"This is my realm," he says. "I make the rules here. Not you."

"That's cheating," says Brad.

Jehova shakes his head slightly. "It's not cheating, Brad. It is playing by the rules. And here, you do not make any of the rules. I do."

Brad sniffles back some tears and lets out the first punch. Jehova's body falls off of the rock and rolls down the side. He tumbles over.

With his bright golden eyes, Jehova wipes at his jaw and grins. "What was that for?"

Brad stands, stunned, for a minute.

He did it. He finally punched God.

His legs begin to twitch with nervous energy, his palms sweat. He makes two more giant fists and runs over to Jehova's side.

Jehova extends a hand to be pulled up. "It's okay, Brad. I forgive you."

Brad punches him again in the face. His knuckles hurt for the first time as long as he can remember. He had gotten used to his strength. He could lift anything, bend whatever, and never be injured.

Never, until now.

He takes a minute to shake off the pain in his hand.

"Brad, you do not understand."

Brad lands one more punch clear across Jehova's nose.

Where Brad expects blood, there is none. No bruises. No pain.

He just smiles, looking at Brad—no, through Brad—as he lies there on the floor.

Brad pulls his fist back. "No, you don't understand. I want my mom back."

Brad pulls his fist forward to hit Jehova one more time but his arm stops in mid air. Pain sparks in his shoulder and he pulls backwards again, trying to relax it.

"Even if you could hurt me, Brad, you are wrong to do so." Jehova pulls himself up into a sitting position. "We can help each other."

"How am I supposed to help you?"

Jehova extends a hand out to Brad. "First, you can help me get up."

"Hell no," says Brad.

"I see this is not working," says Jehova.

A bright light pulses from Jehova's head, washing over him.

Soon, Brad sees nothing but white. He shields his eyes and turns around, bending over.

The light turns warm, intense.

A voice echoes in his head. "Open your eyes, Bradley."

Brad hesitates.

"It is safe," says the voice again.

The voice feels friendly like a smile, but not young. Not like him.

"God?" Brad mumbles.

"Open them," says Jehova. "I command it."

66

The only words that go through Hermes's head is "Not again." He runs with the help of his wings to go faster, fast enough to catch up with Herc and Jamaerah.

He waves his hands. "Herc!" he shouts.

A dark, winged figure launches itself out of the river's surface and brings with it nearly half the river's water.

The shadow hangs in the air, backlit and full opened up. His arms, legs, and wings extended as far as they will go.

"Herc!" shouts Hermes. He points up. "Gabriel!"

Herc waves back, then looks back behind him.

Gabriel's body collides with Herc and Jamaerah, taking them both down into the sand.

Gabriel stands, clutching Jamaerah's body and tosses it to the side.

"You," he says. He seizes Herc's massive neck with both hands.

Herc shakes off the daze and grips Gabriel's head with his own massive hands.

"Me!" he shouts with a smile.

The two squeeze each other to an impasse.

Herc's face glows red as he gets strangled while Gabriel's head turns dark red, almost purple.

Finally, Gabriel screams and punches Herc in the face.

Herc's grip lets up.

Gabriel takes to the air. His eyes are bloodshot, almost golden in the whites. He looks down at Hermes and Jamaerah. "You have no idea what you are up against," he says. "I do not care if I get the throne of Heaven now. Now, I just want to finish you."

Gabriel looks over to his left and smiles.

"I am not the only one," he says.

Hermes flies up to the air, just below Gabriel's height.

"Holy shit," he says.

An army—or maybe a few armies—of police cars and maybe a few tanks sit at the edge of the town's border.

Lights flash red and blue. The engines start almost all at once.

Then, they begin to roll onto the city.

"We're in trouble," says Hermes. He drops to the ground and points at the city's border.

Herc stands up and looks over at Hermes's hand. "We have humans at the border. Well, official humans. With guns."

Herc shrugs. "Who cares. Bullets cannot kill me."

"Maybe, yes," says Hermes. "We are not exactly at our full capacity."

Herc flexes his bicep. "Look at this and tell me that."

Gabriel lands at the beach and draws his sword. It catches full flame and he points it at Herc. "Today, I may return you to Hell myself."

Herc poses, his hands on his hips and his shoulders pulled back. "Ha! Better men than you have tried."

Hermes gives Herc a tap on his shoulder. "How long have you been saving that one up?"

Herc keeps his smile, but says from the side of his mouth. "A little while. Too much?"

Hermes nods. "A little."

Jamaerah rushes to Herc's side. "We can take him if all three of us battle at once," she says.

"All three?" says Hermes.

"He is the Deus Vox. He has much respect and worship in the Christian and Catholic communities. He is perhaps stronger than us."

"Perhaps?" Hermes takes a step back.

Herc pushes him in front. "Stay and fight already."

Hermes's feet dig into the sand.

Gabriel does not wait for a chance to fight, but throws his sword at the Herakles.

The sword cuts at Herc's shoulder. Herc breathes in, deep and sharp, to dull the pain of the searing cut.

"You okay buddy?"

Jamaerah leaps up into the air and charges at Gabriel. "Now! While he is unarmed."

The sword flies out past from behind Jamaerah, slicing at her wings and returning to his hands. He smiles. "One down."

"Not so much," say Herc. HE stands up, wobbles, but keeps his hand on his left shoulder. "It's not my good arm," he says. "I'm good."

Hermes nods.

Just how do you know if you have a good arm? Does Hermes have any good arms, not having been in a full out war before?

The gods of the past were the ones who moved humans to do their dirty work. Seldom did they ever have to war it out themselves.

This is why the transition of the religions were mostly bloodless. Deities do not get their hands dirty.

It is much more becoming of a future god to let the humans do the dirty work themselves.

And now, Hermes sees just how human he has become. Manipulated. Crying. In pain. Weak.

"Soon I will have what I'm looking for, and the whole of humanity will be rendered in permanent chaos. This is the path you chose with your ignorant and pathetic use of free will. Turning your back on God."

"Don't get mad at us," says Herc. He rushes toward Gabriel.

Gabriel takes the sky yet again, this time, just out of Herc's range.

Herc stops, kicking up sand in a tidal wave.

Once he stops, he leaps up into the air.

Jamaerah leaps into the air as well.

Their arcs, if they meet, will land directly with Gabriel in the middle.

Hermes watches on as the Gabriel turns to his side and holds out his hands, his sword extended out at Herc's jump.

"No," says Hermes.

Hermes flies upwards, angling his path toward Gabriel's feet.

Jamaerah is the first to meet with Gabriel's arms. She feels the brunt of his punch, but gets a good punch directly into his side before flapping away.

Perhaps, Hermes hopes, to come back and hit him again.

Herc lands second, clasping onto Gabriel's arm and shoulder and pulling him downward.

Gabriel's wing flap harder and creates a wave the pushes Hermes downward back to the ground.

Hermes leaps up again.

This time, he sets his sights on the angel's boots.

Herc manages to turn Gabriel in the air, but his weight on the angel's ability to stay into the air pulls him down gradually.

Hermes looks up and measures again.

He can only really mess this up once.

The wind blows at Hermes's face. Sand grits against this clenched teeth, the thick, dry, and salty taste of beach sand coats the tip of his tongue, sticking out through the side of his mouth.

He has to focus.

Focus.

Gabriel's feet come into zone and Hermes snatches the tips of both of his boots and pulls him back.

Gabriel's body trembles in the air until he falls face first into the sand. Herc lands on top of him.

"This is for Sophie," says Herc. He grips each of Gabriel's wings with his hands and snaps them in half.

67

B rad's eyes open and the entirety of the garden is gone. The grass, so green it was almost blue, disappeared from underneath his feet. Instead, he stands on a white stone pedestal that is wide enough for him to sit down if he felt the need.

The pedestal, however, appears to hover in the middle of the air. Everything tastes pure, like water vapor and rain, and what isn't covered in clouds is a pure yellow light up over his head that fades into a clear blue sky down below.

"Where are we?" Brad says.

Brad looks over his shoulder. The boy has also disappeared. No where to be seen. Even his robe, the rock. Gone.

Brad turns around completely. He's greeted with a bright white and yellow circles. Three of them, concentric and layered inside each other.

Brad turns his head and swears he may see a face, but the brightness of the sphere is too much for him to catch one.

"Jehova?" says Brad.

A voice pierces the insides of his head like a needle through a jello mold. "Yes, Brad."

"Is this what you really look like?" he says.

The sphere pulses. Yes.

Brad stands up. He realizes the distance between the two makes him just out of Brad's reach.

He can't hit and punch his way out of this one. Now he needs to do what Hermes would have wanted him to do all along.

Talk it out.

"Why are you doing this?" says Brad.

The golden spheres stay still. Brad waits for an answer, taps his feet.

"Why do you make humans do bad things? Why do you let bad things happen to people?"

Brad waits again, pulsing his foot.

The spheres pulse. "I need you, Brad."

"You don't need me," says Brad. "You can do whatever you want. You are the one in control down there. Not me. Not my uncles or my brothers. Just you."

"You do not understand. I am in trouble."

Brad sits down, then stands back up. "What kind of trouble could you really be in? You're God for crying out loud."

In the middle of the awkward and continuous silence between them, Brad smirks that he almost said "For God's sakes," but didn't.

Would that have been rude of him?

"Just like you," says the spheres. "I need people to believe," he says. "I need people to want me in their lives and worship me."

"So you're a needy child?" says Brad. "When I don't get my way, I don't go and make my mom regret it. You can't just pitch a fit and hope that everyone comes right back to you. Sometimes you have to be nice to them."

"I tried that," Jehova says. "And it didn't work out. I was betrayed."

"Then get over yourself," says Brad. He folds his arms and then unfolds them. Having a limited amount of space gives him a strange sense of claustrophobia, except not all closed in.

Brad looks around and considers maybe jumping to a cloud.

Like he sees on TV or in Mario games. The clouds were always strong enough to hold the characters.

Maybe they could hold him. He needs to move.

"If they suffer, they will believe. They will need me. Like I need you."

"You keep saying that, but why do you need me?" says Brad. "Do you need me to believe in you, too?"

The spheres—Jehova—pulses. Yes.

"Too damn bad," says Brad. He throws his hand to the side.

"You are a precocious little one," says Jehova. "Wise and yet so naïve."

"Hermes says we demigods grow faster than mortal boys." Brad snarls. "And stop trying to change the subject," he says. "You want them to believe in you, to need you, and you think just having problems in their lives will do that?"

Silence.

"Well look how well it's worked out for you."

The concentric spheres appear to grow smaller for a moment, then pulls back to their original size.

"You need them to love you, but you won't love them back," says Brad. "You show that you don't trust them by testing them. If you don't trust them to come back, how do you know they were really faithful?"

"Do not speak to me about faith," says Jehova. "You are the one who has no faith. Faith in himself or his family. You see your gifts as a curse. A reason to hide who you really are."

"I am Brad, Son of Zeus," says Brad proudly.

"And you are a little boy, who was not strong enough to stop me from hurting your mother."

Brad's fist clench tight. "You?"

The spheres pulse.

"I needed to test you," Jehova says.

"Life shouldn't be one big test," says Brad. His vision blurs as tears override his entire eyeball. He blinks and the tears drip steadily down the sides of his nose and into the corners of his mouth. He licks his lips, the saltiness of his own tears surprises him.

"This is a war, Bradley," Jehova says. "You are ill equipped to understand that."

"Oh, I know what war is," says Brad. "I play video games."

"This is no game," says Jehova. "Your mother can die at any moment. All it takes is one thought from me."

Brad's legs shake and he collapses to the ground.

"So as you see, Brad, if you are not well equipped for this war, then you really have no reason to come to my domain, my realm, and make demands of me."

Brad's jaw and lips tremble as he tries to speak. He looks up at the sphere and bows his head again. "What do you need from me?"

"I need you and the other gods to want me and need me. I need for all of you to recognize me as the new religion and the new power. I need all of you to accept me."

Brad stands up again. "Good luck. I can't give that to you."

"There is no mercy in war, Bradley. I am warning you now."

"You want to see war? Look down below. Look at the suffering done in your name."

Brad peers over the ledge of the podium.

"Your angels are destroying the Earth realm because they think they cannot hear you."

"But they are correct. They cannot."

Brad freezes. "What? Why? If you need us so much, why turn your back on your own angels?"

"They have grown comfortable. They have grown to disdain humans."

Brad shrugs. "So? Talk to them. Let them know they're wrong. Be a good parent for once."

"This goes beyond being a parent," says Jehova. The spheres pulse and twirl around, pulsing again. "Your mortal eyes cannot understand."

"No my half-mortal, half-god eyes see just fine, thank you very much. If you want them to love you, you need to step up."

"You are much too naïve."

"And you risk losing the people you need to keep you in power,

Jehova. You're going to lose your powers and someone else might come in."

The first image that Brad has is of his father, Zeus, shackled somewhere in Hell. Maybe a bird eating his liver, if they still did that sort of thing down there.

The sphere pulses again. "Fine, Bradley. You win. I will save your mother, but it will cost her."

68

Gabriel reaches out for the empty sand in front of him, his hands now angled and pointed like claws. An animal reaching for his last chance for life.

He's hiding it, Hermes thinks. He's trying to keep from feeling any pain. That it doesn't exist.

"This is bullshit," Hermes says.

He stares at Herc, who just lets the asshole climb away to safety.

"What are you doing, you oaf? Crush him."

Herc stares. He's been known to cause his opponents pain and to play with them. Is this a game to him? He helped to destroy the very thing that he loved.

Hermes flies to Gabriel's back and stretches out his already bleeding wings. The golden droplets that seep from his feathered flesh leaves a metallic flavor in his nose.

When he lands onto the bleeding angel, the taste of nickels and dimes floods the back of his throat.

He coughs, gagging.

Gabriel tries to flip around, but the weight of Hermes keeps him only flapping around like a fish out of water.

"Stay where you are, butcher," Hermes says. He grips the wings again, twisting them as he takes off into the air. Hermes flips around completely, twirling with the wings in his hands.

Dancing with the wings like feathered partners.

He lands back onto Gabriel's back.

Gabriel screams and claws at the sand. He screams again, spitting blood in his spittle.

"You will pay for what you did." Hermes can barely see out of his own eyes, the tears taking up too much of his vision. This alabaster and golden blurry figure beneath him tries to escape the little god's wrath, but there will be no chance.

Hermes will go to the ends of the earth if he manages to escape.

Hermes flips the angel over, surprised by his own strength.

Gabriel's hands flap onto the sand.

And Hermes hops onto his chest and pelts him with his tiny, lighting-fast fists.

Left.

Right.

Left.

Right.

Soon, the golden blood covers Hermes's hands. They shine in the setting sunlight, looking pink and golden like liquid metal.

And he keeps punching.

A hand yanks him off of Gabriel's chest. The hand dangles him from the air.

Hermes's hands and feet swing around in the air.

"Let me go, you ass," says Hermes.

"Not until you calm down," Herc says. There is a concerned but calm tone in his voice.

Hermes almost misses the fact that Gabriel barely moves. He just sits in the sand, his chest pumping up and down slowly. Catching every painful breath and wheezing as he exhales.

"Are you trying to kill him?" says Herc.

"I am trying to feel better," says Hermes. He roars into Herc's face. "Now let me down!"

"Not until you calm down."

"He wanted war," says Hermes. "He got war."

"You're not the killing type, kiddo."

"Stop calling me a kid." Hermes takes a swing at Herc's cheek and barely misses.

"I'll forgive that since you're not yourself."

Hermes's shoulders feel heavy as boulders so he stops swinging. His hands and legs just dangle, lifeless, from Herc's grip.

"Fine," says Hermes. "I am fine now."

"I don't believe you just yet." Herc begins to whistle some pop song Hermes remembers from the radio.

"You know I hate that song."

"I know."

"It will only make me more angry."

"I know."

"So stop singing."

"You can leave when you calm down, wingfoot."

Hermes crosses his arms and pouts. "You know I hate you."

"I know."

Jamaerah lands onto the sand next to Herc. She watches with a smile as Hermes waves, then continues to pout again.

"The humans are much closer than we thought," she says. "This town could be in danger soon."

"How much danger," says Herc.

"Big metal monsters with wheels danger. And a big barrel gun."

"I told him already," Herc says pointing at Hermes, "the guns won't hurt us."

"Perhaps they will not hurt you, but the angels that have turned sides, they probably will."

"Angels have turned sides?"

"They are leaderless now. Many have heard of Gabriel's blasphemy. If he is truly cut off from the gift hearing Jehova, then he is not who they thought he was. As it stands, they are looking for a leader."

"Then what about Michael?" says Hermes.

"Michael would be the best choice," says Jamaerah. "But he has been out of touch as well. We have all lost hope."

Hermes throws up his hand. "Great, so why not have a little coup in Heaven as well, too."

"Wait, wait, wait," says Herc. "As far as we know, both of those leaders are alive and well. Probably in control."

"Just absent," says Jamaerah. The way she says the words and eyes Hermes, it's as if she is wanting to make it known that Heaven has not lost. She's still rooting for her team.

"Absent or not, He needs to get a better grip on his generals."

Jamaerah huffs and turns her back on both of them. "I will return to Heaven and see what is taking Brad so long."

"Take him with you," says Herc, turning around and pointing at him with his thumb. He still holds Hermes in his tight grip, who pretends to just walk away with him.

"What do you think is happening up there?" says Herc.

Hermes shrugs. "I hope someone is watching over him."

69

The golden spheres pulse while they float just above Brad's line of sight. The bright, sunlight yellow almost masks the warm glow of the spheres.

"Your mother will live," the voice tells Brad, "but the others must die."

"But you said you would help them," says Brad.

The spheres pulse and wait.

Brad taps his foot. He measures the distance between his podium and the spheres.

If he has to, he can make this a physical confrontation. Leap onto the sphere and beat him into submission.

"This is cheating," says Brad. "You want them to love you."

"This is a war, and here you do not make the rules," says Jehova.

"Your rules are stupid," says Brad.

"Your mother could die and I could return you back to Earth without any hope of seeing her again."

Brad's heart nearly stops beating, then speeds up. He inches toward the edge of the podium. There would be no room for getting a running start. No hope of finding anything in there to jump off of.

All he wants to do is destroy. Punch and kill and destroy those sphere. To destroy Jehova for everything he's done to him and his mother.

"You may go back. Your mother will heal from her injuries. The others must die."

Brad swallows. "Mom will be okay?"

"She will be better than okay," he says.

The sphere pulses a warm light.

Brad nods.

He takes a step back from the edge of the podium.

He takes a deep breath.

"So everything on Earth will be okay?" Brad says.

The sphere pulses again.

Brad nods, smiling.

Then he waits. The other pulses always meant a yes. The sphere's way of affirming Brad's thoughts.

But this time, Brad feels the pinching in his gut like a sudden rush of stomach acid all over him.

"Will the Earth be okay or not?"

The sphere twirls and lowers to come face-to-face with Brad.

"This isn't an answer," says Brad.

The sphere comes within arm's reach. He makes a tight fist but locks his shoulders into place. No punches yet. Not when he's come so far.

"You will get what you want most."

"Stop your cryptic bullcrap," Brad shouts.

"This is a war," says Jehova. The mind-voice pulses in Brad's ears and head at the same time, sending Brad a headache and pressure like his eardrums are being squeezed from the inside of his head.

"This is a war, and you're too busy being afraid to do anything about it. You just sit up here and wait it out. At least Zeus would go out and fight with his family."

The skies turn from golden yellow to blue and black. "If you are done testing my patience, boy, you will leave me now."

"But you never told me. Will the Earth be okay?"

"You will get what you want most, Brad. And then, when you

have free will after getting what you want from me, let's see if you are willing to give back. Let's see if you are willing to play fair."

Brad feels the bottoms of his feet tilt forward. He barely hangs on to the top of the smooth, marble podium. His shoes refuse to grip onto the surface.

He begins to slide off.

Why couldn't he just give me a door, he thinks.

Brad looks down and feels his stomach and intestines rush to his lungs.

This might just hurt.

70

He doesn't remember the trip down, but as Brad's feet touch the ground, he gets the distinct feeling of just waking up. He stretches and rubs his eyes and realizes, he's not in his bedroom.

Birds flutter from branch to branch in the trees just above him.

The air smells of cold wind, cutting into his nostrils and lungs. The sun has set already.

If hard pressed, Brad couldn't tell you just when he got to Heaven, or for how long he had gotten there.

But across the street from where he stands, yellow lights come through rectangular windows. Saraday's emergency room.

The hospital clinic.

Brad runs across the street, but it feels different. The rocks on the sidewalk and road cut into hit feet, prickling him but not breaking his skin.

He looks down. His feet are bigger. His legs longer.

He holds out his hands in front of him. The baby fat he had along the backs of his hands, the softness of his skin. All of it gone.

He peers up at the sky. "What did you do to me?"

Brad's steps get slower into the grass. The dew covers the

bottoms of his bare feet and he slips along, barely even having to lift his feet to move quickly to the front of the hospital.

The doors barely hang onto the front entryway. They do not open up automatically, the way they did when he brought his mother here.

After the accident.

The closed doors give Brad a chance to catch the reflection of a older boy staring back at him.

"Can you open this for me?" he says.

The voice sounds unfamiliar to him. Almost cracking as he spoke.

"Are you mocking me?"

The boy's mouth moves when his does.

He touches his face, gripping his forehead and his eyes. His nose and his mouth.

He feels the faint pokes of stubble along his cheeks and chin. Long blond hair, a little darker, hangs from his face, just above his eyebrows.

"Facial hair?' he says.

He taps onto the door and it falls off the hinges.

The noise gets everyone's attention, but they say nothing to him. The people inside the waiting room sit on padded chairs, once broken by Brad himself during a tussle with angels. A little girl and a little boy stop playing their handheld video games to catch a glimpse of Brad's taller, older body.

He does not ask for help from anyone. The counter is empty of any nurses or secretaries or whoever they were. The doors are unmanned.

Brad pushes through the door. The bare, uncarpeted floors go cold underneath him. White tiles that look more bluish under the harsh electric lighting. He can hear them hum in the ceiling above him.

As a matter of fact, everything feels louder to him. More intense.

The noises down the hall, the screeching of metal carts, the changing of channels on the television sets. Everything comes to his ears as loud as lightning crashes into his brain.

He comes to his mom's room.

He doesn't know why, but he hesitates. He wants nothing more than to see his mother, but right now, he doesn't know how much time has passed. If any has passed at all.

Will she recognize him?

Will he recognize her?

Is she really okay?

He opens the door with the tip of his pointer finger and the door slides open.

The room is empty. The bed's sheets pulled up, ready for another patient.

He turns from the room.

"Excuse me, miss?" Brad says. "The woman in the room over there. Where is she?"

The nurse in the maroon scrubs doesn't look familiar. Maybe a night shift. Maybe someone called in for more help.

Brad reaches for her arm and squeezes too tight.

"Where is my mother?"

"She's gone," says the nurse. But with no remorse in her voice. No bedside manner.

"Gone?"

Brad drops down to the ground, kneeling, his hands in his hair.

"Get up, son," she says. "She's gone outside to the garden out back."

Brad hugs her, too tightly he suspects, but releases her and rushes to the glass doors on the side of the hallways.

The cold win brushes against his feet and bare arms again. He looks to the side of the hospital and follows a glowing, flashing light.

Candles?

Tiki torches?

Brad turns to the back and watches as a woman stands above the people, all of them sitting or kneeling before her.

The woman looks up, her head and body glowing with a bright blue halo that softens hers edges, blurring her.

"Brad," she says.

"Mom?"

Sophie stands, still in a hospital gown, and pushes past the people in front of her. Once past them, her steps turn to bigger steps until she runs into Brad's arms.

"You recognize me?" he says.

"I'll always recognize my baby boy." She hugs Brad with both arms tight around his shoulder.

Brad's arms rush around Sophie's waist, but something rubs up against them. He jumps backwards and stares.

"Wings?"

Sophie nods. Her eyes appear to blur, and a crystalline blue drop falls from her eye.

"Are you dead? Alive?"

Sophie shrugs. "I am new," she says. "I am better than I ever felt. And I've been helping these people."

Sophie grips Brad's hands and she turns to pull him toward the group.

"Everyone," she says. "This is my son. He helped to fight off the angels."

The group shares confused looks amongst themselves.

"I was younger then," says Brad. He can feel the bass in the back of his voice, but the occasional squeaks make him blush instantly.

"You're so grown up," says Sophie. Her hands caress the sides of his face and she looks into his eyes. "Is this what He did to you, too?"

Brad shrugs, then nods his head. "Yes. Or no. I don't know."

Looking into Sophie's blue eyes, he sees a reflection of himself, but feels something missing.

Not something in him. Something in her.

"Mom, do you feel all right?"

Sophie smiles and kisses his cheek. "I feel perfectly fine," she says.

Brad lets go of her hand and lets her return to the group of injured and sick, who pine after her to help them.

Brad turns from the group and stares at the moon coming just over the trees he woke up from.

In the distance, a large man followed by a tiny dot fly in the air.

Hermes and Herc.

Brad's stomach burns inside. He wishes he predict their behavior.

He looks back at his other, who smiles and looks well, but there is something less about her. Something he misses.

This is not his mother. God had lied to him.

This is not what he wanted.

Brad waves his arms up into the air and catches the faint smell of acrid body odor. This is how Herc smelled after a few sparring matches.

Brad turns his head away and puts his arms down.

Hermes and Herc land on the front lawn of the hospital. Herc hits the ground in a light sprint and slows to a steady walk into the building.

Brad runs around the building, yelling out their name.

"Hermes! Herc!" he waves at them, bent elbow this time, and looks down at the ground.

"It's me," he says.

Hermes walks slowly at first toward Bradley. "Who?"

"Me," Brad says. "It's Brad."

Brad looks up and pushes his hair out of his face. "See?"

"Oh my goodness," says Hermes. "You are old. Like, a lot older."

Brad nods. "You said demigods grow faster."

"Not like this." Hermes waves for Herc to come over.

"You look good, son," he says. Herc slaps Brad's back and lets out a burst of hearty laughter. "You look like a fine young man."

Hermes taps on Brad's muscular shoulder. "You seen your mother? Is everything okay? Did we win?"

Brad opens his mouth, but nothing comes out. He tries again. "Sort of," he says.

Hermes grips Brad's shoulder again, but pauses, squeezing it and makes a face that says he's upset that he's now the smallest of all three of them.

"Okay, let us slow it down, then. Is your mother okay?"

Brad nods.

"Is everything okay?" Hermes asks slowly.

Brad shrugs.

"What does that mean?" Hermes shrugs. "That? What is that?" He shrugs again.

Brad shrugs. "This," he says. "It means this." He shrugs. "I mean look at me."

Hermes pats him on the shoulder again. Again, his face goes to a rolling of the his eyes and a groan of disbelief.

"I need to go check on your mother." Hermes disappears behind the glass doors of the entryway.

"Hermes!" Brad shouts. "She's over here."

71

Brad turns around the corner and stops, biting his tongue.

Hermes grabs Sophie by the shoulder, but holds her at arm's length. "What the hell happened to you?"

Hermes looks over his shoulder. "What did you do to your mother?"

Brad shrugs. "She's better, but I don't know. God said I would get what I wanted most."

"You made a deal with God?" says Herc. "That's ballsy."

"I don't even know what I bargained for," says Brad. The time up in Heaven becomes fleeting in his head. And disappearing as fast as he can try to remember what happened exactly.

Brad pulls his feet up from the wet grass and onto the patio. His toes scrape the cement. He barely feels the pain. His toes, almost numb. He knows he's touching something, but the old sensations of pain and cold and heat mean nothing to his brain.

A sound catches his attention. Something rustles, then whispering.

He walks over to the edge of the sidewalk and listens, blocking out the whispers and exasperated questions of his step-brother Hermes.

"Will you quiet down?" his mother says to his brother.

Brad steps off the sidewalk completely and walks toward the edge of the building. In the hedges along the wall Brad sense more rustling.

He takes another step and feels a small hand on his shoulder.

"I need to go," Hermes says. "I'll go check on Lilith. Maybe she's back in Hell."

"Have the angels gone?" Brad says.

Hermes nods. "Yes, probably. Gabriel is gone. Jamaerah is dragging him back to Heaven as we speak."

Brad nods and taps Hermes's hand. "Good luck."

Hermes takes to the air and disappears in the dark sky above them.

Herc comes out from behind them. "Those are some really nice sick people."

"You're not upset?" Brad says.

"No." Herc shrugs. "Why should I be?"

"I don't know," says Brad. He keeps his eyes on the bushes and hedges. A foot sticks out from near the roots. "I feel like I just royally screwed up."

"Maybe you did. But right now, I can't tell."

Brad smiles. "Thanks."

He then puts his finger to his lips and takes a quiet step toward the bushes.

"Come out, come out, wherever you are," says Brad. He reaches into the bushes and pulls it right out the ground.

The smell of fresh dirt and herbal roses kicks Brad in the nose.

But the huddling mass of women—two beautiful women dressed in white cloths—cowering behind the non-existent shrubs.

"Who are you and why are you cowering?" says Brad.

Herc kneels down and squints. "Oracles?"

The women look up, confused.

"Holy shit, it's the Oracles?" says Herc. He turns around as if Hermes still stands behind him. "Wow, it's the Oracles. Wait," Herc pauses and looks around. "Where is he?"

A deep sigh comes from around the corner and across the street.

A tall figure walks across the street in a rare confidence. His leather jacket sheens in the moonlight, his shoes some kind of animal or reptile leather.

He wears a cowboy hat that sparkles in the light. "Never send women to do a man's job," he says.

"Don't let Artemis hear you say that."

The figure reaches the end of the street and takes his hat off. He holds it over his chest and nods. His skin seems dark, even the moonlight, but his blond hair glows like a solar-powered halo.

"Bah, who cares what she thinks?" the figure says.

"Apollo." Herc rushes to his sidewalk and gives Apollo a giant bear hug.

Apollo turns his head away. "Geeze you stink."

Herc smells himself. "Sorry." He then slaps Apollo's chest. "Where the hell have you been hiding?"

Apollo looks past Herc's shoulder and stares directly at Brad. "You," he says.

Brad looks to the side. "Me?" he points to himself.

Apollo shoves Herc to the side. "What did you do?" he says.

The women rush to Brad's side. They wear white sunglasses over their eyes. Their shirts and fabric pants—not jeans, but something shinier—appear gray in this limited moonlight.

"I didn't do anything. My mom's safe. Everything's good."

"Good?" Apollo says. "Good?" He screams it out across the night sky. "You will get us all killed, you ignorant son of a bitch. How's that for good?"

Apollo jumps out at Brad, clutching him in his hands by Brad's shirt. He pulls back a punch and lets it fly into Brad's nose.

72

The gate is free of angel control. The grass around the rock, however, is downtrodden and struggling to stand up tall and grow.

Hermes knows the feeling.

With a step into the doorway, he lets his hand guide himself along the cold, stony wall down the dark path. The light from Purgatory only a flickers a little, barely there.

Hermes prefers to walk down the rocky steps. Flying is faster, but when looking out for your homicidal and crazy ass ex, sometimes faster is not always better.

Slow. Steady. Prepare for the worst. Hope for the best.

When Hermes and Brad had to save Sophie's soul yet again, the path seemed longer and more treacherous. Today, it only seems short, narrow, and dark. So very dark.

Hermes's eyes have gotten used to being out of Hell for a year. Not having to look into the dark, he fears that maybe he's lost or losing his godly powers yet again.

The light from the bottom of the ragged, stony steps begins to light up brighter, even flaring every few steps.

Someone or something is stoking the fires up down there.

He breathes in the deep humid cold of the caves. He used to miss this smell, but since he's been topside for nearly a year, he can honestly say that he needs to have the warmth and sunlight. The light and clouds, just like home used to be.

Before the eviction by God himself.

When Hermes gets to the bottom of the steps, he hears the rustling of feet and something stamping onto the dry ground, reddish from the ore and hellish dirt.

Last he checked, Limbo was a pretty laid back kind of place. It is lit, but gray. Muted. The kind of almost happy that occurs.

This was God's idea, to rob the souls of their perfect Heaven by making it just subpar. That clever bastard may have been on to something.

Nearly everyone there, mostly regular Greek and ancient civilization folks, bums around in a mild so-so fashion. No smiles, no excitement.

At the same time, no anger and no sadness, either.

Just blah.

Part of Hermes likes this idea, but could never stay there very long.

Whenever he had to travel to Hell and back, it was through the River Acheron, where he could bypass Purgatory and Limbo altogether.

It gave him the creeps, though he would never admit that to many people other than Herc.

Well, maybe not Herc. He has a mouth as big as his biceps.

Hermes rounds out to the end of the hallway and stops just short of the grand opening into Limbo proper.

He peers around the corner and notices that it's empty. Not a literal soul in sight.

He flies into the castle with seven doors and peers through a window. Nothing but gray stone walls and stagnant furniture that hasn't been used or slept in for days. Probably longer.

Hermes looks over his shoulder.

This cannot and should not be happening.

Where can everyone go?

Hermes flies to the edges of Limbo and even Minos is gone. His ruling stick, however, the measurement of where the souls would spend their eternity lies on the ground, cracked along the top edge.

Hermes peers up and follows the rivers that flow to the center of Hell.

But at the beginning of the Second Circle, the echoes of stomping feet, dozens if not hundreds, gives Hermes reason to pause.

In the terrible, ripping winds that blow the lustful back and forth without stop, a shadow of an army emerges from the rain and falling stones.

These souls are clad in black armor, fashioned like ancient medieval armor, with a red hue that seems to catch the Hellish light from the ground.

The winds blow a rock nearly sideways. Hermes watches it travel from one soldier to the end of the line.

"Dammit," he whispers to himself.

His heart nearly stops. Can they hear him? Are they close enough to hear anything in that storm?

The shadows emerge completely from the storm. They march in unison, holding ebony spears that absorb all light. The soldiers look as if they hold shadows in their hands. Sharp, deadly shadows.

A voice, a female voice, screams over the soldiers to halt.

Marching across the field is a centaur holding a black spiked shield and a ebony blade that glows dark purple in the light.

The woman general sits on her back.

Hermes knows already who this is without even having to wait for her to turn her head.

"We take no prisoners," the woman says. She turns her head and Hermes confirms it.

That bitch, Lilith, leads her own army.

All of this time, she had been looking for a new general. Waited too long and took it for herself.

Hermes steps backward and hits the stairs with his Achilles tendon.

He pauses.

The soldiers grow silent.

"Hermes?" Lilith shouts over the storm. "I thought you weren't coming home?"

Hermes flees up the stairs.

Lilith's hellish laugh echoes in the hallways, almost pushing him out of the caverns.

Hermes emerges out into the South Carolina air.

He takes a second to rest, putting his hands on his knees and taking a deep breath.

First Sophie.

Then Brad.

Now this.

Hermes flees back to the hospital. He follows the light of the crescent moon, taking to the air.

Who cares if he gets seen. In a matter of a few hours, it won't matter anyway.

AFTER BEING CAST out of his Mt. Olympus home by God, Erigan finds himself at the service of Lucifer, Lord of Hell. His duties: menial. His boss: a bitch. His life: sucks.

So when he pisses off his supervisor and is exiled from coming back into Hell, Erigan isn't too upset. But when he discovers a plot that threatens the very fabric of the world, Erigan must decide to side with family or watch the world go down in flames.

WE'D LIKE to thank you for reading our books. If you loved this one and want to receive notices of when our next books are to come out, head on over to http://eepurl.com/ZOcPL and sign up for our EvilGenius Newsletter.

TO BE CONTINUED...

Book III of **The War of Gods** Series
Across the Realms

Hell's recent shake-up thanks to Hermes and his friends, Heaven declares victory in the War of Good and Evil and lays claim to the Earth Realm. Meanwhile Sophie is shot trying to save her son Brad, leaving Hermes with a mess as he deals with Lillith's sudden arrival. As if things couldn't get worse, the angels declare war against humans on Earth and Brad is the Earth's only hope.

Check out his books at www.akusaipublishing.com

WANT MORE?

Thank you for reading The War of the Gods series. If you enjoyed this as much as we did, please consider offering a review to help other readers find this story.

Get a free copy of David Gearing's dark urban fantasy novella BEDLAM when you sign up to get news, updates, and info on new releases.

Get Your Free Book

Exiled From Hell Copyright © 2015 by David Gearing.

THE WAR OF THE GODS copyright © 2015 by David Gearing

Legal Notice and Disclaimer:

All rights reserved. Printed in the United States of America. No part of this book may be used or reproduced in any manner whatsoever without written permission except in the case of brief quotations embodied in critical articles or reviews.

This book is a work of fiction. Names, characters, businesses, organizations, places, events and incidents either are the product of the author's imagination or are used fictitiously. Any resemblance to actual persons, living or dead, events, or locales is entirely coincidental.

This ebook is licensed for your personal enjoyment only. This ebook may not be re-sold or given away to other people. If you would like to share this book with another person, please purchase an additional copy for each recipient. If you're reading this book and did not purchase it, or it was not purchased for your use only, then please purchase your own copy. Thank you for respecting the hard work of this author.

For information contact:

David Gearing - davidgearing@akusaipublishing.com

Book and Cover design by Kevin Johnson-Vindiola

Cover photo by Stefan Kellara on Pixabay

ABOUT THE AUTHOR

David Gearing is an educator and author of over 30 novels across multiple genres and pen names. He specializes in fiction with an LGBTQ twist and supernatural edges.

His psychology degree helps him delve deep into the anima and animus of the human mind, where he loves to stare off into the shadows. He doesn't mind when the shadows stare back.

He lives in the Pacific Northwest, but has lived all over the United States, but is mostly inspired by the Southern Gothic stories of the Deep South.

You can sign up for David's newsletter here and visit him at his website, davidgearingbooks.com, or his Publisher's website.

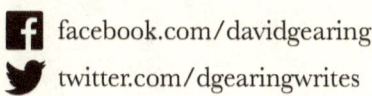

facebook.com/davidgearing

twitter.com/dgearingwrites

ALSO BY DAVID GEARING

Akusai Publishing specializes in LGBTQ centric stories, often with a supernatural edge.

Do Ya Like Dark Fantasy or Godpunk horror?

Join Hermes and Heracles in the **War of the Gods** series

Exiled from Hell (Book 1)

Reign from Heaven (Book 2)

Across the Realms (Book 3)

A Jono Grey Dark Fantasy Mystery

Apocalypse Nigh

Psychological Horror

Savior

Gifted

Mad Maddy

House of Braddock

Echoes

Mr. White

Wannabe

Like Sci-Fi?

For the Republic

Reset

LGBTQ

Just a Thing

Pride and Glass Unicorns

Like Thrillers?

Patient Zero

Tartarus

Short Stories

Unwanted

Touched

Evaluation

Writing as KD Johnson

The Shattering Series

Sword of Stone (Book 1)

Shapes of Clay (Book 2)

Halls of Shadows (Book 3)

Ray of Light (Book 4)

Man of Fire (Book 5)

Orb of Light (Book 6)

Omnibus 1: Collection of Books 1 - 3

Young Adult

Method Acting

www.ingramcontent.com/pod-product-compliance
Lightning Source LLC
Chambersburg PA
CBHW020933260626
47169CB00006B/1700